CLUB TIMES

For Members' Eyes Only

Astral Rejection!

Angela Mason, Mission Creek's famous profiler, and I were both waiting for our hair to dry at the salon. I'd been doing some reading about spirits, crystals and otherworldly things, and thought, might as well ask Angela how to cleanse my aura. She told me to go buy a bran muffin. Her hairdresser, Jorge, whisked her away before I could come up with a snappy comeback. Some people are so huffy.

I will say that Angela has fantastic taste in men. While doing my weekly lawn-chair stakeout on Main Street, I saw Ms. Profiler on the arm of that scrumptious Ricky Mercado. Mr. Tall, Dark and Handsome Mercado is one fine specimen who really should have his own calendar. I just hope Angela's ex-husband, Sheriff Justin Wainwright, doesn't get wind of this pairing. Better not tell him, either, members. I get the feeling

that Justin carries a torch for his ex, and you don't want to make a Wainwright mad. Trust me on that one.

Last note, for those pranksters who made rude shapes on some of the deck tables, using Yellow Rose Café coleslaw, we are not amused. Our fine Lone Star chefs worked long hours, shredding that cabbage. In the future, let's all try a little harder to get along, shall we?

Come to the Lone Star Country Club, your weekend getaway, every day!

D0816312

About the Author

METSY HINGLE

is the award-winning, bestselling author of series- and single-title romance novels. Known for creating powerful and passionate stories, Metsy's own life reads like the plot of a romance novel—from her early years in a New Orleans' orphanage and foster care to her long, happy marriage to her husband, Jim, and the rearing of their four children. She recently traded in her business suits and fast-paced life in the hotel and public-relations arena to pursue writing full-time.

She was thrilled to be invited to participate in the LONE STAR COUNTRY CLUB series because it allowed her an opportunity to work with old friends and other authors whose books she'd enjoyed for ages. She was intrigued by the entire concept for the series right from the start. What truly enamored her to the series was that at the heart of each story is the message that real wealth lies not in money and acquisitions, but in the bonds of family and the healing power of love. She had a wonderful time working with the talented authors and editors on this series. She fell in love with Justin and Angela in *The Marriage Profile*. She hopes you do, too.

Metsy loves hearing from readers. For a free bookmark, write to Metsy at P.O. Box 3224, Covington, LA 70433 or visit her Web site at: www.metsyhingle.com.

METSY HINGLE

THE MARRIAGE PROFILE

Published by Silhouette Books
America's Publisher of Contemporary Romance

Special thanks and acknowledgment are given
to Metsy Hingle for her contribution
to the LONE STAR COUNTRY CLUB series.

SILHOUETTE BOOKS

ISBN 0-373-61362-8

THE MARRIAGE PROFILE

Visit Silhouette at www.eHarlequin.com

Printed in U.S.A.

Welcome to the

LONE STAR
LSCC
COUNTRY
CLUB
EST. 1923

*Where Texas society reigns supreme—
and appearances are everything.*

*It's a race against time as the search
for baby Lena continues....*

Justin Wainwright: The last thing this rough-edged sheriff wanted was to team up with his former bride to work baby Lena's case. But would keeping a tight rein on his smoldering desires be his toughest assignment yet?

Angela Mason: This investigation was a matter of life and death, and if her tough-as-nails ex-husband thought he could intimidate her out of this job, he had another think coming! It would just be her little secret that he still stirred her womanly passions like no other man alive....

Mission Creek rumor mill: Hmm...what's star profiler Angela Mason doing on the arm of the good-for-nothin' Ricky Mercado? Is she aligning herself with the underworld? And will the search for baby Lena lead to another dead end...or could it bring back presumed dead mob princess Haley Mercado to the family she despises?

THE FAMILIES

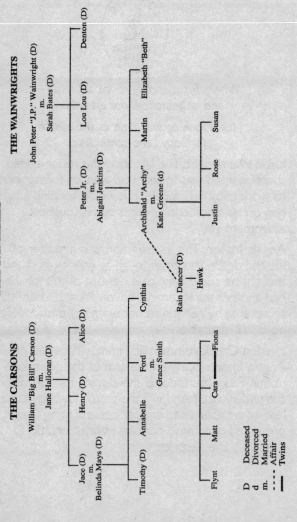

THE CARSONS

William "Big Bill" Carson (D)
m.
Jane Halloran (D)

Jace (D)
m.
Belinda Mays (D)

Henry (D)

Alice (D)

Timothy (D)

Annabelle

Ford
m.
Grace Smith

Cynthia

Flynt

Matt

Cara

Fiona

THE WAINWRIGHTS

John Peter "J.P." Wainwright (D)
m.
Sarah Bates (D)

Peter Jr. (D)
m.
Abigail Jenkins (D)

Lou Lou (D)

Denton (D)

Archibald "Archy"
m.
Kate Greene (d)

Martin

Elizabeth "Beth"

Justin

Rose

Susan

Rain Dancer (D)

Hawk

D   Deceased
d   Divorced
m.   Married
- - - Affair
▬▬▬ Twins

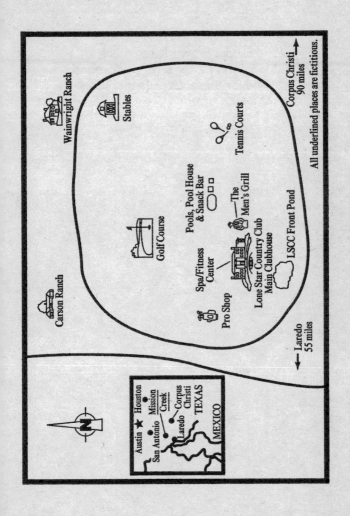

Wainwright Ranch

Stables

Tennis Courts

Corpus Christi
90 miles

All underlined places are fictitious.

Golf Course

Pools, Pool House
& Snack Bar

The Men's Grill

Spa/Fitness
Center

Carson Ranch

Pro Shop

Lone Star Country Club
Main Clubhouse

LSCC Front Pond

Laredo
55 miles

N

Austin ★ Houston
San Antonio Mission Creek
Laredo Corpus Christi
TEXAS
MEXICO

For my Texas Pals
Sandra Brown, Karen Young,
Mary Lynn Baxter & Peggy Moreland
And for the fabulous fans in Texas

One

"They aren't going to show."

Ignoring his deputy's remark, Sheriff Justin Wainwright kept his eyes trained on the entrance of the Mission Creek Memorial Hospital and watched as one by one the movers and shakers of Lone Star County, Texas, strolled indoors. It seemed no one wanted to miss the dedication ceremony of the hospital's new state-of-the-art maternity ward, Justin mused as he noted members of his own family and an equal number of the Carsons file through the doors.

"We're wasting our time here, Sheriff. Mercado and Del Brio aren't going to show for this shindig."

Justin cut a glance to Bobby Hunter, the strapping young man he'd hired as his deputy less than two months ago. "They'll show," Justin assured his impatient deputy. His voice held the same conviction now that it had when he'd promised Dylan Bridges that he would bring to justice the person responsible for the death of Dylan's father. He intended to make good on that promise. The fact that he had in custody the hit man who'd offed Judge Bridges fulfilled only part of that promise. He still had to find the person who had contracted Alex Black to kill the judge. According to the story Black had given him, the not-too-bright gunman hadn't known who had hired him. He'd been contacted by phone, then given instructions via a tape recording. Payment for the job had been in cash and placed in a trash can in the park for Black to retrieve later.

As far-fetched as it had sounded, Justin had believed the man. Maybe Black hadn't known who was behind the order to kill the judge, but Justin had a pretty good idea who was responsible. His every instinct as a lawman told him that the hit had been ordered by someone inside the Texas mafia—someone who was using the Mercado Brothers Paving and Contracting business as a shield for their illegal activities. And he'd wager a month's salary that that person was either Ricky Mercado or Frank Del Brio. Both men had axes to grind with the judge. The trick was linking one of them to the triggerman. Since conventional methods had failed, he saw no option but to try a less conventional route—namely, he intended to take advantage of tonight's social event to rattle both men's cages without their lawyers dancing interference. "They'll show," Justin said again, determined to keep his word to Dylan Bridges. And once this case was closed he could redouble his efforts and find the baby whose kidnapping had rocked his county.

"You sound pretty sure about that, Sheriff."

"I am sure," Justin replied.

"Don't see why," Bobby said as he plucked a chicken wing from a passing tray and all but inhaled the thing. "From what I hear, Mercado and Del Brio aren't exactly what you'd call civic-minded members of the community."

"You heard right. They're not." Far from it, Justin thought as he declined a glass of wine with a shake of his head and continued to survey the guests' arrival.

"So what makes you think they'll come to this dedication shindig?"

"Because neither one of them will be able to stay away."

Bobby scratched his head. "Come again?"

"The whole purpose of tonight is to acknowledge Carmine Mercado for his generous bequest to the hospital in his will. Ricky will come out of respect for his late uncle and for the Mercado family name."

"And Del Brio?"

Justin smiled as he thought of the beady-eyed thug with the vicious temper. "Del Brio will come because he's paranoid. He may have beat out Ricky as Carmine's successor, but he doesn't trust Ricky. So he'll show up here tonight and flex his muscles just to make sure that Ricky and anyone else who thinks that a Mercado should be running the family business thinks twice before challenging him. He wants everyone in the family to see that he's the boss now and that he isn't going to tolerate any disloyalty."

"Well, if they're going to show, I for one wish they'd do it soon. I haven't eaten dinner yet."

"There's plenty of food here," Justin pointed out, noting the half-dozen finger sandwiches and appetizers the deputy had piled onto his plate. He didn't bother pointing out that the younger man had already consumed enough to feed several people.

"This stuff?" Bobby countered as he devoured one sandwich and then another whole. "Barely enough to put a dent in a two-year-old's belly. I need something that will stick to my ribs."

Since the guy was built like a running back for the Dallas Cowboys and had a good three inches and twenty pounds on his own five-foot-eleven frame, Justin reminded himself to be grateful that he wasn't responsible for feeding his deputy. "Try eating some of the cheese or fruit," Justin suggested.

Bobby obliged by scooping several chunks of cheese from the buffet spread, along with a handful of crackers, then followed Justin away from the table. "Any chance I can talk you into taking me over to the Lone Star Country Club for a meal when this thing is over?"

Justin snorted. "You'd have better luck winning the lottery," he told the younger man. "I haven't forgotten that you conned me into buying you a lunch there last week that nearly bankrupted me."

"Hey, you were the one who offered to buy."

"Yeah. Before I realized you had a hollow leg that needed filling," Justin teased. "Sorry, cowboy. When we're finished here, you might want to try Coyote Harry's or the Mission Creek Cafe. There's no charge for seconds on the specials."

"Yeah, but the food at the club's better."

Justin cocked his brow and studied his deputy. "You sure it's the food at the club that's caught your interest?"

"What do you mean?"

"I mean is it the Lone Star Country Club's food you find so attractive, or is it that little blond waitress I saw you talking to?"

"What waitress?"

"You know, that one they call Daisy."

For the space of a heartbeat Justin could have sworn he saw a flicker of alarm in the other man's eyes. Then Bobby scratched his head and gave him a perplexed look. "Daisy? She the one with those sexy dimples?"

"No, that's Marilee, and she's a brunette," Justin informed him.

Bobby's lips spread into what Justin considered a college boy's grin. "Whoever she is, she's a real looker."

"She's also real married to a fellow who rides bulls for a living. You might want to steer clear of her."

"No harm in looking, is there?"

"Not as long as all you do is look," Justin advised the younger man.

"Whatever you say, boss."

Justin nodded, taking a sip of the plain soda he'd been nursing since his arrival before discarding it on the tray of a passing waiter. When several moments ticked by with no newcomers arriving, he found himself growing impatient. "I'm going to move around a bit, see if I can pick up on anything. You might want to do the same."

"Will do," Bobby told him. "Want me to start over there where Johnny Mercado's holding court?"

Justin followed the direction of his deputy's gaze, frowning as he noted that Bobby was right. Surrounded by several members of the crime family and speaking emphatically about something, Johnny did seem to be holding court—which didn't fit with the older man's normal fade-into-the-background demeanor. Justin had concluded long ago that Johnny Mercado hadn't been cut out for the business of crime he'd been born into. He was too weak willed and lacked the ruthlessness of his late brother, Carmine. Unfortunately, that criminal gene hadn't bypassed Johnny's son, Ricky.

As he studied Johnny, Justin couldn't help feeling sympathy for him. Never a man to stand out in a crowd, Johnny was an easy man to overlook. And since the death of his wife, it was as though he'd disappeared within himself. He seemed to have aged overnight and had lost what little spark he'd once had. Or at least that had been the case until recently, Justin amended. Staring at Johnny now, he couldn't help but notice the difference in the man's demeanor. He was more intense, almost angry, Justin thought.

"Looks like you were right," Bobby said. "Del Brio just walked in."

Justin shifted his attention to the doorway where Frank Del Brio strutted into the reception flanked by two of his henchmen. Tracking his progress, Justin watched him make his way over to where Johnny and his cohorts had gathered.

"Want me to see if I can get closer and find out what they're talking about?" Bobby asked.

"Not yet," Justin told him, noting the adversarial body language between the two men. "Let's see what happens first."

Del Brio leaned in and said something to Johnny. Nearly a half-foot taller and leaner than Johnny, Del Brio blocked the older man's face momentarily. But when Del Brio straightened, Justin caught a brief glimpse of Johnny's furious expression—just before Johnny lunged at Del Brio. "Aw, hell," Justin muttered. "Let's go."

Intent on moving in before things got ugly, Justin had taken no more than a half-dozen steps when he spied Johnny's pals restraining him and halted midstride. Bobby nearly collided into his back. Justin held up a hand and said, "Hang on a second." Still poised to step in if necessary, he waited several seconds until a smug-looking Del Brio sauntered off, leaving an angry Johnny Mercado staring daggers at his back.

"You want me to tell him and Del Brio to leave?"

"No," Justin replied. "It looks like Johnny's friends have him under control. Besides, the whole point of this thing tonight is to pay tribute to Johnny's brother, Carmine, for his donation to the hospital. It wouldn't look too good to kick Johnny out."

"Wonder what Del Brio said to set old Johnny off?"

"I was wondering the same thing. I think I'll go have a little chat with Johnny and see if I can find out. In the meantime, you keep an eye on Del Brio."

"Will do. I—" Bobby's jaw dropped. He let out a low whistle. "Oh, man, how come these wise guys have all the luck when it comes to women?"

At his deputy's comment, Justin turned to see what had put that dumbstruck look on Bobby's face.

And his own jaw dropped at the sight of Angela.

Feeling as though he'd been sucker punched, it took Justin a moment to regain his breath as he watched his ex-wife greet one of the hospital's board members. Emotions stormed through him at breakneck speed—anger, disbelief, regret. He stared at her, noted that her hair was shorter now than it had been five years ago, a cap of sexy dark curls that framed her face and emphasized her cheekbones and those incredible blue eyes. She was thinner, too, he decided, as he followed the lines of the little black dress that skimmed her breasts, her waist, the curve of her hips. Disgusted by the unmistakable tug of sexual attraction, Justin scrubbed a hand down his face.

Get a grip, Wainwright.

He and Angela had both moved on with their lives since their disastrous attempt at marriage. She was a hotshot profiler now, and he was the sheriff of Lone Star County. And they had even less in common now than they had had when they'd split, he reminded himself.

But damn if just the sight of her didn't still have the power to make his blood heat, his body ache for her. And if he wasn't careful, he'd find himself falling under her spell all over again. Infuriated by that realization, he swore. "What in the hell is she doing here?"

"If by 'she' you mean the hot number with the legs, she came in with Ricky Mercado."

Justin looked across the room at Angela again. A red haze of fury rushed through him as he stared at that scumbag Mercado whispering something in Angela's ear, placing his hand at her back.

"Sheriff?"

Justin flexed his hands into fists, fought the primal urge to storm over to the two of them and tear Ricky's hands away from Angela. She was no longer his wife, he reminded himself. He no longer had any rights where she was concerned.

"Sheriff, you all right?"

"I'm fine." Justin ground out the lie as he struggled to regain control of himself.

"So I take it you know the lady?"

"Yeah, I know her." At one time he had thought he knew her as well as he knew himself. He'd loved her, had hoped to spend his life with her, create a family with her.

"So who is she?"

"Her name's Mason. Angela Mason."

"Angela Mason," Bobby repeated. "Why does that name sound familiar?"

"Because she's a hotshot profiler out of San Antonio," Justin explained as he watched Ricky lead Angela over to where Johnny and his friends were huddled. "She's helped out in a number of high-profile kidnapping cases and has been in the news off and on this past year."

"Yeah. Now I remember. She helped locate that politician's kid about eight months ago—the one whose little boy was strapped in the back seat of the family car when they stopped for gas and were carjacked."

"That's right." Justin had read about the case, and had watched Angela downplay her role in the boy's recovery.

"There was a lot of hype about her. The congressman and the media all credited her with saving his kid's life."

"That's because she did save his life," Justin pointed out to his deputy. Knowing Angela, he figured she would have driven herself relentlessly, forgoing food and sleep in order to find that child and bring him back safely to his family. "She's good at her job, probably among the top profilers in the country."

"Makes you wonder what a woman like her sees in a guy like Mercado."

Justin remained silent, but it was a question he had asked Angela more than once during their marriage. The truth was he had never understood Angela's loyalty to the likes of Ricky Mercado. Her friendship with the thug had been one of the sore spots between them. And, Justin admitted, he'd nearly driven himself crazy after he and Angela had split up, because he'd worried she would take up with Mercado. As far as he knew, she never had. But then she'd been living in San Antonio, while he had remained in Mission Creek.

"You ever work with her?"

"A time or two," Justin replied.

"So," Bobby began, a lazy grin curving his mouth, "seeing how you and she are old friends, maybe you could introduce me."

Justin frowned. "Forget it."

"Aw, come on, Sheriff. I'd really like to meet her."

"I said forget it, cowboy."

"How come?" Bobby persisted.

"For starters, she's too old for you."

Bobby grinned. "I like mature women."

"Then I suggest you go introduce yourself," Justin said, more irritated than he had a right to be.

"But I bet a good word from you would go a long way."

"Trust me, you'd do better without any recommendation from me."

"But I thought you said you and she were old friends."

"I'm not sure 'friends' is the term I'd use to describe our relationship." He and Angela had been colleagues, lovers, husband and wife, and at the end, they had been enemies. But he wasn't sure they had ever been friends and doubted that they ever would be.

"All right, so you were more like acquaintances. But you do know her, right?"

"I guess you could say that."

"What do you mean?" Bobby asked.

"I mean I know Angela about as well as any man can claim to know his ex-wife."

"Let me look at you," Johnny Mercado told Angela, holding her hands in his following their greeting. "Why, I still remember when you were just a skinny teenager. Now look at you, all grown up."

Puzzled, Angela said, "But it hasn't been that long since you've seen me, Mr. Johnny. Don't you remember, until about five years ago I used to live here in Mission Creek?" She didn't bother adding that it had been during her marriage to Justin.

"That's right," he said, a look of confusion in his faded eyes. "And you're still as pretty as a picture."

"Thank you," Angela replied while he continued to clutch her fingers in his weathered palms. "And it's really good to see you again. I was sorry to hear about your wife."

Something dark and dangerous flashed in the older man's eyes, and his fingers tightened their grasp on hers for a moment. "My Isadora. She was a good woman. She didn't deserve to die the way she did. I should have taken better care of her. If only I had protected her—"

"Pop," Ricky said, and placed a hand on his father's

shoulder. "Mama had a heart attack. Remember? There's nothing you could have done."

"I—" Johnny clamped his mouth shut, but not before Angela noted the murderous look he'd cast across the room. "Yes. Yes, you're right, of course," Johnny told his son. Releasing her fingers, Johnny took a step back so that Ricky's hand fell away. But Angela couldn't help but notice how the older man had averted his gaze. It didn't take psychic abilities for her to recognize that something besides grief was troubling the usually easygoing Johnny Mercado.

"I saw Del Brio talking to you when I came in. He giving you a hard time about something?" Ricky asked, an edge in his voice.

"Del Brio is a yellow-bellied snake. He doesn't scare me."

"I didn't ask if he scared you, Pop. I asked if he was giving you a hard time."

"No," Johnny told his son.

But Angela didn't believe him. There was an aura of darkness about Frank Del Brio that she'd picked up on the moment she'd entered the room. And it was obvious that something Del Brio had said or done had set off the older man. Or was she imagining things? Angela wondered. Maybe the undercurrents and shadows she sensed were of her own making and had nothing to do with the Mercados or Frank Del Brio. After all, she hadn't exactly been herself since she'd agreed to come back to Mission Creek.

Because you knew coming to Mission Creek meant seeing Justin again.

Angela let out a shaky breath at the admission. Even after all this time just the prospect of seeing him again still had the power to tie her up in knots. It had been that way from the first moment she'd set eyes on him at the police academy when she'd been a new recruit and he'd been the handsome deputy assisting in her training class. She'd looked up into those green eyes and the world had shifted beneath her feet. It didn't seem to matter that they were all wrong for each other. That he was a member of the prominent Wainwright family, and she was the estranged daughter of a farmer who could barely make ends meet. She'd fallen for Justin like a ton of bricks, and when he'd asked her to marry him she had accepted.

Overcome by a wave of sadness, Angela attempted to shut off the memories and the ache that always came when she thought of Justin. Hardening her resolve, she reminded herself of all that she'd accomplished since leaving Mission Creek. Not only had she carved out a career for herself as a profiler, but she'd saved dozens of lives and reunited families. And she'd done it by finding a way to put the curse she'd been born with to good use. As much as she'd hated the visions that had made her different, they had served a purpose. *She* had served a purpose. She had made a difference—at least in the lives of those people she'd been able to help.

Did Justin know? Had he followed her career as she had followed his?

Probably not, she conceded. Why should he when he'd made it plain that he never wanted to see her again the day she'd told him she was leaving. Angela whooshed out a breath as she recalled how angry he'd been. She'd hurt him. Or perhaps it had been his pride that she'd hurt. She'd never been quite sure. All she had known was that Justin wasn't a man used to failing at anything, and by choosing her as his wife, he'd failed big time. He certainly wasn't going to be happy to have her showing up on his turf now.

And he was going to be even more unhappy when he found out the reason why.

"Sorry about that," Ricky said as he rejoined her. "You see what I mean about Pop being different?"

"He did seem distracted."

"For a while after my mother died, he sort of shut down. You know, just didn't seem to care about anything. But then he started making noises about how maybe Frank was right about my sister, that Haley really was alive. And I thought he was better. But now since I got back he's changed. He's gotten... I don't know. Almost secretive."

"Are you sure?" Angela asked. "He seemed sad, maybe a little lonely and confused, but sometimes that comes with age. He remembered who I was, even that he knew me as a teenager."

"He's only sixty," Ricky pointed out. "But it's not a memory problem. He remembers well enough. It's some of the stuff he says. Not all of it makes sense. Like that business about him protecting my mother. She died of a heart attack. How could he have protected her from that?"

"I don't know."

"I'm worried about him, Angela. I can feel Pop slipping away little by little each day. And I'm afraid if I don't do something soon, one morning I'm going to wake up and find he's gone over the edge."

"I know," Angela replied, and patted his arm.

Ricky shoved a hand through his dark hair, then pinned her with anxious eyes. "You've got to help me, Angela. If Haley is alive and Pop's right about that missing kid being hers, it could make a difference. You need to find that baby."

"Ricky—"

"Please," he pleaded when she started to withdraw. "Just hear me out."

"All right, but I'm not sure there's anything I can do. I'm here to work up a profile on a kidnapper."

"You're here to find that missing little girl."

Angela neither confirmed nor denied his claim. "What is it you want?"

"When you find her, I want you to let me see her before you call in the authorities."

"You know I can't do that," Angela insisted, taken aback by the request.

"I'm not asking you not to tell the cops you found her, just let me see the kid first."

"Why?" she asked.

"Because since I've been back, I've been watching my pop die right before my eyes little by little. He needs a reason to go on living. That baby could be it."

"He has you," Angela pointed out.

"All I've ever been for him is a headache, someone he doesn't understand. Hell, even I don't understand me. But Haley…Haley was his favorite. If the rumors are true, if my sister didn't die in that boating accident and that missing kid is hers, it would make all the difference in the world to Pop. He'd have a grandchild who needed him, a piece of my sister again. He'd have a reason to live again."

"Ricky, what you're asking—"

"Is a lot. I know that," he said, and caught her hands in his. "But I'm desperate, Angela. I'm desperate."

The weight of Ricky's plea enveloped her like a shroud, and Angela pulled her fingers free. She wrapped her arms around herself. "I can't make you any promises. I'll tell you the same thing I told the FBI and the police chief—

you shouldn't pin your hopes on me. Justin Wainwright's a good sheriff. He'll have followed every possible lead to find that missing child. So will the Bureau. If they haven't been able to find her by now, the chances are I won't be able to find her, either."

"You'll find her," Ricky said with the utmost conviction.

"Ricky, I'm not a miracle worker. I'm a profiler," she protested.

"We both know you're more than a profiler. My mama said you had a special gift. Second sight, she called it. You can see things, sense things that other people can't. Like that time when I was supposed to make that truck run to Mexico and you called me, insisted you had to see me that night. It's because you knew what was going to happen, didn't you? Somehow you knew about that crazy hitchhiker, that he was going to kill the person driving the truck that night. That's why you made sure I canceled the trip. You did it to save me."

Angela remained silent as the memory of that day six years ago came back to her. She'd seen Ricky in the Mission Creek Café at lunchtime that day, and when he'd given her a hello hug, an image had flashed into her mind's eye of a dark roadway, of the sign indicating the Mexican border thirty miles away, of the body of a dark-haired man lying beside a truck with a bullet in his temple. When Ricky had told her he was leaving that afternoon for Mexico, she'd panicked. She'd known at once that he was in danger. So she'd called him, made up an excuse that she needed to see him that night after she was off duty and begged him to cancel his trip. And he'd done as she'd asked. Regret washed over her anew as she realized she'd been so caught up in first saving Ricky and then later defending her meeting with Ricky to an angry Justin that she hadn't thought to ask Ricky if he'd arranged for someone else to take his run. And because she hadn't asked him, a man had died.

"You used your gift, or whatever you want to call it to save my life that night. Now I'm asking you—begging you—to use your gift again. Only this time use it to save my father's life by finding that baby."

Her gift, Ricky had called it. But for as long as she could remember, she'd considered her visions a curse, not a gift. "Marked by the devil" her father had claimed. And she'd believed him, believed she'd deserved to be isolated from her family, to grow up without the love and affection she'd craved. Even Justin, who had claimed to love her, had been uncomfortable when she'd tried to tell him, to explain to him about the visions. And because she'd loved him so desperately and feared losing him, she had gone along with him when he'd chalked up her uncanny knack for knowing things as female intuition. A cop's instinct. A coincidence. Yet here was Ricky, a man with a questionable reputation and ties to the Texas mafia, a man with whom she'd shared nothing more than friendship, accepting without question that she could see things he didn't. Know things others wouldn't. Not only was he accepting it, but he was asking her to use her ability to help him. "I'll try," she finally told him. "That's all I can promise."

"And that's all I'm asking." He pressed a brotherly kiss to her forehead, then suddenly tensed.

"What's wrong?" she asked.

"I just caught sight of your ex heading this way. And judging by his expression, he's not a happy cowboy." He stepped back, eyed her closely. ''Want me to head him off for you?''

Despite the knot in her stomach, Angela shook her head. ''I need to see him sooner or later. It might as well be now.'' She paused, wet her lips. ''Maybe it would be better if I spoke with him alone first. Would you mind?''

''You sure you want to do that? The man looks mad as hell.''

''I'm sure.''

''All right. I wanted to have a chat with Sal, anyway, see if he knows what's going on between Pop and Del Brio. But I'm going to keep my eye on you. And if Wainwright starts giving you a hard time, I'm coming back whether you want me to or not.''

''Thanks,'' Angela murmured.

Ricky winked at her, then headed to the corner of the room where his father and his cronies were gathered. Bracing herself, Angela turned around and waited for Justin to make his way to her. When he got waylaid by the town's mayor, she took advantage of the moment to study him. Despite the sedate business suit and neatly combed hair, there was still something untamed about Justin Wainwright, an energy and restlessness about him that made her think of gunslingers and lawmen of the Old West. And blast her foolish heart if just the sight of him didn't make her pulse quicken now as it had all those years ago.

As though sensing her scrutiny, Justin looked up, locked eyes with hers. Within moments, he was excusing himself from the mayor and heading toward her again. Angela's heart pounded faster with each step he took. And as he drew nearer, she noted the changes in him—the new lines that creased the corners of his eyes, the hint of gray mixed in with the dark blond hair at his temples. She stared at his mouth, that incredible mouth that had always made her knees go weak when he smiled at her, that had made her skin burn when he'd kissed her, that had whispered promises of love and forever in her ears.

"Hello, Angela," he said, his voice deadly soft.

"Hello, Jus—"

"You want to tell me just what in the hell you're doing here?"

TWO

Angela sucked in a sharp breath, taken aback by the stinging remark. Determined not to be intimidated, she hiked up her chin. "It's good to see you again," she said, and extended her hand.

For a second, something hot flashed in those green eyes before he looked down at her outstretched hand. But when he lifted his gaze to hers, those eyes were as cold as his voice as he said, "Too bad I can't say the same."

Angela's smile died, along with any hope that Justin would make this easy for either of them. She dropped her hand to her side. "I'm sorry you feel that way. I know we didn't part as friends, but I had thought…" She swallowed, tried again. "I had thought that after all this time we could at least be civil with each other."

"Then you thought wrong."

"Apparently," she conceded. "Still, I had hoped…"

"What? That maybe I'd forgotten how you walked out on me five years ago?"

"I didn't walk out on you."

"Funny, that's sure how it looked to me when you packed your bags and hightailed it off to San Antonio."

"I asked you to come with me," she reminded him.

"Because you knew I wouldn't go."

It was true, Angela admitted in silence. She'd known he would never leave Mission Creek. So she'd run away to save both of them from hurting each other even more.

"Evidently you forgot what I told you when you left here."

"I didn't forget," Angela told him. It was a scene she would never be able to forget no matter how hard she tried. Just as she'd never forget that look of shock and disbelief on Justin's face when she'd told him she was taking the job in San Antonio. Nor would she ever forget seeing that shock turn to desperation when he'd pleaded with her to pass on the job, to stay in Mission Creek with him and work out the problems in their marriage. Even now she could still hear the lie trip off his tongue as he'd insisted that her being unable to have a baby didn't matter to him. And when his attempts to reason with her had failed, his passionate pleas had turned into a white-hot anger that bordered on disgust and had left her chilled to the bone. She pressed a fist to her heart at the ache that came as she remembered the frigid way he'd looked at her and the coldness in his voice when he'd warned her that if she walked out that door, their marriage was over and he never wanted to see her again. Two weeks later she'd saved him the trouble and had filed for divorce.

"Then you know you're not welcome here. Go back to San Antonio, Mason. You don't belong here."

Angela tipped her chin up a notch higher, met his cool gaze. "You don't own Mission Creek, Justin. And you certainly don't own the hospital. I have as much right to be here as you do."

He narrowed his eyes. "Since when do you give a damn about Mission Creek? You wanted the bright lights of the big city, remember?"

"That's not why I left, and you know it," she told him, irritated with herself for letting him goad her. "We both know why I left Mission Creek."

"Yeah. You left to get away from me," he said, his

voice bitter, his expression hard. "So I'll ask you again, Mason, what are you doing here? Better yet, when are you leaving?"

His words stung, hurting her more than she'd ever thought they would. But after growing up in a household where her visions had made her a frequent target for her father's verbal and physical lashings, she'd learned long ago that it was better not to show pain or fear. So she lifted her gaze and met Justin's chilling green eyes. And with an aplomb she thought worthy of an acting award, she said, "In answer to your first question, I'm here as a guest. As to when I intend to leave, I'll go when I'm ready. Now if you'll excuse me—"

He blocked her path. "No. I won't excuse you. I don't want you here."

He was so close, Angela caught the woodsy scent of his aftershave and spied the muscle ticking in his jaw. "You've already made that clear. Unfortunately, we don't always get what we want."

Johnny Mercado clamped a hand down on his son's shoulder. "Ricky, quit badgering Sal here and go see to your lady friend. Looks to me like the sheriff is giving her a rough time."

Ricky shifted his gaze to where the woman in question was in what appeared to be a heated discussion with Sheriff Justin Wainwright. "Angela can handle herself," Ricky informed him.

"What kind of talk is that?" Johnny countered. "The lady came with you, didn't she?"

"Angela Mason's no schoolgirl, Pop. She knows what she's doing. Give it a rest."

When Ricky started to turn back to Sal, Johnny cuffed the back of his son's head—something he had done many times when Ricky had been a teenager, hell-bent on getting into trouble. "You show some respect for me, and for that girl."

Ricky smoothed a hand at his nape, eyed his father warily. "I'm sorry. I didn't mean any disrespect."

Johnny sighed. "I know you didn't," he said, softening toward this dark-haired, dark-eyed stranger that was his son. It had always amazed him that such a handsome and fierce young man had actually come from him and Isadora. Ricky had always been so much braver, so much stronger than he had been, Johnny thought. He still didn't know what the hush-hush military mission was his son had just returned from, but he had no doubts that it had been dangerous. Ricky had never shied away from danger. And whatever this mission was his former commander sent Ricky on, it hadn't frightened his son. Ricky hadn't hesitated to go. Since his return, the boy had seemed different, more serious. But Ricky had said little about what had happened. Perhaps if he himself had been half the man his son was, Johnny thought, his Isadora would still be alive.

"Pop, you okay?"

Johnny shook off thoughts of his many failures. "I'm fine. Now, quit fussing over me like an old woman and go see about your lady friend."

Ricky hesitated a moment, his gaze shifting from Johnny to Angela and back again. "All right. But you and I are going to talk, Pop. And I need you to be straight with me. I want to know what Del Brio said that's got you upset."

"Who says I'm upset? Do I look upset to you?"

"Cut the act, Pop. Sal told me you and Del Brio had words. I want to know what it was about."

Johnny eyed his friend. "Salvatore doesn't know what

he's talking about. Now, go see about little Angela and quit fussing over me. I can take care of myself.''

''Pop—''

''*La Madre di Dio! Basta!* Leave it alone, Ricky. Just leave it alone,'' Johnny commanded, and stalked away from his son toward the bar.

By the time the bartender handed him the glass of red wine, Johnny's hands were no longer trembling from the rage that had been burning inside him for weeks now, ever since he'd put two and two together and had realized the truth—that Frank Del Brio had played a hand in Isadora's death. Mixed in with the rage was shame. Shame at his own cowardice. He stared at the glass of red wine, remembered the sight of his Isadora lying in the hospital bed all battered and bruised. What kind of man was he to have gone along with Isadora's claim that she'd been mugged when in his heart he'd known the truth? She'd been beaten as a warning because he had not followed Del Brio's orders.

He hadn't been a man at all, Johnny conceded. He'd been a coward, a yellow-bellied coward and a weakling. And because of him, Isadora was dead. He took a swallow of the merlot and squeezed his eyes shut as he thought of his sweet, tiny wife who had never had an unkind word for anyone.

Forgive me, Isadora. Forgive me.

How could he have been so blind? Johnny wondered as he left the festivities and wandered outdoors, away from the noise, away from the lights, away from the memories. He stared up at the sky, noted the dusting of stars, the half-moon. Yet his thoughts remained on Del Brio. How could he have failed to see before now how truly evil the man was? And to think at one time he had even condoned the man's offer and allowed him to become engaged to his daughter, Haley.

Haley. My pretty, smart Haley. You knew what he was, didn't you? That's why you disappeared. It's why you pretended to drown and let us believe you were dead. But all these years, all these years, your mama knew. She knew you were alive. And that baby girl, the little one called Lena that was kidnapped, she's your baby, isn't she? My granddaughter. My flesh and blood.

"I'm going to get her back for you," Johnny murmured. And once Haley's baby was safe, he would make Del Brio pay. He would pay for destroying his family. For forcing his daughter into hiding. For what he'd done to Isadora. Johnny clutched the now-empty wineglass between his palms as anger festered inside him. And when the pig was pleading for his life, when he was begging that he not be killed, Johnny would show the dog the same mercy that he had shown Isadora. None.

"Johnny, I'm sorry," Sal said as he came up behind him. "That boy of yours, he tricked me. He said you'd told him you and Del Brio had had an argument. So I thought he knew."

Johnny held up a hand to stem his friend's apology. "It doesn't matter. Ricky's a smart boy. Both he and his sister have always been smarter than their old man."

Sal frowned at him. "You talk as though Haley's still alive. I thought you said you didn't believe all that stuff Del Brio's been spouting off, you know, about her not dying in that boating accident."

"I don't believe it," Johnny lied, and silently cursed his slip of tongue. It was bad enough that he'd persuaded his son that Del Brio was right in his suspicions that Haley was alive. Now he wished he hadn't. While he was convinced that the nun the nurse reported seeing in Isadora's room shortly before her death had been Haley, he'd probably have been wise to keep that to himself. "Sometimes I get confused and forget that she's dead. Too much vino, I guess," he explained, holding up his empty glass.

Apparently satisfied, Sal nodded. "So, you going to tell Ricky what you found out? You know, that stuff about Del Brio ordering that potass…that potass…"

"Potassium chloride," Johnny said, supplying the name. He'd read up on the subject after learning that Del Brio had taken a keen interest in the substance shortly before Isadora's death. He'd also discovered that potassium chloride was one of the four electrolytes found in the body, but if injected into an IV in large doses it would be lethal and cause a victim to suffer a heart attack. His Isadora had never had a heart condition. That she had suffered a heart attack within a week of her hospital stay was reportedly a coincidence. Well, he'd lived too long and seen too many people he cared about hurt to believe in such coincidences. "And no, I have no intention of telling Ricky. I don't want him involved. This is between me and Del Brio."

Sal's eyes darted around, searched the shadows. "Talk like that will get you killed," Sal hissed in warning.

"I'm not afraid of Del Brio." And he wasn't, Johnny admitted silently. For the first time in his life, he wasn't afraid.

"Then you should be. You know what kind of man he is, Johnny. He sees shadows when there are none. He thinks you're out to get him, and he won't hesitate to kill you."

"Not if I kill him first."

Sal swore. "You're my oldest friend, Johnny. I'm godfather to your son. I'm begging you to listen to me. Forget about this plan of yours," Sal pleaded. "You're no match for Del Brio. Not only is he almost half your age, he's

dangerous, and he has the power of the family behind him.
His taking over for Carmine the way he did instead of
Ricky, it only made him more dangerous. For you to even
think of taking him on would be suicide.'' He placed a
hand on Johnny's shoulder. "Let it go, Johnny. Forget
what I told you about Frank ordering that drug. It's too
late to help Isadora now. And she wouldn't want you to
do something stupid that could get you killed.''

Johnny shook off Sal's hand and whirled around to face
his friend. "You think I really care what happens to me
now?''

"You should,'' Sal told him. "Frank isn't like your
brother, Carmine. He's ruthless. He'll kill you, Johnny.
He'll kill you without blinking an eye.''

"I told you, not if I kill him first. I intend to have my
vengeance. An eye for an eye.'' *Una vita per una vita.* A
life for a life, he added silently.

Sal looked furtively around them again. "We shouldn't
even be talking about this, not here. You know as well as
I do that the shadows have eyes and ears.''

"I don't care.''

"You should. Maybe you've lost Isadora and Haley, but
you've still got a son, Johnny. And Ricky's still part of
the family.''

"This doesn't have anything to do with Ricky,'' Johnny
said, and stared at Sal Nuccio, a man much like himself.
Someone who had been born into the life of corruption
and had followed the dictates of the ruling family all of
his sixty years. It wasn't the life he'd wanted for either of
his children. Haley had been smart enough to try to get
out. But instead of escaping, Ricky had used the skills he'd
learned as a marine to grow more entrenched in the family
business. It was one of his greatest regrets, Johnny admitted. Maybe if he could make things right now, find Haley

and her little girl and take out Frank Del Brio, Ricky would finally break away, lead an honest life, the life that he and Isadora had wanted for their son. "This is between me and Del Brio."

"Do you really think that will matter to Del Brio?"

It would, Johnny promised. Just as soon as he found Haley and his granddaughter, he'd make sure that Del Brio never hurt anyone in his family again.

He was being a real bastard, Justin admitted. Though she'd tried to hide it, he hadn't missed Angela's wince before she had lowered her gaze. Disgusted with himself, he didn't have to stare into those blue eyes of hers to know that he'd hurt her. He could remember all too well that bruised look she got when he'd hurt her feelings in the past. Hell, he'd been haunted by the memory of those sad blue eyes of hers for more years than he'd wanted to admit. Just as the woman herself had haunted every corner of his life for the past five years.

When she'd first walked out on him, he hadn't been all that sure he would get over her. Those first few weeks had been a real bitch. But eventually time and burying himself in work had helped to dull the pain.

He'd gotten over Angela Mason. Or at least he'd thought he had gotten over her—until she'd walked through the doors of the hospital for tonight's party. And now in less than an hour after seeing her again, she had him all tied up in knots.

He didn't want her here. At least he'd been honest with her about that. What he hadn't told her, and had no intention of telling her, was that he didn't want her here because he didn't want to remember what it was like to be with her, to hold her, to touch her, to taste her.

Justin shoved a hand through his hair. Dammit, he didn't

need this kind of grief. Not now. Not when he had so much on his plate trying to train a rookie deputy, finding the judge's murderer, dealing with Del Brio and finding that missing baby. Having Angela show up now would only screw up his head, something he could ill afford at the moment. She would simply have to go, Justin reasoned.

"Justin? Are you all right?" she asked, and touched his arm.

Justin stilled even though his body went on full alert. Angela had always had that affect on him, from day one when he'd first seen her at the police academy. With a look, the brush of her fingers, one little word, she set off some primal instinct in him—an instinct that had caused him to practically bully her into marrying him because his need to bind her to him had been so strong. It was also an instinct that invariably led them to bed where the sex had been mind-blowing. And thinking about having sex with Angela was the worst thing he could do. He jammed his fists into his pockets to keep from reaching for her as that instinct kicked in again now. "Go away, Mason," he told her, his voice deliberately hard. "Just go away."

"I'm sorry," she said softly, in much the same way she had that day when she'd told him that their marriage wasn't working and that she was taking the job in San Antonio. "Truly, I am." There was regret in her voice and in her expression as she turned away from him.

It was like déjà vu, Justin thought, watching her walk away from him. Five years ago, he'd been a lovesick fool. He had swallowed his pride and pleaded with her to stay. When she'd refused and kept right on packing, he'd resorted to threats and then anger. But nothing had worked. She'd walked away from him, anyway. He'd almost gone to San Antonio after her—until what little pride he had left kicked in and kept him from making a bigger fool of himself. And it was that same stubborn pride that kept him from going after her now. Pride and the fact that he wasn't the same lovesick fool he'd been all those years ago.

But not even pride could stop him from tracking her movements as she crossed the room. And pride didn't have a thing to do with that kick in his gut when he saw her hook up with Ricky Mercado again. Irritated with both Angela and himself, Justin marched over to the bar.

"What can I get for you, Sheriff?"

Justin glanced up at the petite redhead he recognized from the Lone Star Country Club. "Erica, isn't it?"

"That's right. Erica Clawson," she replied, and gave him a smile that was a shade too saccharine for his taste. Not at all like Angela's warm smile, he thought, then chastised himself at once for thinking of her again.

"You got anything besides soda pop and wine back there, Erica?"

"What did you have in mind?" she asked, tipping her head to one side flirtatiously.

"Whiskey, neat," Justin said, choosing to ignore the come-on. Besides the fact that he wasn't interested, he'd heard noises that little Miss Butter-wouldn't-melt-in-her-mouth Erica Clawson had been keeping company of late with Frank Del Brio.

"Here you go." She slid the glass toward him, gave him a soulful look.

"Thanks," he murmured, taking the drink and turning his back to her. He tossed the whiskey back, welcomed the fiery burn down his throat and the way it spread like acid in his stomach. Like radar, his gaze sought out Angela. She was still with Ricky, their heads bent close together, the two of them in what appeared to be a deep conversation. Justin tightened his fist around the glass, wishing it was Ricky Mercado's throat. Agitated with himself for letting her get to him, he turned away and slapped the empty glass down on the bar.

"Another one?"

"Yeah." He had the glass halfway to his mouth, was already anticipating the fiery kick, when he noted Ricky leading Angela toward the exit. In the blink of an eye, he had an image of Ricky sliding into the car next to Angela, reaching across the seat to touch her face, to taste her mouth.

Unable to shake the image, Justin slapped his glass on the counter. Ignoring the slosh of whiskey, he started to get up and follow them when a firm male hand clamped down on his shoulder. "You might want to let your head and your blood cool before you go after her," Hawk Wainwright told him.

Justin narrowed his eyes, stared into the sun-darkened face of his half brother. Although he'd been aware of his father's long-ago affair with the Native American beauty who had been Hawk's mother, only recently had he and Hawk acknowledged the blood bond between them. The relationship was tenuous at best, and there were old wounds that needed time to heal. But tonight he was feeling too edgy to mince words with Hawk and blurted out, "That a Native American thing? You being able to tell what's going on inside a man's head?"

Hawk smiled, something Justin realized that he could rarely recall the other man doing. "More like an observation."

"Then you have some pretty amazing observation skills," Justin told him, and went back to nursing his drink.

Hawk declined a drink with a shake of his head and urged Justin away from the bar. "Not all that remarkable. I remembered that the woman you watch with hot eyes was once your wife."

"*Was* being the operative word here. We're divorced now, have been for more than five years."

"There are still strong feelings between you."

"Not the kind you're talking about," Justin assured him. "Whatever Angela and I had ended a long time ago."

"Who are you trying to convince? Me? Or yourself?"

"Neither. And since discussing my ex isn't exactly one of my favorite things to do, I'd just as soon drop the subject."

"Whatever you say."

Noting his brother's stoic gaze, Justin asked, "What?"

"I was just wondering if you'll be able to shut off your feelings for her as easily."

"What are you talking about?" Justin asked.

"I'm talking about the green-eyed monster that eats at your heart now as you think of your woman with another man."

"She's not my woman anymore," Justin insisted.

"But you want her to be. Or am I wrong?"

Justin gritted his teeth and met Hawk's steady gaze, refusing to answer the question even to himself. "It's not that simple."

"It's not that complicated, either."

"You don't understand," Justin told him.

"Maybe I understand far better than you realize. I may have Apache blood in my veins, but I also have Wainwright blood," Hawk explained. "I know what it is to want something, to want someone, until that want becomes a hunger that burns like fire in the belly. And I know what it is to feel the steel talons of pride digging deep into the soul until it's pride that rules one's tongue and actions instead of what's here," he said, thumping a fist against his heart.

But Justin didn't need to be reminded that Hawk had

spent much of his life wanting to be accepted, to be acknowledged as Archy Wainwright's son and not merely the bastard half-breed who had been at the root of Archy and Kate's divorce. Even now Justin couldn't help but feel a measure of shame at the callous way their father had treated Hawk. Justin also couldn't help but feel shame of his own, as well as regret, for not doing more to bridge the gap that had long existed between Hawk and the rest of the Wainwrights. Not only had Hawk lost all those years, but he and the rest of his family had lost, too.

"I nearly let pride cost me the thing I wanted most—Jenny," Hawk told him, referring to the interior designer who'd recently become his wife. "Don't make the same mistake I almost did and let pride cost you what you want most."

"I wouldn't drink that if I were you," Audrey Lou Cox told him the following morning as Justin prepared to take a sip of the coffee he'd just poured himself.

"Why? You lace it with arsenic so you can have my job?" Justin teased the stern-faced secretary he'd inherited along with the sheriff's office. Somewhere between the age of fifty and eighty, the woman had served more than twenty-five years under a string of Mission Creek sheriffs. "You don't have to kill me to get the job, you know. I keep telling you, the folks in this town would vote you in over me in a heartbeat."

"And why on earth would I want your job?"

"You'd get to wear a badge," Justin offered.

The woman didn't even crack a smile. "I got all the jewelry I want already. Besides, somebody has to keep this place running, and it don't look like that person's going to be you if you keep spending all your time traipsing from one end of the county to the other."

"You got me there," Justin told her, and took a sniff of the coffee.

"Heard there was quite a turnout for the dedication of the maternity ward at the hospital last night."

"Yeah, I think half the county was there. You should have come," Justin told her.

Audrey Lou sniffed. "And why would I want to spend my evening eating puny little sandwiches, drinking watered-down punch and listening to long-winded speeches from politicians when I could eat a nice hot meal, put my feet up and watch my favorite crime show?"

"When you put it like that, I guess I can't think of any reason." Justin certainly wished he had skipped the ceremony last night. If he had, he wouldn't have seen Angela and might have actually managed to get some sleep. As it was, he'd barely slept a wink. Soured by thoughts of Angela, he stared at the inky contents of his cup. "So what's wrong with this stuff?"

"That boy you hired made it about an hour ago, and he put enough grinds in the thing to make six pots."

"Strong, huh?"

"I wasn't about to drink any to find out. I was waiting for a free minute so's I could come in here and throw the stuff out and make a fresh pot. But since you're here, you can do it. I've got work to do." And on that note, she turned and exited the little kitchen.

Desperate for the caffeine, Justin took a sip. And he nearly gagged. Audrey Lou had been right. While he generally liked his coffee black and strong, he drew the line at drinking brew that could pass for tar. Not that the extra caffeine would hurt, Justin admitted as he went about the business of measuring coffee grinds and water. After his chat with Hawk, he'd driven around and thought about what his brother had said. Hawk's remark about pride had hit close to the mark. Too close.

More than once after Angela had left him, he'd missed her so much that he'd almost gone after her—until pride had kicked in and he'd abandoned the idea. Hawk had also hit the nail on the head about his feelings for Angela. Seeing her with Ricky had made him jealous, he admitted. And it had been that jealousy that had been the driving force behind his anger toward her last night.

As he waited for the coffee to finish dripping, Justin grimaced as he remembered swinging by the town's two hotels, intent on apologizing to her for his behavior. Only there had been no Angela Mason registered at either establishment. He'd gone home to the ranch wondering if she'd driven back to San Antonio or if she was spending the night with Ricky Mercado. And it had been thoughts of Angela with Ricky that had kept him awake most of the night. Sometime during the early hours of the morning, he'd finally fallen asleep, only to dream about her. The way she'd looked at him on their wedding day in the small church when she'd pledged her love. The sweet, shy smile that curved her mouth on those mornings when he'd awakened her with a kiss. The way she'd gasped his name as he filled her when they'd made love. The way he'd felt when he'd been inside her.

Justin scrubbed a hand down his face. Was it any wonder he'd awakened with a dull, throbbing ache in his head and a painful hard-on for his ex-wife?

"Sheriff, the mayor's on the line for you and your sister Rose wants you to call her, something about a dinner party," Audrey Lou told him.

"Thanks," Justin said, and forgoing the coffee, he headed for his office.

More than an hour later when Justin hung up the phone,

the dull throbbing in his head had escalated into a bruiser of a headache. And he wasn't at all sure how much of it had to do with his sleepless night or the workload. Rubbing the muscles at the base of his neck, Justin sat back and stared at the piles of paperwork and messages that covered his desk.

Maybe now was a good time for that coffee, Justin decided. After pouring himself a mug of the no-longer-fresh brew, he went back to his desk and began sorting through the endless reports and files and messages. For a county that he had always considered small by Texas standards, Mission Creek had certainly been a hotbed of activity lately, he thought as he sorted the open case files jammed with reports.

He opened the file containing a report on the abandoned baby girl named Lena who had been found on the Lone Star Country Club's golf course last year—the same little girl who had since been kidnapped and he had yet to find. Picking up the snapshot of the smiling sweetheart that Josie Carson had taken only days before the kidnapping occurred, he traced her tiny face with his fingertip. Once again he felt that familiar pang as he thought of the little angel being snatched from the Carsons. And on the heels of that ache came frustration and anger. Anger with the person who had taken her. Anger with himself for failing to find her. Whooshing out a breath, Justin put the photo aside and reminded himself that as sheriff he couldn't afford to let his emotions become involved. Anger and resentment weren't going to help him find Lena. Only solid skills and dogged determination would do that.

And he would find her, he promised himself. He had to. Because it sure didn't look like the FBI was going to be able to do it. If anything they only hampered his own efforts.

Thumbing through the file, he scanned the DNA tests that had been run on select members of the country club and the final paternity test that had revealed Luke Callaghan as the girl's father. He couldn't even begin to imagine how Luke must feel, returning home from some sort of business trip out of the country during which he'd been blinded. And then discovering he not only had a daughter he knew nothing about, but that the girl had been kidnapped. What still puzzled him was how Luke could be the baby's father and not know who the mother was. Justin rubbed a hand along his jaw. Had it been any other man, he'd have sworn the guy was lying. But not Luke Callaghan. He didn't doubt for a second that Luke had told him the truth.

For the next twenty minutes Justin fielded calls while he went over the notes on Lena's kidnapping. And once again he found himself with more questions than answers. Closing the file, he picked up the next folder in the stack and sighed at the sight of the label that read "Bridges, Carl—Murder Case." He didn't even have to open the file on this one because he could recite the details of Judge Carl Bridges's murder from memory. The fact that the case remained unsolved gnawed at him almost as much as Lena's kidnapping. As he made a note to follow up with a call to Dylan Bridges that evening, he snatched up the ringing telephone.

When he hung up the phone fifteen minutes later, Justin reached for the next file, which was not only the oldest working file in his office, but the thickest by far because it contained information on the Mercado crime family. Since Carmine Mercado's death eight months ago and the shifting of power within the organization to Frank Del Brio, Justin hadn't been able to shake the feeling that something was brewing within the family ranks. From all accounts, Johnny Mercado had been acting strangely of late. That scene he'd witnessed between Johnny and Del Brio last night attested to that fact. But it was more than that, he admitted. There was something about that look in Johnny's eyes, his sudden spirit, that nagged at him like a splinter under his skin. Maybe now that Ricky was back in town, he should pay the younger Mercado a visit, ask him what was going on between his father and Del Brio just so Ricky knew that the sheriff's office had an eye on them.

And what if Angela is with him?

Justin gritted his teeth at the taunting voice in his head and shut his eyes to block out the images of Angela with Ricky last night.

"Sheriff," Audrey Lou called from the doorway, her voice impatient. "Something wrong with your hearing, son? Bobby's on the line for you. Said it's important."

"Wainwright." Justin all but barked out his name as he grabbed the telephone.

"I'm afraid I've got bad news, boss."

Just what he needed, Justin thought. "All right, spit it out."

"I lost Del Brio."

Justin swore. "What happened?"

"He pulled a switch on me."

"I told you not to let him out of your sight."

"And I didn't," Bobby contended. "I tailed him to Mercado Brothers Paving and Contracting this morning just like you told me. And I'm positive it was Del Brio that I followed when he left there. I stayed with him all morning through this string of back roads outside of Mission Creek and all through Goldenrod—even down some private road—until he went back to his spread. Only when he reached his place and got out of the truck, it wasn't him. It wasn't Del Brio. It was a dude dressed up just like him, and the truck was a dead ringer for the one Del Brio was driving."

"If you were following him the whole time, how could he make the switch?" Justin demanded.

"The only thing I can think of is that he arranged to have the dummy driver in a look-alike truck waiting around one of those curves. Because I swear that's the only time the man was ever out of my sight."

Trying to contain his frustration, Justin wiped a hand down his face. He'd ordered the tail on Del Brio after that exchange with Johnny last night—in part because he didn't want a full-scale war erupting between the Mercados and Del Brio and his men, and in part because there was a rumor on the street that a big deal was about to go down.

"I know I screwed up. I'm sorry, Sheriff."

"Don't sweat it," Justin told the kid. "It happens to the best of us. Del Brio didn't get where he is because of his brains. He's got the instincts of a cat. Evidently he spotted your tail. I just wish I knew where he was going that he felt the need to shake you."

"You want me to see if I can pick him up again?" Bobby asked.

"No. We've got too much to do. We can't afford to spend any more time playing games with the likes of Del Brio. Come on back to the office. The phone's been ringing off the hook all morning, and I swear the paperwork is multiplying faster than rabbits."

"Boss, there's something else you should know," Bobby told him.

Justin paused, sensing he wasn't going to like what his deputy had to say. "What?"

"I wasn't the only one tailing Del Brio. So was Johnny Mercado."

Justin scowled, not at all happy to learn his own instincts had been right. Something was brewing between Johnny and Del Brio, and whatever it was, it could only mean trouble. "I was afraid of that."

"You think Johnny plans to fight Del Brio for control of the family?"

"No." At least Justin hoped that wasn't the case because Johnny, even with this newfound spirit he'd shown, didn't stand a chance against a ruthless thug like Del Brio. His son, Ricky, however, was another story. "But something's going on, and I intend to find out what it is."

"You going to go see Johnny? Try to talk to him again?"

"No. The old man is playing his cards close to the vest. I was planning to pay Ricky a visit later. But I think maybe I'll drive out to the Mercado place and have that little talk with Ricky now. I'll see you when I get back."

After hanging up the phone, Justin shoved away from his desk and headed out of his office. He grabbed his hat and paused in front of Audrey Lou's desk. "Bobby's on his way in, and I'm going out to Johnny Mercado's place. I need you to hold down the fort for me until I get back."

The woman didn't so much as bat an eye. "What do you want me to tell your sister? Rose has called for you twice already."

"Tell her I'll call her when I get back."

But when Justin got back, after striking out on catching either Ricky or his father at their place near Goldenrod or the Mercado Brothers Paving, Audrey Lou was manning two phone lines and Bobby was taking down Mrs. Elkinson's weekly complaint about the randy bull on the neighboring homestead bothering her milk cows. Wanting no part of that scene, Justin reached for the stack of phone messages Audrey Lou held out to him and headed for his office when Audrey Lou hung up the phone.

"That was Dylan Bridges's office returning your call."

Justin looked up from the messages he'd been skimming. "He still in his office?"

"No. That was his assistant who called to say he's tied up until late this afternoon, wanted to know if he could call you at home tonight. I said I didn't see why not since you don't do much of anything but work and sleep, anyway."

Justin ignored the dig at his lack of a social life. "Anything else I need to know?"

"Nothing except that you've got yourself a visitor. I put her in your office to wait."

"Damn! She's here already?" Justin asked, assuming it was his sister. Granted he'd called her from his vehicle and agreed to meet with her back at his office, but he'd told her he needed at least an hour. Evidently Rose decided not to wait. Which seemed to be par for the course where his younger sister was concerned this past year—starting with her running off to Aunt Beth's in New York and shocking everyone when she came back with the news that she'd married Matt Carson of all people and was expecting his child. While the wedding hadn't sat well with either the Carsons or the Wainwrights, the early arrival of the baby and the illness that had threatened both Rose and the baby had not only scared everyone but it had eased some of the tensions between the two families. However, his sister didn't appear to be content with the strained truce. No, now that the danger was past, the darned female seemed hell-bent on ending the feud between the two families that had spanned seventy-six years. And for some reason, she had decided he was to be a key player in her fence-mending plans.

"You knew she was coming?"

"Sure. I talked to her about twenty minutes ago and told her to come by. Of course, I told her to give me an hour to return some of these calls. Obviously, she didn't hear that part," Justin said, but he wasn't really irritated. He both liked and loved his sister, and he especially liked getting a chance to see his nephew.

"Well, you might have seen fit to tell me she was coming," Audrey Lou sniffed. "And she might have told me you was expecting her instead of just saying she needed to see you and that she didn't mind waiting."

"She probably thought you knew," Justin said, not wanting Audrey Lou angry with Rose. "She got the baby with her?"

"You mean to tell me she's got herself a baby?"

Justin frowned. Obviously his sister Rose wasn't the woman waiting in his office because everyone in Mission Creek, for that matter, half of Texas, knew about the recent birth of Wayne Matthew Carson and the danger that both the baby and Rose had faced. It had been the near loss of his sister's life and the birth of the baby that had prompted Archy Wainwright to begin making amends with the Carsons, Hawk and even with his ex-wife, Kate. From what he'd seen the previous night, Justin suspected his parents were well on their way to a reconciliation—three decades after their divorce.

"Well, she never said a thing about any baby."

"Audrey Lou, why don't we start over? I take it that that's not my sister Rose waiting in my office."

Audrey Lou blinked, her big brown eyes magnified by the wire-rimmed glasses, reminding him of an owl. "Who said anything about Rose?"

"No one. My mistake. So who—"

The phone rang and she grabbed it. "Lone Star County Sheriff's Office. Audrey Lou speaking."

Justin strove for patience as he waited for Audrey Lou to finish the call. She'd no sooner hung up when the phone rang again. When she started to reach for it, Justin grabbed the receiver. "Lone Star County Sheriff's Office. Hold on a minute. Now," he said after punching the hold button on the phone, "who am I going to find waiting in my office?"

The woman gave him a look so stern, he felt like an errant schoolboy who needed to apologize for his poor manners and not the county's sheriff and her boss.

"Thought you just said you was expecting her," Audrey Lou told him with a sniff.

"Audrey Lou..."

"It's your wife."

Three

"Ex-wife," Justin corrected. "We're divorced."

Angela tensed at the sound of Justin's voice just outside the door. Despite a sleepless night and the lecture she'd given herself this morning, she was every bit as anxious at the prospect of working with Justin now as she had been when she'd agreed to take the assignment. But even if she could convince the FBI and the police chief to release her from her agreement to work the case, her conscience would never allow her to walk away. That meant she had to face Justin now and try to make him see that this wasn't about them, but about the welfare of a missing little girl.

Bracing herself, Angela turned away from the window she'd been staring out of and watched Justin saunter into the room with that same purposeful stride she'd noted the first time she'd set eyes on him. His air of self-confidence had always fascinated her. Perhaps because she'd had so little self-confidence growing up and throughout their marriage. It had only been in the past few years that she'd begun to feel more sure of herself.

She hadn't been mistaken in her impressions of him last night, she mused. Age hadn't diminished Justin's looks in any way. If anything, he was even more handsome in the slate-gray sheriff's uniform than he had been the previous evening in the expensive suit. The silver badge pinned on his shirt gleamed beneath the office lights. With his service revolver strapped to his waist and the Stetson in his hand, he could have stepped right off the pages of some slick magazine showcasing lawmen hunks of the Southwest. Right down to the forbidding scowl on his face. She wasn't sure if that grim set of his lips was due to her presence or to Audrey Lou's reference to her as his wife. Probably both, she decided.

"For what it's worth, I did try to explain that I was your ex-wife," Angela told him. "And the truth is, I was surprised that Mrs. Cox even remembered me, let alone the fact that we were once married."

"Audrey Lou's got a memory like a computer chip," Justin informed her as he made his way over to his desk. "The woman doesn't forget anything when it comes to the citizens of Lone Star County. And there's very little that goes on in this town that she doesn't know about."

The mention of how everyone knew everyone's business made her smile. "I guess I forgot what a small town Mission Creek can be at times," Angela offered.

"It's not all that small of a town. But then I suppose that depends on the person and what they want."

Angela knew it was a dig at her because she'd opted to move to the big city of San Antonio instead of remaining in Mission Creek and trying to salvage their marriage. Since Justin had refused to admit five years ago that the real problems at the core of their marriage had little to do with their careers and everything to do with their relationship, she doubted that rehashing her reasons for leaving would serve any purpose. Deciding to let the remark pass, she said, "Well, I'm sorry, anyway, about the confusion and any embarrassment it caused."

"The confusion was of my own making. I thought you were Rose," he explained as he dropped his hat on the corner of the paper-laden desk. "As for embarrassing me, you didn't."

"I'm glad. That I didn't embarrass you, I mean," she added nervously. "But I suppose I should have made sure Mrs. Cox understood."

"She understood, all right. But whether we'd been divorced five years or fifty, it wouldn't have made a difference to Audrey Lou. As far as she's concerned, you're still my wife."

"I take it she's not too fond of divorce?"

He made a dismissive sound. "That's like asking if water is wet. The woman thinks the only time a marriage ends is when one of the pair dies. As far as she's concerned, 'until death do us part' means just that. And since she's been married to the same man for over forty years, I guess I can understand why she feels the way she does."

"I suppose so," Angela offered, feeling more awkward by the second. "The idea of two people spending their lives together, well, it is a lovely sentiment."

"I guess that would depend on the two people and whether or not the marriage works out. In our case, it didn't."

While he didn't say "because of you," Angela could almost hear the words he'd left unsaid. Uncomfortable, she stared down at her clasped hands a moment. She'd long ago accepted blame for the failure of their marriage. Looking back now, she could see so clearly that their marriage had stood little chance of succeeding. How could it? Even without the added strain caused by Justin's family's objections to his choice of her as a wife and her inability to conceive a child, the marriage had *mistake* written all over it from the start. Someone like her wasn't meant to be anyone's wife—especially not the wife of a man like Justin Wainwright. Yet knowing that, she'd been too blinded by her love for him to say no when he'd proposed. And because she'd been selfish, she had married him and had made them both miserable.

Shoving aside the sad thoughts, Angela lifted her gaze again and found Justin's eyes on her. And as had so often been the case during their marriage, those cool green eyes of his gave away nothing of what he was thinking. Growing more stressed by the minute, she decided the best thing to do was to get this over with and tell Justin the reason she was there. "Justin, I—"

"Listen, Angela, I—"

He chuckled.

So did she. And she let out a breath as some of the tension eased. Even though she realized that she was simply delaying the fireworks that her announcement was sure to set off, she said, "Go ahead. You first."

"I was about to say that considering how our conversation ended last night, I'm surprised to find you here."

"I realize I should have called you first, instead of just showing up here like this," she said, feeling defensive. "But to be honest, I wasn't sure you'd agree to see me. So I decided to just take my chances and come by."

A hint of red burnished the sharp lines of his cheeks. "Yeah, well, can't say that I blame you. I didn't do such a good job of handling things last night. Seeing you...well, it took me by surprise. I was out of line."

Angela knew what a proud, stubborn man Justin was, so the unexpected admission that he was wrong left her reeling. She opened her mouth, then closed it, unsure what to say.

It was Justin who spoke. "Anyway, I apologize for the way I acted last night."

"Apology accepted," she finally managed to say.

"I'd have apologized to you sooner, but I couldn't find you at either of the hotels."

"I didn't stay at a hotel."

"Yeah, I figured that much," he said, a slight edge in his voice. "And I don't suppose you drove all the way back to San Antonio last night and then turned around and drove back here this morning."

"No, I didn't."

His lips tightened at her response, but he made no comment. And the short break in the tension between them evaporated as quickly as it had come. Once again Angela rued her decision to accept this assignment. "May I?" she asked, motioning to the chair in front of his desk.

"Suit yourself," Justin replied, and once she was seated, he sat down in the black swivel chair behind the battered mahogany desk.

Striving to smooth the way for the bombshell she intended to drop on him, she said, "For what it's worth, I didn't make the decision to attend the dedication ceremony at the hospital until the last minute. Otherwise, I would have called and warned you that I'd be there."

"As you pointed out last night, I don't own Mission Creek and you're no longer my wife. Where you go and who you go there with isn't any of my business."

The cool reminder stung. "True. But considering that we share a history, telling you that I'd planned to be there would have been the courteous thing to do. I'm sorry that I didn't."

"Fine. Now that we've both got our apologies out of the way, you're going to have to excuse me because I need to get back to work." Without waiting for her answer, he reached for the stack of mail in his incoming basket. "You can just leave the door open on your way out."

His dismissal stunned Angela almost as much as it irritated her. "Believe it or not, I didn't come here because

I felt I owed you an apology or because I expected one from you.''

"Whatever you say. But I can't imagine anything else we have to discuss and I really do need to get back to work." Obviously believing the matter was at an end, he went back to perusing the papers in front of him.

Angered by his arrogance, Angela shoved to her feet. "Aren't you even the least bit interested in knowing why I'm here?''

"Not particularly," he told her without so much as a glance in her direction.

Suddenly Angela's patience snapped. She came around the desk, slapped her hands down on the papers in front of him. "Dammit, Wainwright, look at me!''

Slowly he lifted his gaze to hers. And the heat in those green eyes sucked the breath right out of her. "All right, Mason. I'm looking.''

Angela's pulse jumped. Her head began to spin, and she tried to remember exactly what it was she'd been about to say to him.

"As much as I enjoy looking at you, Angel, I'm pressed for time. So if you've got something on your mind, I suggest you spit it out.''

Angela felt a sharp pang at Justin's use of the pet name he'd given her during the early days of their courtship. She started to speak, but her throat seemed impossibly tight, and she closed her mouth again. She couldn't think about the past now, she reminded herself.

"You going to tell me why you're all worked up? Or am I supposed to guess?''

Angela swallowed, tried to clear her head. But before she could answer him, he shoved away from the desk and walked away from her, only to whirl around and march back over to stand in front of her.

"Since you seem to be at a loss for words, why don't I tell you why I think you're here," he began, his mouth hard, his expression even harder. "I think you're here because you want a little payback."

"Payback?" Angela repeated.

"Yeah, payback. I gave you a rough time about the divorce, and last night you decided to pay me back by flaunting your relationship with Ricky Mercado in front of me and everyone else in this town. Well, it worked. I blew my cool last night when I saw the two of you together. But that was last night. It isn't going to work today. You're not going to be able to use Mercado to push my buttons."

"Is that really what you believe? That I would do such a thing?"

The look he gave her could have melted ice. "You saying it isn't? Are you going to stand there and deny that you wanted to rub my nose in the fact that you're sleeping with Mercado?"

Taken aback by his accusation, Angela remained speechless for several moments. While Justin had never liked nor understood her friendship with Ricky, she had always believed it was because of the Mercado's family business and Ricky's ties to organized crime. It had never crossed her mind that Justin might have seen Ricky as a romantic rival. Staring at the man she'd given her heart to so long ago, she wondered how she could have been so blind. "You're jealous of Ricky," she murmured more to herself than to him as realization dawned. Which made no sense—especially now when Justin had all but said he wanted nothing to do with her.

"The hell I am!" He jammed a hand through his hair, paced the length of the room. "I just don't like seeing you hooked up with a scumbag like Mercado."

"But you're wrong. Ricky and I—" She swallowed,

deciding she needed to be blunt. "Justin, I'm not sleeping with Ricky."

He whipped around, pinned her with those stormy eyes. "You expect me to believe that when I know damn well that you didn't stay in a hotel last night?"

"Believe whatever you want," she told him while she tried to convince herself that what Justin thought about her didn't matter. "But the truth is I didn't spend the night with Ricky. I spent the night in my own bed."

Justin narrowed his eyes. "That's quite a trick since you've already said you didn't go back to San Antonio."

"But I did return to my condo. Or perhaps I should say to my new condo—the one that I'm leasing, which happens to be located just outside of Goldenrod and is the place where I spent the night in my own bed, alone."

Justin marched back over to her. "You're lying."

"Why would I lie about something like that? It's easy enough for you to check. I moved into the place two days ago."

"Why?" he demanded, eyeing her warily.

"Because I didn't want to be living out of a suitcase while I'm working here."

Justin's head snapped up at that. "Working here? On what?"

"Finding the baby that was kidnapped from the Carsons' ranch. The FBI said they'd had a request for my help."

"The hell they did," Justin shouted. "There's no way that I asked for you, and if anyone in Lone Star County had, I'd know about it."

"Evidently, someone did," Angela replied, recalling her conversation with her FBI contact and her dismay upon hearing no one had advised Justin about her involvement in the case.

Justin snatched up the phone. "Audrey Lou, get the person we had as a contact with the FBI on the phone for me. Now." When he slammed the receiver back down, he said, "I'll speak with the Bureau and have them take you off the case."

"I don't want off the case."

"No offense, Mason, but I don't need your help."

"No offense taken, Wainwright. But you obviously do need my help. So does the FBI. From what I understand, the little girl's been missing for almost three months now. And you and I both know that in a kidnapping every day that goes by without her being found makes the chances of getting her back even slimmer."

"I'm well aware of that fact."

"Then maybe if you'd get past your anger at me, you'd see that you're not getting anywhere on your own. I can help you find her, Justin," she said, trying to ease the tension so that working together wouldn't be more difficult than it had to be. "We can help each other find her."

"I prefer working alone."

His rebuff hit her like a slap. But Angela reminded herself she had a job to do—to find the missing little girl—and that meant she didn't have the luxury of running away and licking her wounds. "Suit yourself," she told him, and picked up the handbag she'd placed next to the chair. She walked toward the door, paused and turned back to face him. "But whether you like it or not, I'm on this case now, too. I'd prefer working with you because I think our chances of finding her are better. But I'll work alone if I have to. It's up to you. Either way, I don't intend to leave until I find that little girl."

"And how are you planning to do that? Hope that one of your dreams tells you where to find her?"

Angela stiffened. During their marriage, Justin had always skirted the issue of her psychic abilities and chalked up her uncanny accuracy as woman's intuition. And because the memory of her family's rejection had been so painful, she'd allowed him to do so. Not anymore. "I intend to use any and all means available to me to find her—including my psychic abilities. I've already made arrangements to visit with Flynt and Josie Carson tomorrow, and I've requested copies of the Bureau's files on the case. I'll want to take a look at your files, too."

Justin shot across the room, slapped his hand against the door she'd started to open and sent it slamming shut again. "Let's get something straight here, Mason. This is my case. Mine."

"Then I suggest you have that chat with the Bureau because they don't see it that way. Now, get out of my way," she said evenly, and reached for the doorknob. When he made no move to allow her to leave, Angela looked up at his hard face, noting the grim set of his mouth.

A muscle ticked in his jaw as he stared down at her. "I've been searching for that little girl for months and have hit one dead end after another. So have the feds. You think just because you've had some success tracking down a few missing people, you can waltz in here and tell me to turn over my files? That I'll let you take over my case?"

Angela sighed. She didn't bother telling him it wasn't his case—that officially it was a federal matter. She knew Justin well enough to know that once a case was his, it remained his. Not even the head of the FBI himself would be able to convince the stubborn man otherwise. While he might have made noises about cooperating with the FBI, Justin would have continued to work the case on his own. "It doesn't have to be this way, Justin. I've offered to work with you. I'm still willing to work with you on this case.''

''Right. You expect me to put my faith in the woman who walked out on me? Better yet, I'm supposed to tell the Carsons to put their faith and hopes of finding Lena into some psychic mumbo jumbo?''

Angela flinched at the barb. Her father had made her an outcast in her own family, subjecting her to brutal lashings of both his tongue and his belt, claiming it was the devil that enabled her to see things others couldn't. It had taken her years to learn to control her own tongue, to not let others know about her visions. But no matter how hard she had tried, sooner or later she would slip and earn her father's wrath. She hadn't thought it possible for anyone else's rejection ever to hurt her so much.

She'd been wrong.

Justin's jibe about her psychic abilities had been just as sharp, just as painful, as Horace Mason's leather belt had been all those years ago. Feeling the hot sting of tears behind her eyes, she blinked hard, determined not to cry in front of him.

''Angel.'' He said her name softly and started to touch her. ''I—''

''Don't,'' she said firmly. And because she felt so vulnerable, because she was afraid if he touched her the tears would start and not stop, she deliberately pulled open the door. ''I want copies of the files, Justin. I'll leave my number with Mrs. Cox. Have her call me when you have them ready and I'll come by to pick them up.'' Then before he could respond, she walked out the door without looking back.

Justin pulled his truck up to the curb across the street from Angela's condo and shut off the engine. After turning off his headlights, he sat in the darkness and stared at the place Angela had moved into several days earlier. Located on the outskirts of Goldenrod, it was one of the newer developments that had gone up in Lone Star County during the past year. There were six units in all, moderately priced and small by Texas standards. The limestone facade still had that new look about it. He supposed the small trees with their less-than-lush branches had been the developer's attempt at landscaping. They didn't even come close to the massive century-old oaks found on the Wainwright ranch. But he had to admit the rows of azaleas that lined the front of each unit and the walkways were a nice touch. No doubt it had been those rose-colored blooms that had sold Angela on the place. She'd always had a weakness for flowers, Justin remembered.

Instantly an image of Angela came to mind. As though it were only yesterday, he could see her kneeling in the flower beds of the ranch-style house they'd bought during the last year of their marriage, her cheeks streaked with dirt and those blue eyes of hers bright with excitement as she described how beautiful the azaleas would be when they bloomed, all the different flowers that would be pushing up through the earth when spring came. At the time he would have sworn the two of them would have grown old together in that house. They'd already started trying to have a baby and he'd envisioned kids racing through those flower beds with a couple of dogs at their heels. But a hard winter freeze had destroyed the azaleas, and by the time spring arrived, she'd been gone. A sharp pang stabbed through him at the memory. Justin found himself wondering now if the couple he'd sold the house to had ever seen any of Angela's flowers bloom or if they'd filled in the garden with concrete and made other use for the space.

When a light came on in an upstairs room of Angela's

condo, Justin blinked. Shaking off the memories and the melancholy that accompanied them, he shifted his attention to the window. Although the drapes had been drawn shut, evidently the fabric wasn't lined because there was no mistaking the feminine form on the other side of those curtains—or the fact that the woman was undressing.

He had no business watching this.

Justin knew it, told himself not to watch her. Yet he did watch—mesmerized by the sight of Angela's silhouette on the other side of that flimsy curtain unbuttoning her blouse, stepping out of her slacks. When she arched her back and unhooked her bra, Justin's mouth went dry.

"Damn!"

Gripping the steering wheel with both hands, he rested his head against it, all too aware of the burgeoning ache against his zipper. Disgusted with himself, he lifted his head and drew in a ragged breath. He was a grown man of thirty-five and the county's sheriff, not some adolescent at a peep show. Besides the fact that the woman was his ex-wife, she was a cop, he reminded himself. And it was the cop he'd come here to see, not the woman.

Determined to get things over with, he scooped up the file folder from the passenger seat of the truck and shoved open the vehicle's door. Gravel from the side of the road crunched beneath his boots as he crossed the street and started toward the condo. Judging from the darkened windows of the adjacent units, either Angela's neighbors turned in before nine o'clock or the other condos remained unoccupied. Suspecting the latter, Justin frowned at the idea of Angela or any woman living out here all alone.

Not smart, Mason, he thought. Isolation would make anyone more vulnerable, but especially a woman. Even a woman like her who had been trained to take care of herself wouldn't be immune to the dangers of living alone.

More than likely her training would only place her at greater risk, because knowing Angela as he did, he didn't doubt she would be inclined to handle any threat to her safety on her own.

Reminding himself that Angela Mason was no longer his responsibility, Justin approached the front door of the condo. And that was when he heard the music. Immediately he recognized the female harmony and country rock tune as the Dixie Chicks' newest release. He couldn't help but smile. His and Angela's tastes in music had always run along the same lines, and to this day he'd yet to meet another woman who could follow his lead on the dance floor so perfectly. Pushing the doorbell, he recalled the many times during their marriage when they'd been in the midst of some chore and a song would come on the radio. All he had to do was take her hand, and regardless of where they were or what they'd been doing, he'd dance her around the floor. In the living room, in the bedroom, even in the kitchen. And as they moved to the music's rhythm, as thigh brushed against thigh, as chest pressed against chest, they would invariably end up making love. Suddenly realizing the direction of his thoughts, Justin sobered and punched the bell again.

"Coming," Angela called out from somewhere inside the condo. The music stopped, more lights were flicked on, and moments later he heard the snick of the locks and she opened the door. "Justin?" She said his name in a breathless rush.

Justin stared at her. In one sweeping glance he took in everything about her. The tennis shoes. The threadbare gray sweatpants. The strip of flesh between her waistband and the frayed bottom of the ugly San Antonio Police Department sweatshirt. The arms left bare by the ripped-out shirtsleeves. The short tousle of dark curls along her neck and forehead. The flushed cheeks. The wariness in those haunting blue eyes.

Even void of feminine frills and makeup, Angela was still the most beautiful woman he'd ever set eyes on. And just looking at her still had the power to make him ache with wanting. Furious with himself for his weakness where she was concerned, he said, "I'd have thought a woman trained in law enforcement would have the sense to at least find out who's on the other side of a door before she opens it."

Angela's mouth thinned. She hiked up her chin, making him all too aware of that long, slender neck. "Not that it's any of your business, but I checked you out through the peephole before unlocking the door."

Now that she'd called his attention to it, Justin noted the hole in the door that he had failed to see when he'd first approached the condo. That he had missed it only drove home the fact that being anywhere near the woman tied him up in knots. The realization did nothing to improve his mood or alter his belief that working with her was a lousy idea.

"So did you drive out here at this time of night just to insult me? Or are you here for some other reason?"

The snap in her voice helped to clear his sex-charged brain. "I talked to the feds."

She crossed her arms, met his gaze evenly. "And?"

"They informed me that you'll be working independently of them, but keeping them apprised."

"That's right."

"Wrong. I've decided to take you up on your offer and have you work the kidnapping case with me on one condition."

She arched one dark brow. "Which is?"

"Nothing you learn about this case gets back to Ricky Mercado or anyone in his family."

Angela sighed. "I suppose that means you know that Ricky believes his sister, Haley, is still alive and that the baby belongs to her."

"I'm aware that there's a rumor to that effect. But so far that's all it is—a rumor. I don't have any proof to substantiate it," Justin informed her. "And until I do, I want the Mercados kept out of this. So do we have a deal?"

"All right. You have my word. I won't share any information with Ricky. Any other conditions?"

"No. That's it."

"I guess I should be grateful that you didn't try to have me taken off the case," she said, some of the stiffness going out of her. "When I left your office, I was sure you'd use your influence to have me removed."

"I tried," he admitted. "But I was voted down. The Carsons and Luke Callaghan were the ones who wanted you brought in."

"Luke Callaghan?"

"He's the little girl's father."

"But I thought... Then the mother..."

"Luke doesn't know who she is. It was a one-night stand. It's all in here," he said, and shoved the file at her. "There's a copy of everything I have on the case so far."

"Thanks," she said, taking the file from him. "But I would have come by your office to pick it up. You really didn't have to drive out here to bring it to me," she said, her expression softening, along with her voice.

He shrugged. "It was no big deal," he said, far too

aware of her for his own peace of mine. "I figured it was probably more detailed than what you got from the feds, and I knew you'd be itching to get started on working up a profile of the kidnapper, so I decided to drop it off."

"You're right. I am eager to get started. Thanks again for bringing it out."

Justin nodded. "Well, it's getting late. I'll go and let you get back to…to whatever it was you were doing."

She looked down at her clothes, then back up at him. "I was trying to make myself work out. And trust me, I was glad to have an excuse to stop," she informed him, and almost smiled. "Would you like to come in? I mean, if you have the time. I'd really like to talk about the case."

Justin hesitated. "I think you'll probably find the answers to any questions you have in there," he informed her, indicating the file folder she held.

"But what I won't find are your perceptions and theories about the kidnapping."

Justin remained silent, eyed her cautiously.

"You were always a good lawman, Justin, and a good judge of people. I'd be foolish not to take advantage of those facts and pick your brain a little. And while I realize you don't think much of my methods, I know you want to find that little girl every bit as much as I do. Getting your impressions could save me some time and might help us find her faster."

Her mention about his lack of respect for her abilities reminded him of his earlier behavior. Embarrassed, Justin rubbed the back of his neck. "Listen, about that crack I made earlier in my office, I—"

Suddenly headlights flooded the darkened road as a sedan turned onto the street. Justin fell silent as the vehicle pulled up and parked in the driveway of the corner condo, two units over from Angela's. Moments later laughter spilled out into the quiet night air as a man and woman exited the car. The giggles and laughter died as the pair engaged in a steamy, groping kiss that, in Justin's opinion, went on and on and on.

"They're newlyweds," Angela explained.

Just what he needed, Justin thought, as the passionate duo locked lips again and made no attempt to move it inside. It reminded Justin of the erotic thoughts that had been occupying his own mind since seeing Angela again.

"Maybe we should finish this conversation inside," she suggested when the man backed the woman up against the car and began to sample her neck.

Instead of arguing, Justin followed her into the condo and did his best to wipe away the memory of the early days of their own marriage. Like Angela's neighbors, the two of them hadn't been able to keep their hands off of each other, either.

"Would you like something to drink?" she offered after leading him into the den.

"Got any beer?"

Angela made a face. "Afraid not. I'm sure I have some wine, though. Or I can offer you iced tea."

"Tea's good."

"Still drink it sweetened and with lemon?"

"Yes," Justin replied, surprised that she'd remembered, because he'd been sure she would have done her best to forget everything about him. Still, he was pleased that she hadn't.

"Make yourself comfortable," she told him, motioning to the couch. "I'll only be a minute."

But instead of sitting down, Justin checked out the room. It was larger than he'd first suspected. The walls had been painted a basic white, but big leafy green plants had been tucked in strategic corners. And an eclectic mix of paintings provided splashes of color ranging from sunset orange to midnight blue. Two overstuffed chairs and a couch with an afghan tossed over one arm had been grouped around a marble-and-glass coffee table that was stacked high with books, photos and candles. Huge throw pillows lay on the floor in front of a stone fireplace and gave the room a cozy, welcoming touch. Angela may have moved in only a few days ago, but the place already had a lived-in, homey feel to it.

"Here we are," Angela said as she entered the room carrying a tray with a pitcher of tea, two glasses and a dish of extra lemons.

"Let me get that for you," Justin offered, and took the tray from her and placed it on the table.

"Thanks," she said politely.

Following her lead, Justin sat down. The awkward silence that had hung between them in his office earlier that day reared its head again while she poured them each a glass of tea. Worse, there was a sense of intimacy at being alone in the softly lit room with her that made him far too aware of Angela as a woman and the fact that he was still attracted to her. Determined to say his piece and get out of there as quickly as he could, Justin began, "About that crack I made back in the office about your dreams...I didn't mean it the way it sounded."

"So you think my psychic mumbo jumbo might actually help us to find the baby, after all?"

Justin grimaced. "Don't put words in my mouth, Mason. Just because I don't buy into the psychic stuff doesn't mean I don't recognize that you're good at your job. You are. I doubt there's another profiler in the country who's better. I'm sorry if it sounded otherwise."

She arched her brow and watched him over the rim of her glass. "Two apologies from you in one day? That must be a record."

Shame had heat climbing his neck. "I don't usually need to apologize," he said defensively. "And I try not to make a habit of offending people, particularly women."

"Then it must be me," she said, a hint of unhappiness in her voice. "Apparently I bring out the worst in you."

"Maybe we just bring out the worst in each other."

"Maybe we do," she conceded, and stared down into her glass of tea as though it held all the answers to life's mysteries.

She looked so unhappy, so alone, he was tempted to reach out, tip up her chin and rub his thumb along the curve of those sad lips. Realizing the dangerous direction of his thoughts, Justin stood abruptly and stalked over to the fireplace—away from Angela. Away from temptation. He remained silent for one beat, then another, and only when he'd marshaled the wild thoughts she had set off in him did he turn around to face her. "This isn't going to work."

She tipped her head to the side, gave him a perplexed look. "What isn't going to work?"

"Us. You and me. There's no way we're going to be able to work together on this case. There's just too much history between us." He jammed a fist through his hair. "Why don't you make it easier on both of us, Angel? Call the feds and tell them you have to pass on this case."

"I can't."

"Sure you can," he insisted as desperation set in. "It's not like you have any ties here. And you haven't invested a lot of time in this case yet. No one's going to think less of you if you say you've changed your mind."

"You don't realize what you're asking. I can't just walk away."

"Why not?"

"Because somewhere out there is a baby who's been taken from everyone she knows and loves. You said yourself the FBI has come up empty and there's been no ransom demand of any kind. So whoever has her isn't going to just give her back. She needs me... She needs us to find her."

"Don't you think I've been trying? That I'll keep on trying?" Justin fired back. "There hasn't been a single day that's gone by that I haven't spent hours going over every detail again and again, checking out every lead I get." Frustrated and afraid he'd revealed too much of the turmoil inside him, Justin turned away and stared into the cold hearth.

He heard only the whisper of movement, and then Angela's voice was behind him saying, "I know you've tried and that you won't stop trying to find her. But together we can find her faster." When he said nothing, she continued. "Put yourself in Luke Callaghan's shoes, Justin. Suppose I had been able to give you the child you'd wanted, imagine how you'd feel if it was our little girl who had been stolen."

Her words caught him by surprise. It had been more than five years since he'd even allowed himself to think of what it would be like to be a father. In his arrogance, he'd assumed that when he was ready to start a family, he and Angela would simply make a baby. Their inability to conceive had been a source of major tension and frustration during that last year of their marriage. The specialists, the fertility drugs, the shots and in-vitro procedures had taken all the joy and pleasure out of their lovemaking, and it had left them both feeling like failures. By the time the third in-vitro attempt failed, Angela had completely withdrawn from him and within weeks she'd been gone from his life.

"If Lena was our daughter, wouldn't you be willing to do anything, use every resource available to you to try to get her back?"

Justin turned around, stared into the stark blueness of her eyes. "You know I would."

"Then use me."

He knew her statement wasn't meant to be provocative, but that didn't stop him from experiencing that one-two punch of desire again. Dammit, he didn't want to want Angela.

"Please, Justin," she said, touching his arm. "Please, let me help you find her."

Justin locked his eyes with hers. And when her gaze lowered to his mouth, he sucked in a breath. But instead of steadying him, her scent—that hint of apricots, mixed with sweat and female—had a familiar tightness settling in his loins.

And because he was tempted to cup her jaw and taste that mouth, he shoved his fists into his pockets and took a step back. "All right. We'll work the case together. But we do it my way, on my terms. Understood?"

"Yes."

"Go over the file," he instructed her with a nod toward the folder on the coffee table. "When you've finished, we'll meet in my office and decide where to go from there."

"All right. But I have a couple of questions—"

"Read the file first, then we'll talk. I've got to go," he insisted, and headed for the door. And it wasn't until he reached his truck and got behind the wheel that he realized his hands were shaking.

Four

"Thank you for allowing me to take these," Angela told Josie Carson, indicating the baby blanket and little stuffed lamb that the other woman had given her following her request for something belonging to Lena. "I promise I'll take good care of them and return them to you soon."

"Keep them as long as you like. Just find Lena for us," Josie pleaded, her green eyes bright with the threat of tears.

"I... We'll do our best," Angela amended, eager to take her leave of the Carsons before Josie's fear and distress overwhelmed her completely. Although Angela had tried to shield herself, she hadn't been able to block out the woman's emotions. It was always one of the drawbacks of being psychic—this hypersensitivity to the people she was trying to help. While she'd become better at controlling it in recent years, for some reason she hadn't been able to do so with Josie. As a result, the woman's pain was now her own.

"Thanks again, Flynt, Josie," Justin said with a nod of his head, then he followed Angela outside.

Flynt Carson stood on the porch beside his petite wife, placed his arm around her shoulders. "I know Lena is Callaghan's daughter, but we'd appreciate it if you'd keep us informed," Flynt told Justin.

"Consider it done," Justin replied, then guided Angela toward his truck.

As Angela walked beside him in silence, she tried to

make her mind go blank, to draw the emotions ricocheting through her into the imaginary box where she could store them away and deal with them later.

When they reached his truck, Justin opened the passenger door and assisted her inside. "You all right?" he asked.

Not trusting herself to speak yet, Angela nodded.

For a moment she thought he would call her on the fib. And she was relieved when he simply shut her door, walked around and climbed into his side of the truck and drove away from the Carsons' house.

But her relief was short-lived when a few miles after they'd exited the Carson Ranch, Justin pulled the truck into a cluster of trees at the side of the road and cut off the engine. He turned to face her. "You want to tell me why you look like someone just ran over your dog?"

"I…" Angela brought her hand to her throat, wondered how to explain to a man who didn't believe in things he couldn't explain logically that she'd been struck by the emotions coursing through Josie Carson.

He tipped up her chin, forced her to look at him. Despite his somber expression, there was no mistaking the concern in those deep green eyes. "Did Josie Carson say something to upset you when the two of you were alone in the baby's room?"

"No," Angela managed to say.

"Then what's wrong?"

"I… Nothing."

"It's not nothing if it has you this upset. You can trust me, Angela. Talk to me. Tell me what's wrong."

The husky note in his voice and the way he was looking at her made her want to crawl into his lap and let him comfort her. But to do so would only complicate things. And the situation between them was already rife with complications. "It wasn't anything she said. It's what she was feeling. When she picked up the stuffed lamb, she was remembering how much Lena loved it, remembering the way the baby's face lit up the first time she saw it. The empty nursery is a constant reminder that Lena's gone."

"She tell you that?" Justin asked.

"No," Angela told him, and braced herself for his skepticism.

Instead Justin simply said, "That baby might not be their flesh and blood, but I suspect they love her all the same. Besides being worried about her, I imagine they're carrying around a lot of guilt, too."

"They are. Especially Josie."

"It makes sense. Seeing as how the baby was kidnapped while she was in their care, Josie probably blames herself."

"She does. And the guilt's eating away at her," Angela said.

"I'll talk to Flynt, make sure he's aware of how Josie's feeling, suggest he keep her away from the nursery."

Evidently he read her surprise in her expression because he said, "What?"

"I didn't think you would believe me, that you'd understand."

"Why not?"

"No reason. I just know how you feel about my psychic ability."

Justin made a face. "Sorry to disappoint you, but there's nothing psychic going on here that I can see. It's simply a matter of observation. That, and doing what you suggested—putting myself in somebody else's shoes."

For a moment Angela had actually thought that Justin might at last be willing to acknowledge that her abilities weren't based in anything tangible, that he could accept that she was different. That he hadn't shouldn't have disappointed her, but it did.

"If you're not feeling well and want to hold off on going to see Luke Callaghan," he began, breaking into her thoughts, "I can give him a call and arrange for us to go to his place another time."

"No. I'm okay. And I'd really like to talk to him today."

"All right," Justin told her, and started up the truck. "I should warn you, though, Luke is different than you might remember him."

"Different how?"

"He's blind," Justin advised her as he pulled the truck back out onto the road.

"Blind?" The good-looking millionaire had always struck her as invincible. "What happened?"

"Some kind of accident while he was out of the country."

Angela realized at once that it must have happened during the hush-hush military mission Ricky had told her about. She also realized that Justin remained unaware of Luke's governmental activities. "Is it permanent?" she asked.

"I don't think Luke or the doctors know."

"It must be very difficult for him," Angela mused aloud. "I can only imagine how he must feel—losing his sight and having his daughter kidnapped."

"Yeah. Just keep in mind that it's only recently that he even learned that he has a daughter. I don't think you should bank on him being much help."

"As I've told Justin, I doubt that I can be of much help," Luke Callaghan told her a short time later.

Seated outside on the picturesque patio of the Callaghan

estate, Angela studied Luke. Ever since Ricky had con-
fided in her about the secret military mission for which
Luke had been the leader, she found herself viewing Luke
through different eyes. Knowing of his military activities,
she noticed minor things now—like the way he had posi-
tioned himself so that his back faced the wall. And while
he appeared relaxed, there was an air of alertness, a read-
iness about him. Though this demeanor could be attributed
to his blindness, Angela didn't think that was the cause.
During her marriage to Justin, she had crossed paths with
Luke at the Lone Star Country Club a number of times.
More often than not, she'd pick up a serious, almost secretive vibe about the man that, at the time, had seemed
at odds with his playboy image. Now, at least, she knew
why.

He waited until the houseman had finishing pouring
them coffee, and not until they were alone once again did
he continue. "As Justin's probably told you, I've been out
of the country for the last few months on business. It's
only since I got back that I even learned I have a child."

"I'm aware of that," Angela told him. "What I'm hoping is that you might be able to tell me something about
your daughter's mother."

Luke's mouth hardened, and despite the fact that she
knew those blue eyes pinning her like lasers from behind
the dark glasses were sightless, Angela had to stop herself
from shrinking away. "As I'm sure Justin's told you, I
don't know who the woman is."

"I understand."

"Do you? Because I sure as hell don't." He shoved a
hand through his dark hair. "Despite my reputation, I'm
not casual about sex. I certainly don't make a habit of
going to bed with a woman I don't even know and bring-

ing an innocent child into the world. But obviously, that's exactly what I did.''

Justin clamped his hand down on the other man's shoulder. ''No point in beating yourself up over this, Luke. It's done.''

''He's right,'' Angela told Luke. ''The important thing now is for us to find your little girl. So if there's anything, anything at all, you can remember about the woman, even something that might seem insignificant, it could help us to identify her and possibly find your daughter.''

Luke sighed, seemed to stared off into the distance. ''She was a blond, but not the typical pale-eyed, fair-skinned girl-next-door type. She had olive skin and the most exotic-looking dark eyes—sad, lonely eyes, that seemed to look right into a man's soul.''

Angela didn't have to be psychic to know that Luke had felt something for this woman and that she continued to haunt his thoughts. ''Do you have any idea of how old she was?''

''She could have been in her late twenties, but I suspect she was closer to my age. Thirty-four.''

''What about her height? Weight?''

''She was about five foot six, slender but not skinny, curves in all the right places,'' he said.

''Is there anything else you can remember about her?'' Angela asked. ''Maybe an accent or something she said that might indicate where she was from?''

''We didn't do a great deal of talking,'' Luke informed her, his mouth going flat. ''She had an English accent or did a pretty good job of using one when we first hooked up, but as the night wore on, I picked up a hint of a Southern drawl.''

''You never mentioned that to me,'' Justin told Luke.

''I didn't think about it until now.''

"Any idea what part of the South?" Angela asked. "Louisiana, Alabama, Mississippi?"

"Texas would be my guess," Luke replied.

Angela couldn't help but notice Justin's frown. Haley Mercado had been from Texas. Could Ricky be right? That his sister really was alive, and that the child might be hers? But surely Luke would have recognized the woman if she'd been Haley—even with a different hair color. From what Ricky had told her, Luke had been very close to Ricky and his sister before the boating accident that had claimed Haley's life and ended the two men's friendship.

"You would think that a man my age would have had the decency to at least make sure he knew the name of a woman he goes to bed with," Luke said, his voice filled with self-loathing.

"We're here to find your daughter, Luke, not to judge you," Angela said softly, wanting to ease his torment.

"You don't have to judge me. I've already done that myself. And I can tell you that I don't measure up very well," Luke informed her. "There's no excuse for my actions. Because of me, because of my own selfishness, there's a little girl out there somewhere at the mercy of God knows what kind of people."

"Cut yourself some slack, Callaghan," Justin told him. "It doesn't sound like the woman needed much coaxing."

Luke's hands balled into fists. His eyes grew stormy. "She wasn't some cheap floozy."

"I never thought for a minute she was," Justin assured him. "I may not know her, Callaghan, but I do know you. You'd never fall for a floozy."

Seemingly mollified by Justin's response, Luke flexed his fingers. His spine lost some of its stiffness. "She and I... The sparks were just there. The minute I saw her come into the bar, I wanted her. It was as though... I can't explain it,'' he said.

''You don't have to. I know what you mean.''

Something in Justin's voice caught Angela's attention, and she looked over at him. Her pulse quickened when she found his green eyes trained on her with such intensity. But just as quickly he averted his gaze.

''Since there's still been no ransom demand,'' Justin began, ''there's a good chance that whoever took Lena doesn't realize she's your daughter.''

''And what happens when they find out? What do you think the odds are that we'll get her back alive even if I do fork over money? I have enemies,'' he spit out. ''And I'm not talking about the kind you meet over a boardroom table or at the Lone Star Country Club. If they were to find out—'' Removing his glasses, he scrubbed a hand down his face, and when he looked up at them out of eyes that Angela knew could not see, he said, ''You've got to find her before anyone discovers that I'm her father.''

''Not many people know about the connection,'' Justin assured him. ''Anyone who asks is being told that Angela was brought in at the request of the Carsons.''

''There is one other person who knows Luke is the father,'' Angela corrected him, and both men looked at her. ''Lena's mother,'' she explained. ''I understand she left the baby on the golf course, with a note saying that one of your golfing foursome was the father and asking you to take care of the baby until she came back for her. So she obviously knew who you were, Luke.''

''She's right,'' Justin added. ''Unfortunately, we don't know who *she* is. What I still haven't been able to figure out is if the woman knew who you were, why she didn't just come right out and tell you about the baby from the get-go? Why go through the pregnancy and have the baby without saying anything to you, only to leave her on the golf course for you to find her?''

''Maybe she didn't feel she had any other choice,'' Angela said.

''What do you mean?'' Luke asked.

''From what Josie and Flynt Carson told me, the little girl had been well cared for, loved. It doesn't sound to me like she was unwanted. So maybe the mother never intended to tell you about the baby.''

''Only something happened and she couldn't keep her a secret anymore,'' Justin added.

''Exactly. And whatever it was that forced her to leave Lena, she apparently felt it prevented her from contacting you directly for help. So she left the baby on the golf course where she thought you would find her. She wouldn't have had any way of knowing that the sprinkler system would kick on and your name would be obliterated on the note. As far as she knew, you would find the note and the baby.''

''Only I wasn't there to find her,'' Luke said, his expression once again filled with self-reproach.

''From all accounts, your little girl was in very good hands with the Carsons,'' Angela offered.

''I'm her father. I should have been there. Maybe if I had—''

''Don't,'' Angela cautioned. She reached across the table, touched his hand. Choosing her words carefully, she said, ''The night you met Lena's mother, you said that your actions were out of character for you.''

''That's right,'' he replied, and removing his hand from her touch, he slipped the dark glasses back on. ''I don't usually sleep with a woman I've just met.''

''Speaking as a woman, I have a feeling that the same

thing would hold true for your mystery woman. Most women aren't casual about sex, either.''

"What's your point?" Justin asked.

"That maybe Luke and this woman weren't strangers," Angela told him, toying with the possibility that if the woman had been Haley Mercado and she'd changed her appearance somehow, Luke might not have recognized her, but she would have recognized him.

"He's already said he didn't know her," Justin pointed out.

Luke spoke up. "Hang on a second. Maybe Angela's on to something. I mean, there was something familiar about her. She—she reminded me of someone I used to know, a girl I'd once been close to.''

"Could it have been the same woman?" Angela asked.

Luke's expression grew even more somber. He seemed to gaze off into the distance, his thoughts evidently locked somewhere in the past. Then he shook his head as though shaking off some memory. "No. No, that would be impossible. It couldn't have been her.''

"We've taken up enough of your time," Justin said, and shot her a warning look. He stood. "Angela needs to get busy working up that profile, and I need to get back to the office.''

Following Justin's lead, Angela came to her feet, all the while aware of Justin monitoring her. "It was good seeing you again, Luke. I'm sorry it couldn't have been under happier circumstances.''

"Angela, thank you for coming to Mission Creek, for agreeing to help," Luke told her, and extended his hand.

"You're welcome.''

"Obviously I'm of no use in any kind of search," Luke told her, his voice filled with disgust at the reference to his blindness. "But if there is anything you need, anything at all, you need only to tell me. All my resources—money, manpower, anything—they're at your disposal. Just find my baby for me. Please.''

"Justin and I will do everything we can to locate her," she assured him.

"Thank you," he said, and released her hand. "Both of you."

"You hang in there. I'll be in touch," Justin told him, and after shaking Luke's hand, he ushered her away.

"I know what you're thinking," Justin told Angela, breaking the silence that had hung between them since leaving the Callaghan estate. Although she'd said nothing for several miles now, he could almost see the wheels turning in her head.

"Well, that's certainly a switch. Usually I'm the one who's accused of reading people's minds."

Justin slanted a glance across the truck seat, noting the hint of a smile on her lips. "That's the first time I've ever heard you joke about it."

"It?"

"You know, the psychic thing. Usually you just clam up," he said cautiously. The way she had in his office only a few days ago.

Angela shrugged, and the trace of a smile died. "Reflex, I guess. I've spent so much of my life being afraid that if people knew I was different, they wouldn't accept me. I wanted to fit in, to belong. And I learned that the best way to do that was not to say anything, to just keep my thoughts and feelings to myself."

"Is that why you used to shut me out?" he asked, the question tumbling past his lips before he could think better of it.

She stared at him with serious blue eyes. "You're a man

who deals in facts, Justin. For you, everything is black-and-white. The few times when I tried to tell you about my visions, you claimed it was my cop's instincts kicking in, remember?''

''I don't remember you denying it,'' he said, feeling defensive because he remembered all too well that she'd spooked him on more than one occasion with her ability to know the phone was going to ring before it rang, knew who would be on the other side of the door before there was a knock, knew where to find the missing pieces on a puzzling case without any solid reasoning behind it.

''Because I knew it made you uncomfortable. You needed a logical explanation for things—not something as illogical as having your wife tell you that she had psychic visions.''

''You make me sound like some kind of close-minded jerk.''

''I don't mean to. You're a good man, Justin, an honorable one. I knew exactly who and what you were when I married you. The problem wasn't you. It was me. I was the one who was dishonest. I was afraid that if I ever let you see who I really was, what I really am, that I would lose you.''

''You think I don't know that? You think I didn't know that you always held a part of yourself back from me? That you didn't trust me?'' he fired back, unable to keep the bitterness out of his tone. ''You were like some lost, scared kitten, Angela. And I loved you so much that I would have walked through fire for you, done anything for you. I thought if I was patient, that if I showed you how much I loved you, that you would learn to trust me, that you would love me the way I loved you. But you never did.''

''I did love you,'' she told him.

"Well, I guess you just didn't love me enough to have a little faith in me. If you had, we might have been able to work things out. But I suppose that's one of those things we'll never know, isn't it?"

"I guess n— Justin, look out!"

Justin jerked his gaze back to the road, where a big slow-moving rig was blocking the road directly ahead of them. "Hang on," he shouted as he hit the brakes and yanked the steering wheel to the right. His truck slid several feet, kicking up dust and gravel and with it the stench of burning rubber. When the truck finally came to a hard stop a few yards from where the semi was just lumbering by, his head snapped forward and back before his body slammed back against the seat. "Are you all right?" he asked, his gaze raking over her.

"Yes. I think so," she said, her voice a little more than a whisper.

But her eyes were wide, her face pale. And without stopping to think, he unhooked his seat belt, reached across the seat and began running his hands down her torso, checking to assure himself she was okay. When his hand brushed the side of her breast, he went still. The adrenaline rush of the near crash somehow kick-started the sensual awareness that he'd spent all morning trying to keep leashed. Suddenly he realized how close her mouth was. All he had to do was lean forward an inch, maybe two, and he'd be kissing her as he'd wanted to do from the first moment he'd seen her the other night at the dedication.

As though reading his thoughts, she sucked in a breath. Justin lifted his gaze to hers, and the answering need he saw darkening her eyes sent heat firing through his veins like a blowtorch. He started to lower his mouth when the blare of a horn slapped him back to his senses. He yanked himself from the brink, released his hold on her and cursed his own weakness where she was concerned. Frustrated, he punched the steering wheel and found some measure of satisfaction at the jolt of pain that shot up his arm.

After a long moment he said, "I'm sorry. I should have been paying closer attention to the road." And he was also sorry for allowing himself to get worked up as he had and nearly getting them both killed. He was even sorrier for letting his guard slip and coming dangerously close to kissing her. It was a mistake that he didn't intend to make again. Feeling somewhat more in control, he allowed himself to look at her. "You sure you're all right?"

"I'm fine," she said.

Only, he knew she was lying. Already he could sense her retreating into herself once more, shutting him out as she'd done so often during their marriage. Which was just as well, he told himself as he refastened his seat belt and started the truck up again. The last thing either of them needed was to go tiptoeing through the emotional minefields of what went wrong with their marriage. No, the sooner this case was closed and she was on her way back to San Antonio, the better off they'd both be, he told himself. He maneuvered his truck back onto the roadway and aimed it toward Angela's condo.

For the next twenty minutes neither of them said a word. Silence settled inside the truck like a dense fog. Feeling edgy and far too aware of Angela sitting quietly beside him, Justin was almost grateful to have Audrey Lou call him on his radio transmitter. "Wainwright," he all but barked out in answer.

"Sheriff, we've got a fender bender with an overturned horse trailer on Pine Street. The trailer was empty, and the driver's only got a few scratches, but the trailer's blocking two streets and has traffic in a mess. Hank's on the scene, but he's still taking statements. He could use a hand clearing the streets.''

"Tell Bobby to get over there and help him,'' Justin instructed.

"Tried,'' Audrey Lou said. ''But the boy's not answering his radio. I sent him to clear up a scuffle between the Mitchell and Hawkins boys. He radioed in fifteen minutes ago, saying everything was under control and he was heading back here after he made a quick stop. But so far, there's no sign of him.''

Justin swore. "Keep trying until you get him,'' he ordered. "I'm only a few minutes from Angela's now. As soon as I drop her off, I'll be heading back to the office. In the meantime, call Roy and ask him if he'll give Hank a hand.''

"Will do,'' Audrey Lou replied.

"And, Audrey Lou?''

"Yeah, Sheriff?''

"You tell Bobby I want to see him when I get back,'' he said before ending the call. He liked Bobby, thought the kid had potential. But he couldn't shake the feeling that his new deputy wasn't being straight with him. He'd been a lawman too long not to be able to get a sense when something was off. And something was off with his deputy. The kid was hiding something.

He'd been sorely in need of another deputy when Bobby had applied for the job. And although Audrey Lou said Bobby's references had checked out, it wouldn't hurt for him to take a closer look. He made a mental note to put a call in to a friend he had at the capitol in Austin and ask him to run Bobby's name through the system.

"Things sound pretty busy,'' Angela said, breaking into his thoughts. "I should have taken my car and gone to see the Carsons and Luke on my own instead of taking up your time like this.''

''I offered to take you, remember?''

''I know, but it's pretty obvious that you're needed back in town.''

''The town will survive without me for a while,'' he told her, and flicked on his turn signal as he headed for the exit lane. ''Besides, I didn't want you talking to the Carsons or Luke without me there.''

''Why not?'' she asked, and he didn't miss the sharp note in her tone.

''Because I didn't want you saying anything to them about your pal Ricky Mercado's theory that little Lena is his sister's kid. And judging by your questions to Luke, I can see I was right to be worried. That is where you were heading with that line of questions about the woman he spent the night with, isn't it?''

''You heard Luke. He said the woman reminded him of someone he used to know.''

''Haley Mercado died in a boating accident four years ago,'' Justin pointed out as he turned onto Angela's street.

''But from what I understand, the body that was found was so badly decomposed there was no way to make a positive ID. And there were no dental records or other means to prove it was Haley.''

''And you don't know that it wasn't Haley,'' he argued.

''Are you going to sit there and tell me that you don't think it's even a possibility that the woman was Haley?''

''Yeah, I think it's a possibility that the woman was Haley. I also think it's a possibility that she wasn't. So until we know otherwise, we deal in facts. And the fact is that as far as either one of us knows, Haley Mercado is dead.''

"Since when did you become such a close-minded stuffed shirt, Wainwright?"

The accusation hit home. Justin swung the truck into her driveway and slammed the gearshift into Park. Then he turned to face her. "Maybe since I watched Luke's guilt over that accident nearly eat him alive. Or maybe it was when I saw him and Flynt and Spence Harrison and Tyler Murdoch go through that circus of a trial for Haley's murder. Or maybe it was after their acquittal when that psycho Frank Del Brio vowed to get his own justice for Haley's death."

"But—"

Justin got in her face and dropped his voice as he said, "You're the one who's supposed to be the psychic, Mason. All I have to work with is my gut. And my gut tells me that if that little girl is Haley's, there's a real good chance that Del Brio's behind her kidnapping."

"But if you think he's the one who has Lena, then we know where to look. All we need is a search warrant for his home, for his business."

"We can't get a warrant without some evidence."

"Well, I can get one," she informed. "Let me make a call—"

He caught her wrist when she reached for her purse in search of her cell phone. "Listen up, Mason. You aren't going to call anyone. And you aren't going to say a word about any of this until I say so. Understand?"

She jerked her wrist free, tipped up her chin. "I don't take orders from you, Justin Wainwright."

"On this you do," he told her, and damned if he didn't think she looked beautiful with temper heating her cheeks and sparking in her eyes. "There's no way I'm going to let you put two people's lives at risk."

"If you're talking about you and me—"

"I'm talking about Luke Callaghan and his little girl. If Luke thinks Del Brio has his daughter, he's not going to let something like the fact that he's blind stop him from going after Del Brio," Justin explained. "And if Del Brio suspects that Haley is alive and he's kidnapped the kid to get at her, what chance do you think that baby has of seeing her next birthday if Del Brio finds out Luke is her father?"

"I didn't realize," she murmured.

"Now that you do, I want your word that you won't say anything about this to anyone."

"Of course."

"Say it," he demanded.

She looked up at him, met his gaze. "I promise not to say anything."

"To anyone," Justin prompted.

She thinned her lips. "I said I wouldn't say anything to anyone. Whether you believe me or not is up to you."

Deciding he'd pushed her enough, Justin said, "All right." He unhooked his seat belt. "I'll help you bring that stuff inside, and then I need to head back to work," he told her, motioning to the files, baby blanket and stuffed animal.

"Don't bother," she countered, and began trying to unhook her seat belt, which apparently was stuck.

"Let me get it," he told her.

"I can do it," she informed him, temper in her voice. She shooed his hands away, made a frustrated sound when the catch refused to release.

When she yelped because the thing pinched her finger, Justin pushed her hand away. "There," he said as the catch gave, and when he looked up, he found himself close, too close to her. He wasn't sure if he moved that inch or if she did. All he knew was that suddenly they were kissing. She tasted sweet and hot. She tasted familiar and yet new at the same time. He sieved his hands through her hair and drank her in. Her mouth fitted beneath his like it was made for him. Desire raced through him like a bullet. He slid one hand between them to cup her breast, and nearly lost it when he felt her nipple harden beneath the fabric and strain against his palm.

She tore her mouth free and gasped. "Justin, we...I... This is insane. We can't—"

Sanity came back in a rush. He jerked away, dragged in a breath. "You're right. This was a mistake. I don't know what I was thinking," he admitted, irritated with himself, with her. He moved over to his side of the truck, needing some distance and a chance to clear his head. He rubbed a hand down his face.

"It was just a kiss, Justin."

"Right. I know that," he countered. "But it shouldn't have happened. I never meant to—I was out of line. I had no right to subject you to..." He was blabbering like a schoolboy, Justin realized, disgusted with himself.

"I said it's all right," she told him. "It was only a kiss."

But he'd wanted something to happen, Justin admitted. And judging by Angela's response, so had she. Only that was one road neither one of them should travel again— not if they had any sense. He let out another breath and tried again. "You're right," he finally said. "It was just a kiss. But you don't have to worry, I promise it won't happen again."

Five

Angela pushed away from the combination desk and art table that she'd set up as a workstation in her condo and headed for the kitchen. Her stomach grumbled, a reminder that it was already after eight o'clock, long past dinnertime, and she hadn't eaten since breakfast. She pulled open the door to her refrigerator and eyed its meager contents. "Should have gone to the grocery," she muttered, and retrieved a can of soda. Snagging the bag of chips and salsa from the pantry, she headed back to her work.

While she munched on the chips and salsa, she eyed the reports, statements, photographs and other items that she'd spread out across her workstation. But even though she tried to think about the case, tried to figure out what it was she was missing, her thoughts drifted back to Justin once more. In the two days since he'd kissed her outside in the driveway, he'd remained true to his word. It hadn't happened again. But his treating her like a stranger—or trying to—had done little to ease the sensual awareness between them. It was as though some inner radar went off in her every time they were in the same room with each other. Given the way Justin did his best to avoid being near her, she suspected he felt it, too.

The sexual chemistry that had sparked between them the very first time they met in training school was just as powerful now as it had been eight years ago. He wanted her, and didn't like the wanting one bit. The realization stung almost as much as his bumbled apology for kissing her had, Angela admitted as she dunked the flat tortilla chip into the spicy red sauce. And if she had a lick of sense, she would stop thinking about Justin Wainwright and concentrate on this case. Because the sooner she found little Lena, the sooner she could go back to San Antonio and get out of Justin's life.

And maybe, maybe she could forget about him. Forget about the anger and hurt in his voice when he'd told her how much he'd loved her and how she'd shut him out. Forget the way desire had heated his eyes when he'd looked at her. Forget how his mouth had felt, hot and hard and demanding, when he'd kissed her. Forget the feel of his hands on her skin, strong and calloused, yet gentle.

Angela groaned and pressed the cold drink can against her cheek. She had to stop thinking about him. She had to—or she was going to drive herself insane. Putting the soda and snacks aside, she went into the bathroom, rinsed her hands and splashed cool water on her face. And then she headed back to work.

Picking up first the baby blanket and then the stuffed lamb that Josie Carson had given her, Angela made her mind go blank of everything but the little girl to whom the items belonged. "Talk to me, Lena. Talk to me," she whispered. Closing her eyes, Angela held the blanket against her cheek and tried to pick up the dark-haired baby's aura.

It came to her in snatches. Laughter. The sound of a baby's giggles. The wonder at feeling the blond, silky hair. Lena's emotions, her baby's curiosity and joy continued to flash at Angela like strobe lights.

And then she saw her. Lena.

A dark-haired little girl, laughing, her chubby fingers reaching out for something. Angela frowned, tried to see what or who coaxed the child, but she couldn't move beyond those outstretched fingers. Then more emotions hit Angela—surprise, fear, pain from something razor sharp—then darkness. At the sudden blackness, Angela wrapped her arms around herself. Caught up in the child's fear, Angela trembled. Tears ran down her cheeks. Instinctively Angela started to retreat from the overwhelming emotions, but she forced herself not to close the door. She had to relive Lena's fear, to listen to her weeping if she was going to find her.

When she thought her heart would break from the little girl's fear and distress and that she would not be able to go on, she heard it. Music. Soft, dreamy music that sounded like a lullaby. Suddenly new images flashed behind her shuttered lids—horses, a group of beautiful horses. A palomino, a black stallion, another with a snowy mane. A fence, some sort of track, an old wooden structure.

Concentrating, Angela tried to recapture a sense of the little girl. But instead of Lena, a string of new images assailed her, quick flickers that came in flashes. It was like trying to watch a movie with every other scene missing or slides in a projector being run at fast speed. Confused, she caught a glimpse of some sort of cave or cavern. Another clip showed her layers of dust. More slides revealed objects—groups of objects—heavy and rounded like the shape of a coin. Another blip of the screen and there was a cross, an old cup that had lost its patina. Unable to make sense of it, she stopped questioning what it meant. Instead she opened her eyes and did what she always did. She reached for her drawing pad and pencil and began to sketch.

Her fingers raced over the blank pages, trying to recapture what she'd seen in her mind's eye. And when Angela finally put down her pencil and shoved away from the table, she was stunned to discover that nearly three hours had passed. Feeling drained, she stood and stretched her arms up over her head to ease the aching muscles in her back from sitting bent over her workstation for so long.

After getting herself a fresh soda from the kitchen, she returned to her workroom. And as she sipped the caffeine-laden drink, she viewed the sketches she'd made. The cave with the coins and cross, the cup and statues. None of it made any more sense to her now than it had when she'd first seen the images in her head. She set down the can of soda and began flipping through the rest of the pages in her sketch pad. She stopped at the pictures of the horses she'd drawn in a circle. Then she stared at the wooden fence she'd drawn. On still another sheet was the house—only she wasn't sure if it was a house. She shaded in the road she'd seen surrounding the structure. Then she went back to the sketch of the horses in the circle.

"A track?" she murmured. A track where horses were trained? Suddenly her heart began to race. Maybe this was where Lena was being kept, she thought. At some house or a place with a track for training horses. Excited that at last she was on to something, she hurried over and picked up the phone to call Justin. She began to punch in the number to the Wainwright Ranch, then stopped and hung up the phone. It was well past eleven o'clock. She couldn't call him this late, she told herself.

But as she glanced over at the little stuffed lamb on her worktable and remembered how frightened Lena had been, she picked up the phone again and dialed his number.

"Wainwright," Justin answered on the second ring.

"Justin, it's Angela." She waited a second, and when he didn't say anything, she repeated, "Justin?"

"Yeah?"

The gruff response did little to ease her nerves. "I hope I didn't wake you."

"You didn't."

"Oh, that's good," she said, and wondered if she could possibly sound any more inane. She wet her lips, and quickly, before she lost her nerve, she blurted out, "I have something I need for you to see. It's a…picture of where I think Lena is being held. I realize it's late, and this could probably wait until morning, but I'm hoping you might recognize the place. Anyway, I was wondering if you could come over. Or I could come over to your place and—"

"I'll come there. Give me thirty minutes."

And before she could thank him, the dial tone was buzzing in her ear.

Twenty minutes and several broken speed limits later, Justin pulled his truck up in front of Angela's condo. Except for the lights blazing in her place and the one on at the newlyweds', the rest of the block was in darkness. Judging from what he'd witnessed a few nights ago, the newlyweds were probably not asleep.

If he had any sense at all, Justin chastised himself, he wouldn't be thinking about what they were doing. Irritated by the direction of his thoughts, he shut off his lights and engine and exited the truck. He didn't even make it to the front door before Angela was pulling it open for him.

"Thanks for coming so quickly," she said, and ushered him inside.

Justin nodded, trying not to notice the fact that she was barefoot and wearing a pair of worn jeans that hugged her bottom and made her legs look a mile long. But with the light at her back, it was impossible to ignore the view of the curves beneath her shirt.

"I appreciate you coming all the way out here this late at night. I mean, I probably should have waited until the morning."

Justin jerked his gaze to her face and realized now what he hadn't when she'd first opened the door. She was wired. Probably running on fumes, if he had to guess.

"But then I thought—"

"Angela, slow down," he said firmly. "I'm here now. So why don't we go inside and you take your time and tell me about this picture."

"Right. Right," she repeated, and hurriedly shut the door. "I guess I'm a little excited."

She was more than a little excited, Justin realized as he noted the shadows beneath those overbright blue eyes and what he suspected were tear stains on her cheeks. She'd probably been at it for hours and was on the verge of collapse. Not that she would admit to it. She wouldn't. Angela's ability to lose herself in a case had been one of the things he'd both admired and resented about her during their marriage. While he'd appreciated her dedication, he'd also hated the way she would shut herself off from him and everything except the case.

"Well, at first I wasn't sure it meant anything," she began, growing excited all over again as she explained. "But then when I started going back over the pictures—"

She was like a kid, racing ten miles a minute, he thought. "Whoa! You're going too fast. Take a deep breath, Angel," he said, the endearment tripping off his tongue as it had so often in the past. Without thinking, he caught her by the shoulders and ran his hands down her arms.

And just like that, heat exploded in his veins. He released her at once and took a step back. But not before those big blue eyes of hers locked with his. Not before he heard that catch in her breath that told him she'd felt those sparks, too. "You said you had a picture you wanted me to see," he pointed out, annoyed with himself because in less than a minute the past two days of reining in his desire for her was in danger of going up in smoke.

"Yes. It's in here."

Determined to see the picture she wanted to show him and get out of Dodge before he did something stupid, he followed her into the den he'd seen for the first time a few nights ago.

"I suppose it would have made more sense to set up an office in the extra bedroom," she explained, evidently noting his surprise at the changes. "But I liked it better in here."

It wasn't difficult for him to figure out why she'd turned one corner of the room into her work area. The openness of the big room and the picture window on the far wall would have appealed to her. The fireplace, rug and pillows would have given it a cozy feel and made it feel less like an office. Accustomed to sizing up a scene quickly due to his law enforcement training, Justin noted the bulletin board with a map and arrows linking locations that she'd anchored to the wall in front of her workstation. A photo of Lena was pinned at the top of the board, a reminder he was sure, that the baby was depending on her. In front of the bulletin board sat an art table piled high with books, folders and reports. The baby blanket and stuffed lamb that Angela had gotten from the Carsons during their visit two days earlier was beside a stack of files. An open notebook filled with what he recognized as Angela's handwriting sat next to it. At the center of the table lay several art pencils and a sketch pad. "Looks like you've been busy."

"I suppose so," she said, as though only now seeing the worktable and the array of material.

On the edge of the table atop a napkin sat a can of soda that Justin suspected was lukewarm, an open bag of chips and a jar of salsa. Remembering her tendency to fuel up on caffeine and junk food, he chalked up her hyper state to tonight's diet. Walking over to the desk, he gestured to the snacks. "I take it this was your dinner?"

Angela blinked, then looked at the chips as though she hadn't a clue how they'd gotten there. "Actually, it was lunch and dinner," she confessed.

He started to lecture her about taking better care of herself, but reminded himself that Angela Mason and her eating habits were no longer his concern. Instead he opted to ask, "So what is it you've found that's had you too busy to eat a decent meal?"

"Not everyone considers steak and potatoes a decent meal," she informed him, and Justin told himself it was just as well that he'd put her on the defensive. "But to answer your question, I spent most of my evening going over the reports and statements, and didn't come up with much more than you or the FBI already have. Then I tried using Lena's things, to see if I could get a sense of what might have happened to her."

Justin read the challenge in her eyes that he'd heard in her voice, but he remained silent and waited for her to explain.

After a moment she continued, "Josie said the day Lena was kidnapped from her nursery, that she found her gone when she went in to check on her during her nap. I think whoever kidnapped her had staked out the Carsons' place and knew Josie's routine. When Josie put the baby down for her nap, they snatched her."

"We've always suspected as much," he conceded. "But if Del Brio is behind the kidnapping, we haven't been able to link him to it. And believe me, I've tried. Since there's been no ransom demand, we have to also consider the possibility that Lena's mother—whoever she is—is the one who kidnapped her."

"It wasn't her," Angela replied.

"How do you know?"

"Because whoever took Lena used something—a doll or a toy of some kind—as a means to get close to her without scaring her and then they snatched her. Once they had her, they covered her up with something so that she couldn't see. She was terrified," Angela said, her voice little more than a whisper.

The fear in her eyes as she replayed the scene for him had Justin's gut tightening and anger fueling his blood. He clutched his hands into fists at his side and waited for her to continue.

"When she started to cry. They…they drugged her to keep her quiet. It wasn't her mother," she told him. "No mother would put her child through that. Not for any reason."

She stared at him, obviously waiting for him to challenge what she'd said. He didn't because he believed her. Every word of it. He didn't doubt for a second that it had happened just as she had described. A part of him wanted to reason that it was Angela's uncanny instincts and training as a cop as he'd done so often in the past. But he knew to do so now would be to lie to himself. "All right," he said finally. "So where's this picture you wanted me to see?"

"It's right here," she said, and reached for the sketch pad. Her fingers shook as she fumbled through the pages.

"May I?" Justin asked, and took the pad from her. He sat down at the table and began to view her sketches. The first one was of a horse poised on its hindquarters. He flipped to the next drawing of a black-and-white pinto strutting.

"I saw the horses first," she explained from behind him. "The drawings aren't very good, but I think you get the general idea."

She was wrong. They were good. As a man who'd been incapable of drawing a straight line without a ruler, he'd always been in awe of Angela's ability to sketch and paint. Judging from these sketches, he could see her skill had only improved with time. He turned to the next picture. In this one she'd drawn the same horses again but had put them in a circle with a fence surrounding them. He studied the picture a moment longer, then moved on to the next one. "What's this?" he asked at the sight of what appeared to be some type of coin.

"I'm not sure, and I don't know that it has anything to do with the kidnapping. I—I just had these quick flashes and jotted them down."

She leaned over his shoulder, her hand brushing against his as she reached for the sketch pad, and the innocent contact had his entire body on instant alert. Doing his best to ignore her scent, he allowed her to skip through the rest of the drawings until she found what she was looking for.

"This is what I wanted you to see," she told him, her words a warm breath against his neck.

When he turned his head, looked up at her, she seemed to sense the same sparks he did because she moved over to the side of the table and waited for him to look at the picture. Justin stared at the drawing of a house. It was small, with a winding road and a wooden fence that looked almost primitive. There was another house or small building in the rear that could have been a shed, a barn or a garage.

"I realize the drawing is poor, but does it look at all familiar? Do you ever remember seeing a place like that?"

He could hear the hope in her voice and hated to dash that hope. But he had no choice. "First off, there's nothing wrong with the drawing. You're a very talented artist, Angela."

"Thank you, but—"

"And yes, the place does look familiar," he began. Before she got excited, he stood. He caught her hands, held them in his own as he met her gaze. "But there are probably at least a hundred places that look like that one or are pretty close to it in Lone Star County alone."

"But what about the horses?"

"What about them?"

"Maybe the house is on some kind of a ranch that has a place to train horses. Look," she said, pulling her hands free to go back to the sketch pad. "See how they're moving in some kind of a circle? Maybe it's a track where they train horses to race."

"Maybe," he conceded, not having the heart to dash her hopes completely. "But that still leaves a lot of territory to cover. This is Texas. Do you have any idea how many ranches there are with training facilities for horses?"

"Probably a lot."

"A lot," he repeated. "But at least with this," he said, indicating her sketches, "we have a start."

She smiled at him then, a real smile that brightened her eyes and wrapped itself around his heart. "Thank you for believing me about the visions, and for not treating me like I'm some kind of nutcase."

Justin tipped up her chin so that he could see her eyes, and so that she could see his. "I've never thought of you as a nutcase," he told her. "And while I'll admit that I don't understand any of this psychic stuff and I'd probably be more comfortable if you'd told me you just had a gut feeling about that place, none of that changes the fact that I believe you. I've always believed in you, Angel. How could you not know that? Did I do such a lousy job as your husband that you didn't know how special I thought you were? How special I still think you are?"

She shook her head. "It wasn't you," she told him, tears in her eyes. "It was me. I didn't believe in myself. So how could I expect you to believe in me?"

"I guess it comes back to that issue of trust again, doesn't it?"

"It was myself I didn't trust. Not you," she whispered. "I always trusted you."

Her tears ripped at him. "Don't cry," he pleaded, unable to bear the sight of her hurting. "I hate seeing you cry."

She took the handkerchief he offered. After hopping atop the worktable, she swiped at her wet cheeks and then handed him back his handkerchief. "There," she said, lifting her face up for inspection. "See? No more tears."

"Not quite," he said, noting the lone tear that clung to one of her lashes. He moved closer and caught the tear with his thumb. He was so close he could see the damp spikes of her lashes, note the trail made by the tears on her cheeks, smell the scent of apricots in her hair.

Her grin faded.

So did his.

Alarm bells went off in Justin's head, telling him to get out of there, not to look into those liquid blue eyes, not to stroke his thumb along her cheek. Ignoring the warnings, he lowered his head to within a whisper of hers. "This is a mistake," he said, more to himself than to her.

"Absolutely."

"I should go."

"Yes," she told him just before she fitted her mouth to his.

One taste, Justin promised himself as he drank her in. One taste would take the edge off this craving for her. One taste, and he'd stop. But after one taste, he wanted more.

Angela must have felt the same way because she slid her fingers into his hair and deepened the kiss. Desire became a fire in his belly, in his blood. Her hunger fed his. He raced his hands over her curves, ached with need as she raced her hands over him. With every touch, with every sigh, the flames burned hotter, faster, brighter. And when Angela opened her lips under his, the fire inside him exploded.

Angling his head, Justin took the kiss deeper. Mouths fused. Tongues tempted, teased, mated. She wrapped her arms around his neck, pressed herself against him. And with each move, each stroke of her tongue, each nip of her teeth, new aches and new hungers flared to life inside him. Somewhere in the back of his mind the last shreds of reasoning whispered that this was madness. That this was Angela, his ex-wife. That they were working on a kidnapping case together, and the minute it was over she'd be gone. Back to San Antonio. Back to her job. Back to the life she'd wanted without him.

He was searching for the strength to stop when she tore her mouth free and attacked the buttons of his shirt. She yanked his shirttail from his jeans. "Angela," he said, and sucked in his breath at the feel of her fingers on his skin.

"Touch me," she demanded, and flicked her tongue across his throat. "I want to feel your hands on me."

Groaning, he took her mouth. Pulling her shirt from her jeans, he made short work of the buttons, then flipped open the clasp at the front of her bra. He pushed the fabric aside and stroked her nipples with his thumbs. She gasped, and the sound sent a new wave of need ripping through him at lightning speed. The sight of her nipples pebbled and dusky brought him to a flash point. He wanted to drink her in, swallow her whole. And because he did, he forced himself to go slow.

Lowering his head, he circled one nipple, then the other, with his tongue. He heard the hitch in her breath, felt her tremble at his touch, felt her nails bite into his shoulders. Sweat beaded his brow with the effort it took not to rush her. With a patience that cost him dearly, he continued to lave the tender flesh. And then he closed his teeth over the swollen nipple.

"Justin," she cried out.

Yanking him by the hair, she forced his head up. He caught a glimpse of wild eyes the color of smoke. And then she was fastening her mouth to his, kissing him again.

Her hands were everywhere—in his hair, racing down his back, sculpting a swift path over his chest, down his belly to fight with the buckle of his belt. She tore at the snap of his jeans, fumbled with the tab of his zipper.

"Angel," he called out, strangling back a groan as her fingers brushed his straining shaft.

If she heard him, she gave no indication. She continued to pepper his face with kisses while she fought to get his zipper down.

Her eagerness inflamed him. He wanted her. Wanted her more than he'd ever wanted another woman in his life. And he came within a breath of stripping off her jeans and taking her right there. But they weren't two reckless teenagers in the throes of first passion. This was Angela. This was his ex-wife. She deserved better. So did he.

Justin gulped in a breath and somehow found the strength to stop. Capturing her fingers, he brought them up

to his lips and kissed them with a gentleness he was far
from feeling.

She looked up at him, her brows creased in question,
her eyes glazed with confusion.

He dragged in another breath, tried to clear his scorched
senses and said, "Angel, sweetheart, we can't do this. We
have to stop."

Six

Angela blinked as Justin's words roared like thunder in her ears.

"Angel, I never thought—I wasn't planning—"

She shook her head, tried to clear her overloaded senses, not wanting to believe what Justin was saying, desperate to believe she'd misunderstood him.

"We can't."

But she hadn't misunderstood, she realized as she heard the rejection in his voice, read the regret in his green eyes. Justin didn't want her. She'd all but thrown herself at him, and he didn't want her. A strangled cry escaped her lips as pain and humiliation ripped through her. Suddenly aware of her near-naked state, she jerked her hands free and clutched at her shirt. Blinking back tears, she fumbled with the buttons, not even bothering to refasten her bra.

"Aw, hell!"

Ignoring him, Angela tried to get her fingers to stop shaking long enough for her to button her shirt.

"Angel, look at me," he pleaded.

But she didn't dare look at him, afraid of what she'd see if she did. Her eyes burned with the effort it took not to cry. But if the tears started, she wasn't sure she'd be able to stop them. And she had no intention of letting Justin Wainwright know just how deeply his rejection had hurt her.

"Dammit, look at me," Justin commanded. And when

she continued to ignore him, he grabbed her by the shoulders and repeated, "I said, look at me!"

She yanked her gaze up to his. "I don't take orders from you, Wainwright," she spat out, temper taking the edge off her pain. "Now, get your hands off of me."

"Not until you let me explain."

"There's nothing to explain," she informed him.

"Yes, there is."

"Not as far as I'm concerned," she replied, and tried to shrug off his grasp without any success. "I made a mistake—one that I very much regret. And since I'm feeling like a bit of a fool at the moment, I'd appreciate it if you'd leave."

"No."

His flat refusal threw her. She'd never been one to remain angry for long. It simply wasn't in her nature. And already her temper was ebbing, giving way to the hurt. Tears welled up in her eyes again. She blinked hard, tried to keep them at bay. She'd sooner chew nails than let Justin see her crying over him. "Fine. Then you stay, and I'll leave."

When she tried to move past him, he blocked her path.

"Justin, please, I'm not up for this," she told him, wanting to crawl in a hole somewhere when she heard her voice crack. She swallowed and tried again. "You've had your fun. If humiliating me was your intention, you've succeeded. I wanted to make love with you, and you turned me down. There, I've said it. You win. So now, please just go."

"You think what happened between us a minute ago is some kind of game to me? That I stopped because I don't want you?" he demanded, the fury in his voice no match for the storm in his eyes.

"I…" She spied the muscle ticking angrily in his jaw,

noted the flat line of his mouth. "Isn't that why you stopped?"

"No, that is not why I stopped," he said with a fierceness that made her tremble. "I stopped because I didn't come here tonight prepared for anything like this to happen between us, and I didn't have any way to protect you."

Surprise replaced the bitter taste of his rejection and went a long way in soothing the hurt. He had stopped because he'd been concerned for her, had feared he would put her at risk? That he would do so and not simply expect her to be responsible for herself sent a wave of warmth flooding through Angela. In that moment she knew without a doubt that she still loved Justin.

"How could you think, even for a minute, that I don't want you?" He tightened his fingers on her shoulders, dragged her so close that Angela could see the flecks of black in his green eyes. "How could you not see that I want you so damn much I can hardly breathe?"

Angela's pulse leapt at his admission. "I'm sorry," she told him, and wrapped her arms around him.

He groaned and held her hard against him. "You're not the only one." He sighed and loosened the embrace. "I'd better get out of here before I do something totally stupid and irresponsible and try to convince us both that just this one time won't matter." He stroked his hand over her hair, pressed a kiss to her head. "Next time, I promise you I'll be prepared."

But what if there isn't a next time?

The voice inside Angela sent a shiver of unease through her, and before she allowed reason to dictate her heart, she blurted out, "Stay."

"Aw, sweetheart, don't do this to me."

"But it's all right. I mean, there wouldn't be anything irresponsible about your staying."

Justin eased her away from him a bit. His eyes searched her face, and Angela knew that he was remembering that she'd been unable to tolerate the oral contraceptives in the early days of their marriage. As they'd both learned later, she'd had no reason to worry since she'd been unable to conceive. "Are you saying that you're on the pill now?"

"No," she said, lowering her gaze. "That's not what I meant." The truth was she didn't know if she still had an adverse reaction to the contraceptives or not. Since she hadn't been involved with anyone since their divorce, she'd seen no reason to worry about it.

He frowned. "Then I don't understand."

"Don't you remember all the fertility treatments and the in-vitro procedures I went through when we tried to have a baby?" And none of them had worked. Nothing had. Between her recurring endometriosis and her low ovulation she'd been told her chances of ever conceiving were slim to none. It's why after the last procedure failed she'd decided to let Justin go.

"I remember."

"Well, nothing's changed. My doctor in San Antonio said the same thing all the specialists did. That it's not likely I'll ever be able to conceive a child normally." Angela swallowed. "What I'm trying to tell you is that I don't want to wait. I want to make love with you now. Tonight."

"Angela—"

"Please, Justin. Make love with me."

She waited a heartbeat, two, and when he said nothing, she knew that she had lost. He was going to refuse her. Disappointment gave way to resignation. Justin was a man who lived by the book. He followed orders, obeyed rules. He believed in things like responsibility, honor and doing what was right. He was not a man who made reckless decisions. He was not going to make one now. Not for himself or for her. She couldn't blame him. His noble streak was one of the things that made him who he was, and it was also one of the reasons that she loved him, she reminded herself as she started to turn away.

"Where are you going?" he asked.

Angela's gaze shot to his, and what she read there made her heart pound. Taking her face in his hands, he lowered his mouth to hers. He kissed her. Deeply. Tenderly. Thoroughly.

Overcome with emotion, Angela roped her arms around his neck and tried to show him what she hadn't dared to tell him. That she loved him. That she had always loved him. Only him. That she'd missed him. That she wanted him. One kiss spun into another, and then another still, each one deeper, hotter, hungrier than the one before.

Still drugged by his kisses, wanting him to kiss her again, she didn't protest when Justin lifted her and sat her atop the desk. Slowly he began to unbutton her shirt. The heat in his eyes as he looked at her sent a trill of excitement up her spine. The hands that cupped her breasts were hard and calloused, not the hands of a man who sat behind a desk and pushed papers. They were the hands of a man who worked hard, be it helping to herd cattle at the ranch or by risking his own life to keep the county and its people safe. But there was such a gentleness in the way he touched her that it made Angela tremble. She was a grown woman, she reasoned. She'd been married to this man, was no stranger to his touch. Yet each caress, each kiss was somehow sweeter, more special than she'd remembered.

"You're so beautiful, so perfect," he whispered, and took her into his mouth.

The heat that had started in her belly before he'd even kissed her now ran like molten lava through her system. His teeth closed over her nipple, and Angela clutched his head to her, shivered as the waves of pleasure-pain coursed through her. When he lifted his head, the hunger in his eyes sent desire skyrocketing through her.

Justin took her mouth again, savaged it. Tongues tangled. Teeth scraped. Fingers stroked, kneaded. He had her out of her jeans and panties with a speed that would have shocked her had she not been just as impatient to get him out of his clothes. She had just managed to get his zipper down when he cupped her mound and slid his finger inside her. Angela gasped and nearly came apart at the seams.

"Easy, sweetheart."

Flushed, embarrassed at how near the brink she was, she knew a brief moment of annoyance at the smile in his voice. But then he stroked her again. And she couldn't think, could barely breathe. Her vision blurred. She bit down on her lip to keep from crying out as waves of pleasure whispered just out of reach. After a moment when she could breathe again, Angela decided that two could play this game. Easing her hand inside his briefs, she closed her fist around him. And then it was her turn to smile as a groan rumbled through him.

"Where's the bedroom?" he demanded, his voice hoarse with need, his body taut with impatience.

"Too far," she whispered just before nipping the lobe of his ear. "Make love to me, Justin. Here. Now."

He made some sound, part hiss, part moan. She couldn't be sure which. And her heart nearly sank with disappointment when he drew away from her. Then without saying a word, he toed off his boots, shrugged out of his jeans and kicked them aside.

She had to sketch him. The notion popped into her head as she watched him, took in the ripple of muscles, the sun-bronzed skin, the golden hair and gleam in his emerald eyes. Then Justin shed his briefs and the sight of his rigid shaft thrusting up from the wiry dark gold hair wiped every thought from her brain. As he moved between her thighs, anticipation shivered through her.

"Are you sure?" he asked her, his fierce expression belying the gentleness in his voice.

That even now he would still give her the choice only made her love him more. "I'm sure," she told him.

He entered her in one swift stroke that had her clutching at his shoulders and her body poised on the brink once more. With his hands anchoring her at the hips and his mouth on hers, he began to move. In and out, long slow strokes, nearly withdrawing completely before entering her again. Each stroke a little harder, a little deeper than the one before. Each one tantalizingly slow and nearly driving her mad with the ripples of sensation. Impatient, Angela arched her back, dug her nails into his skin, urging him to hurry. Justin refused to be hurried.

"Not yet," he told her, his voice tight, his back slick with sweat.

Knowing Justin as she did, she realized he was holding back for her. He wanted to make this special for her, to ensure her pleasure came before his own. She loved him for that, but she'd never been the patient type. When he slid into her again, she clamped her feminine muscles around him. She knew a moment of satisfaction at his groan, heard his grumbled "Someday I'm going to teach you how much fun it can be to go slow."

"But not today."

"No, not today," he growled before slamming into her again, and again and again. Each thrust was deeper, harder and faster than the one before.

The first waves of sensation hit her, tossed her high, sent pleasure roaring through her like the rushing surf. Wrapping her legs around him, Angela clung to Justin as she went hurling head- and heart-first into the storm. Moments later, his body stiffened and he thrust into her a final time before he shouted her name and followed her into the stormy seas.

"I really had planned to make good on that promise," Justin told her hours later as he lay in Angela's bed with her draped on top of him.

"Unless I'm mistaken, Sheriff, you did make good on your promise. Several times, in fact," she informed him. "Of course, if you're sure you don't need more time to recover—"

Justin laughed and flipped her over onto her back. Feeling totally sated and happier than he had in years, he pinned her beneath him and nipped at her sassy mouth. "I was referring to my promise to make love to you slowly."

"You don't hear me complaining, do you?" she asked, a satisfied smile curving her lips.

He laughed again. He couldn't remember the last time he'd been in bed with a woman who made him laugh. And quick as a snap he realized that the last time he'd felt this way was when he'd been married to Angela.

"Justin?" She said his name on a stifled yawn.

Sobered by the realization, he stared into her sleepy blue eyes. "I wanted to make it special for you, Angel. You deserve for it to be special."

She held his face in her hands, gently kissed him and said, "You did make it special. Making love with you was always special."

Then why had she left him?

He wanted to ask the question, but worried what her answer would be.

She yawned again. "I'm sorry," she said, her eyelids

fluttering sleepily. "But you wore me out, cowboy. I'm whipped."

He pressed a kiss to her forehead. "Then get some sleep," he whispered, and started to ease off of her.

"Will you stay?" she asked, reaching for him.

"Yeah, I'll stay," he promised, and tucked her against his side.

She tangled one of her legs with his and snuggled up against his shoulder. Within moments she was out cold. Smoothing her hair with his fingers, he gathered her in his embrace and contented himself with the sound of her breathing as it settled into the steady rhythm of sleep. While she had changed in some ways, her ability to zonk out at the drop of a hat was not one of them, he thought with a grin. Too bad he couldn't claim that same trait, because he was bone tired and dawn was only a few hours away.

Justin closed his eyes, tried to make his mind go blank. Yet despite the fact that he'd put in a long day and had spent a good portion of the night sating his passions with Angela, sleep continued to elude him. After ten minutes he opened his eyes and admitted it wasn't going to happen. While his body craved rest, his mind refused to shut down. Probably because for the first time in a long time, he was thinking about the future. A future that went beyond his job and family.

Who was he kidding? He was thinking about a future with Angela.

Surprisingly the admission didn't disturb him nearly as much as he'd thought it would. What did disturb him was the fact that he had a great deal going on right now, with the rumblings within the Mercado crime family since Del Brio had replaced Carmine, the open murder investigation of Carl Bridges, the kidnapped baby, the potential ramifications if Haley Mercado really was alive and that missing child belonged to her.

While he had made light of Angela's theory that Haley was the woman Luke had slept with and the mother of the missing baby, he was almost sure it was true. With any luck, he'd be able to confirm those suspicions soon enough. He should tell Angela. He wanted to tell Angela. And he hadn't told her because of Ricky, he admitted.

Justin grimaced. He didn't like the hotheaded Italian, had never gotten along with the man. Perhaps Hawk had been right that it was his own jealousy of Ricky's relationship with Angela that was at the core of that friction. Ricky had known Angela longer than he had, and Angela was fiercely loyal to the other man. Which meant that he couldn't put her in the middle. She would want to tell Ricky, and he couldn't afford for Ricky to know—not without putting a lot of innocent people at risk.

He looked down at the woman sleeping in his arms, felt a fist tighten around his heart. Somehow he would have to work with her to find the child without sharing full information. Angela wouldn't be happy about it when she learned he'd held out on her. But it wouldn't stop her from doing her job. It couldn't stop him from doing his, either. They would find the little girl, he vowed. He refused to believe otherwise. But once her job was done, would Angela want to stay? Suddenly the thought of her leaving rent a hole the size of Texas in his gut.

So he would have to convince her to stay. While he didn't delude himself into thinking that the mind-blowing sex meant Angela was looking for a reconciliation, he knew her well enough to know that she'd never have slept with him unless her feelings were involved. It was a start, he reasoned, and breathed a little easier.

Staring up at the ceiling, he ran his fingers up and down

her spine and considered the obstacles that lay ahead. Eventually, they would have to talk. He'd do his best to put to rest her concerns about the children issue. There was always adoption, and if that didn't appeal to her, he'd be content being an uncle. Rose and Matt Carson had already provided him with one nephew. Between his sister Susan's marriage to Michael O'Day and Hawk's marriage to Jenny, he figured it probably wouldn't be too long before he had another nephew or niece to spoil, as well.

Justin smiled at the idea of a horde of little ones racing around the ranch calling for their uncle Justin. The smile disappeared almost as quickly as it had come as he realized that the logistics of his and Angela's jobs was something else that they would have to work out. Despite all the headaches that came with being sheriff, he enjoyed his work. He liked the feeling that he was giving something back to the community he'd grown up in by keeping the county safe. It was home. His family was here. He'd been born in Lone Star County, and it was where he'd expected to die someday. But Angela didn't have those same ties. Her career hadn't taken off until she'd gone to San Antonio. Would she be willing to give it up to move back here with him? What if she wasn't? His arms tightened around her. Would he leave Mission Creek to be with her? As much as he hated the idea of leaving, he hated the idea of staying and being without her even more.

"What is it?" Angela mumbled sleepily. She lifted her head slightly, her eyes all fuzzy with sleep. "Is it time to get up already?"

"No. It's not time to get up," Justin murmured, and loosened his hold slightly. He pressed a kiss to the top of her head. "Go back to sleep."

Her head drooped down to his chest again. Within moments, she was once more fast asleep. He was a long way from being faced with the decision of where he would live, Justin admitted as he lay there with Angela in his arms. He watched her sleep, wished sleep would come as easily for him.

Sleep did come for him finally shortly before dawn— but only after he'd formulated a plan.

Justin put his plan into action early the next morning. Or at least he tried to, greeting Angela with a kiss. She draped her arms around his neck, nuzzled close and was well on her way to going back to sleep when he said, "Come on, sleeping beauty. Time to get up."

"It's still early," she whined, and didn't even bother to open her eyes.

"It's already after six."

"In the morning?" she said with a groan.

Justin laughed. One more thing about her that hadn't changed. His Angela still wasn't a morning person. "Yeah, in the morning."

"It can't be," she countered. "We just went to sleep. Come back to bed."

"As enticing as that offer is, I'm afraid I'll need to take a rain check. How about some breakfast?"

"Breakfast?" She opened her eyes, pushed up to her elbows and sniffed. "You fixed me breakfast?"

"You should sound surprised. It was obvious from the contents of your refrigerator and pantry that you still consider chips, salsa, ice cream and chocolate the four basic food groups."

She wrinkled her nose at him. "So what did you fix?"

Justin retrieved the tray from the dresser and lifted the napkin he'd used as a cover to reveal a cheese omelet, toast and a pot of coffee.

Angela's face lit up like a kid's on Christmas morning.

"Give me two seconds," she told him and scrambled out of bed, affording him a lovely view of her bare backside before disappearing into the bathroom.

To his disappointment, she was wrapped in a white terry-cloth robe when she exited the bathroom a few minutes later. And she didn't bother removing it before she climbed back into the bed. "This looks great," she told him, and reached for the coffee first. She took a sip, leaned back against the pillows he'd piled up against the headboard and sighed.

"Eat," Justin told her, and held out a slice of buttered toast.

She took a bite, sighed again and closed her eyes as she chewed it. He followed with a forkful of eggs and another bite of toast, alternating until between the two of them they'd polished off the meal.

"Hmm. That was wonderful," she said. "I haven't had breakfast in bed since that time we went to New Orleans for the weekend when we—" She fell silent a moment. The smile slipped from her lips. "When we spent that weekend in New Orleans."

Where they had gone with the intention of getting pregnant, Justin finished in silence. They'd been married for six months and had thought having a baby would be easy. So he'd booked the romantic getaway for them, liking the idea of conceiving their first child in the sultry city. They'd stayed in a ritzy French Quarter hotel, and on their last morning there after a night filled with lovemaking, they had ordered breakfast sent to the room. They'd fed each other buttery croissants, fresh berries dipped in cream and an assortment of decadent pastries in bed. And when they'd finished the meal, they had made love again. From the expression on her face, Justin suspected that Angela was remembering that morning, too.

The smile she gave him was overbright. So was her quipped "Thanks for the room service. If you ever decide to give up law enforcement, you'll have no trouble making it as a chef. Breakfast was excellent."

"Glad you think so," he told her. "But it isn't over yet."

"No?"

"No. It comes with dessert."

She arched one dark brow questioningly. "After breakfast?"

"It's the best time." He took the tray, brought it over to the dresser and then returned to stand beside the bed. Never taking his eyes from her, he stripped off his jeans and joined her on the bed.

Justin kissed her. She tasted of coffee and butter and Angela. Determined to wipe away the haunted look that had crept into her eyes a few moments ago, he kissed her slowly, tenderly, lovingly. And when he lifted his head, he was relieved to see her eyes were all dreamy now, her mouth pink and warm and wet from his kisses.

He wanted to make a new memory for her, one to wipe away the sad one that had stolen its way into their morning. Reaching for the belt of her robe, he untied it and parted the folds. It was like opening a present, he thought as he took in the sight of her body. All that pale, silky skin, the gentle curves, the long limbs. He filled his palms with her breasts, brushed his thumbs over the dusky tips. Desire coiled hot and fast in his gut. It had only been a few hours since they'd made love last, but already he wanted her again. With a herculean effort, Justin reined in the hunger that rushed through his veins like a whirlpool.

He kissed his way down the slope of her hips, across her waistline to her belly. He circled her navel with his tongue, smiled at the sound of her breath hitching and moved lower. He parted her thighs. Taking his time, he kissed the inside of one thigh and then the other. With each touch, each stroke, she trembled. So did he.

When he kissed her at her center, she lifted her hips, curled her fingers into the sheets. He stroked her with his tongue and she cried out, "Justin!"

"Don't fight it, Angel. Take it," he urged her, and continued to make love to her with his mouth. She reminded him of a pagan goddess. All pale skin, midnight hair and those ghost-blue eyes glazed with passion. Sweat pooled between his shoulder blades with the effort it took to hold himself back, determined that he not take his release before she'd taken hers.

"Justin, please, I—"

She arched her back, and Justin gripped her hips to hold her as the first spasms took her. And when she called out for him again, he moved between her thighs and entered her. Justin groaned. Every muscle in his body went taut as he sheathed himself inside her. Angela locked her legs around him, lifted her hips, and the storm inside Justin broke. And as the white-hot sensations splintered around him, he heard Angela shout and he followed her over the cliff.

From inside the neighboring condo occupied by the newlyweds, the woman who posed as a new wife pulled back a curtain and looked over toward Angela's condo. "Hi, honey, it's me checking in as requested."

"Funny, Harte. Real funny," Sean Collins, the FBI agent in charge who'd posed as her husband, fired back. "What's happening over there?"

"Wainwright's truck is still parked outside the Mason woman's place. So my guess is he spent the night."

"Any sign of Ricky Mercado?"

"No," Annabelle Harte told him. "Just the sheriff."

"What about the phone tap? Any calls to Mercado?"

"Not unless she used her cell phone," Annabelle replied. "The only call she made from her place last night was to the sheriff at his home, and that wasn't until after eleven o'clock. She was all excited about some picture she had that she said might be where the little girl is being held."

"All right. Keep her under surveillance, and let me know if she hooks up with Mercado. I'll have our man on the inside keep an eye on the sheriff."

"Collins?"

"Yeah?"

"Do you think there's anything to what the reports said about her being psychic?"

"Damned if I know."

"If she is and really does know where the little girl is," Annabelle began, "maybe I should see if I can get a look at that picture."

"Forget it. With the Mason woman so friendly with the Mercados and obviously sleeping with the county's sheriff, I've got more than enough to worry about right now," Collins told her. "The last thing I need is for you to go sneaking around her place and get caught and jeopardize this entire operation."

"I've got news for you, ace, I wouldn't get caught."

"I mean it, Harte. Keep out of the Mason woman's condo."

Seven

"**D**amn!"

Feeling lazy and content, it took Angela a moment to register the reason Justin was rolling out of bed swearing. Then she heard it, the annoying and incessant sound of a beeper. Since she refused to use one, she knew it was Justin's.

He scrambled around on the floor in search of his clothes, snagged his jeans and shut off the noisemaker. Enjoying the view of him naked, she felt her pleasure dim when she saw the frown on his face. "Problem?"

"I don't know. I need to make a call," he said, and began pulling on his jeans.

"You can use my phone," she told him, indicating the one on the night table.

"Thanks, but I'd better make it downstairs."

Once Justin left the room, Angela grabbed her robe and headed for the bathroom, intent on getting her own show on the road. She'd barely had time to brush her teeth when she heard him running back up the stairs. "Is anything wrong?" she asked, exiting the bathroom.

"Nothing major, but I'm afraid I'm going to have to leave you with the dishes."

"Don't worry about the dishes. They can wait," she told him. "I'm probably going to need about fifteen minutes. Do you want me to meet you at your office or should we hook up somewhere else?"

Justin slid on one boot and then the other and stood. "Actually I'm not sure how long I'll be. There's a good chance I'm going to be tied up for most of the day."

"I see," she said, disappointed and suddenly a little worried that maybe she had misread things last night. While making love with her didn't necessarily mean that Justin loved her as she loved him, she had felt that they had connected last night on some almost spiritual level in a way that they never had before. She'd actually hoped it might be a new beginning for them.

Evidently reading something in her expression, he went to her, tipped up her chin and brushed a kiss across her lips. "I'm sorry to rush off on you like this."

"I understand," she said, and she did, but it didn't stop her from feeling disappointed and unsettled.

"Come on, Angel. Don't look at me like that. If I could stay, I would."

"I said I understood," she repeated, not sure what to make of his seeming agitation. "I guess I'll just talk to you later."

"Wait," Justin said when she started to turn away. He sighed, raked a hand through his hair. "That call I had to make was to Dylan Bridges. I've been trying to see him for nearly a week, and he just got back into town late last night. I'm meeting him in an hour."

"He's Judge Bridges's son, isn't he? The one who got in some kind of trouble and left Mission Creek a long time ago. I heard he's now some kind of investor."

"Yeah. Only Dylan is more than an investor. He's worth millions. And he lives in Mission Creek now. He and the judge patched things up and he moved back just before Carl was killed."

"Carl Bridges is dead?"

"Yeah. He was killed about ten months ago. The lowlife

scum who pulled the trigger is in prison, but I think Frank Del Brio is the person who ordered the hit. But so far, I haven't been able to tie it to him."

"Is that what you're meeting with Dylan about?" she asked.

"Dylan allowed me access to his father's business files, and I discovered that for the past couple of years and right up until his death the judge was in contact with a woman working as a graphic artist in London who went by the last name of Joseph. If you're right, and Haley Mercado is alive, it's possible that this Ms. Joseph is Haley."

Stunned by the information and excited by the possible link, Angela sat down on the corner of the bed. "Then we need to contact her at once and—"

"She's gone. It seems she and her infant daughter vanished and left no forwarding address."

Angela jerked her gaze up to Justin's at the mention of the baby. "It's her, Justin. I know it is."

"I think so, too. It certainly would explain a lot of things." At her questioning look, he said, "Carl Bridges stepped down from the bench to represent Luke Callaghan and his friends when they were charged with Haley's death. When they were acquitted of the charges, Del Brio swore that he'd make all of them pay for his loss. The guy's a loose canon. If he found out that Haley was alive and had somehow faked her own death, he wouldn't rest until he got back what he believed was rightfully his. And the best way to do that is to get rid of the person helping her."

"Carl Bridges," Angela replied.

"Exactly. Del Brio wouldn't think twice about putting a contract out on him."

"But the baby?"

"If this Joseph woman is Haley, she'd know her baby

was in danger. You said yourself that she'd probably left the baby on the golf course with the note for Luke so that he could protect the child."

"Only Luke's name became smeared on the note and Luke wasn't there to take the baby," Angela added.

"Exactly."

"And if we've figured it out, chances are so has Del Brio."

"Yes," Justin replied. "If he did, there's a good chance he did kidnap the little girl and is trying to use her to smoke Haley out. That's why I'm going to see Dylan, to see if he knows anything at all about this Joseph woman, or if he's come across anything about her in his father's personal papers that might lead me to her."

"You mean lead us," Angela corrected him. "I'm coming with you. Just give me time to throw on some clothes."

Justin caught her by the shoulders. "I'm sorry. I can't let you come. I need to see Dylan alone."

"But—"

"You said yourself this is a small town. People think you're here to help find that missing little girl. You go with me to see Dylan Bridges and they'll wonder why. I don't want Del Brio or anyone else involved to realize we might have put the pieces together. All that will do is put little Lena in greater danger than she already is."

While she could understand and even agree to Justin's line of thinking, she didn't like it. "All right," she said reluctantly. "I guess you're right. But you'll let me know what you find out?"

"Yes," he told her, and kissed the tip of her nose. "I've got to go. I'll give you a call later."

"Justin, what about the ranch? The place in my sketch?"

He paused at the door. "Like I said last night, it isn't

going to be easy to find it. There are a lot of places that fit that description.''

"We can find it," Angela insisted. "I know we can."

"All right. But it'll have to wait. After I meet with Dylan, I've got to swing by the office. But as soon as I'm free, I'll pick up some maps and then we'll see where it leads us.''

"But—"

Too late, he was already racing down the stairs. Angela walked over to the window and watched Justin's truck pull off. The problem was that she'd never been good at waiting, Angela admitted as she grabbed a pair of jeans and a blouse from her closet and headed for the bathroom to shower and get dressed.

"After your visit this morning I went through the files and personal papers my father kept at home," Dylan Bridges told Justin at the sheriff's office later that day. "It took me quite a while to go through all the boxes. You wouldn't believe all the stuff he had, some of it more than thirty years old.''

Justin couldn't help think of all the years lost between Dylan and his father because of their estrangement, and with Carl Bridges dead, there would be no years for them to share in the future. He thought of his own situation and the years he'd missed out on having Hawk as a brother. It also made him realize that he'd lost the last five years with Angela, as well. While they still had to work things out, after last night surely she would see that they belonged together.

"He had letters from people he defended when he was practicing law, notes from students he'd helped when he was teaching at the university, cards from families whose relatives came into his courtroom to thank him for his help.''

"Your father was a good man and he had a lot of friends in Lone Star County. He touched a lot of people's lives," Justin told him.

"Yes, he did," Dylan told him. "More than I'd realized."

"I gave you my word that I'd find the person who had him killed. I intend to keep that promise."

"And I intend to hold you to it."

Justin nodded. "Those the files I asked for?"

Dylan stood, then picked up the box he'd placed on the floor upon entering the office and handed it to Justin. The thing was stuffed full of folders with legal documents and correspondence. "It's everything I could find regarding the Mercados. There's also a couple of letters in there from Isadora Mercado that date back to when she must have been in her teens. It's funny, all these years and I never knew my father had been in love with her. I mean, I knew they'd been friends all their lives, but I hadn't realized until I read her letters that he'd wanted to marry her."

"I'm sure your dad was happy with your mother," Justin said, wanting to console Dylan as best he could. He knew from his own father's affair with Hawk's mother how complicated and unsettling it was to see one's parents in a different light.

"Oh, I know that," Dylan replied. "It's just there's so many things about him that I never knew and should have known. Maybe if I had come back and tried to work things out with him sooner—"

Justin clamped a hand on Dylan's shoulder. "The important thing is that you did come back and you patched things up before he was killed."

"Yeah," Dylan said. "I guess there's some comfort in that."

Justin wished he could offer him something more, but already he could feel the clock ticking. "So what did you find?"

"Well, I checked on my dad's computer like you asked me to for any e-mail correspondence with this Joseph woman in London."

"And?" Justin asked, anxious for any lead that might conclusively link the woman in London to Haley Mercado.

"And it looks like my dad didn't believe in saving e-mail correspondence. Either that, or he didn't trust leaving it on his computer. Except for some legal and business stuff, he deleted any personal messages he received."

"I always knew it was a long shot," Justin told him.

"Turns out it was a good hunch."

Justin jerked his attention from the box of files to Dylan. "What do you mean?"

"There were several unopened e-mails to my dad from someone calling herself 'ItalianGirl' that were dated just after he was killed."

The moniker "ItalianGirl" definitely described Haley, Justin conceded. "And?"

"And all of them asked if something had happened to him. Why he wasn't answering her e-mails. The sender was obviously worried about him."

"Did you get a return address on the sender?" Justin asked.

"Yeah, but it's no good. I tried sending a message and it bounced back."

"Damn!" He had hoped that if this Joseph woman was Haley he'd be able to track her through an e-mail address.

"But what I did manage to do was tap into my dad's hard drive and restore the last message he sent the day he was killed." Dylan removed a sheet of paper from inside his jacket pocket and handed it to Justin.

Justin unfolded the paper, and sitting back down in his chair, he quickly scanned the note Carl Bridges had sent.

My dear ItalianGirl,

I'm worried about you. In your last message you sounded very lonely and sad. I know how hard this is for you and how anxious you are for this all to be over so that you can be with your baby again, but promise me you'll be careful. I spoke with S.C. today and expressed my unhappiness at how long this is taking and how concerned I am for your safety. He assures me that they're on top of the situation and that this nightmare will soon be over for you and your family. How I wish your mother was still alive to see that happen. She would be proud of you, as proud of you as I am.

I saw your little girl today, and she appears to be doing fine. So please don't worry about her. She's in good hands. You just take care of yourself. I have to run. Dylan is going to attend the mystery gala at the Lone Star Country Club with me tonight and I need to make sure my tuxedo still fits. Would you believe I'm actually looking forward to going? But then I guess that's because after all these years, I finally have my son back.

Please, please be careful. I'll be in touch soon.

"You think it's her? Haley Mercado?" Dylan asked.

Justin looked across his desk at the other man. "Yeah, I do. And after reading this, I'm sure that Lena is Haley's daughter. It all makes sense now," Justin said as all the pieces of the puzzle fell into place. "Before Haley's supposed death, she was engaged to Frank Del Brio."

"The mob guy you think was behind my father's murder?"

"One and the same. The rumor on the street was that Haley wasn't happy about her engagement to Frank. Faking her death in that boating accident gave her a way out. But to pull it off, she would have needed help from someone who knew the ins and outs of the legal system. Someone who would not only help her, but whom she could trust to keep her secret."

"And my father fit both criteria," Dylan supplied.

Justin nodded. "Because of his affection for her mother, Haley would have felt she could trust him. And as a lawyer and a judge, your dad would have known what would be needed in the way of evidence to convince everyone that Haley was dead. He'd also have had the connections to get her out of the country and set her up with a new identity."

"I could buy it all except for the fact that you said Luke Callaghan and his friends were charged with Haley's murder. I can't see my dad going along with having innocent men facing a prison term for a murder that he knew hadn't even been committed."

"My guess is that neither Haley nor your father counted on Del Brio bringing the murder charges against Luke and his friends. That's probably why your father headed up their defense team. If they hadn't been acquitted, he would have insisted that Haley come forward and admit that she was still alive."

Dylan shook his head. "It just all seems so surreal. I mean, I understand about this guy Del Brio's mob connections. But come on, this isn't 1930s Chicago where the mafia runs the city. Why go to such lengths just to break off an engagement?"

"I know how it sounds. But Haley Mercado wouldn't have felt she had any choice about marrying Del Brio— not if she wanted her father and brother to go on breathing." The truth was he imagined she would have been desperate, and he couldn't blame her. From what he remembered about Haley, she'd been a bright, talented, nice young woman—too nice and too bright for a thug like Del Brio. At Dylan's skeptical look, Justin said, "You've spent the last fifteen years away from here and haven't been back long enough to see Del Brio in action. Trust me, the guy's a real piece of work. He's ruthless and has a warped sense of his own importance. He wouldn't think twice about threatening to kill her family unless Haley agreed to marry him."

"The man sounds like a psychopath."

"I think he is." He'd heard too many tales of Del Brio's cold-bloodedness to believe otherwise.

"Then why haven't you locked him up?" Dylan demanded.

"Because psychopath or not, Del Brio's no dummy. He gets someone else to do his dirty work—men like Alex Black. And he makes sure they can't be tied to him. I'm more convinced now than ever that he's the one who had your father killed. This—" he indicated the e-mail he held in his hand and the box of files "—this is the connection that I was missing. Del Brio already held a grudge against your father for getting Luke and his friends acquitted in Haley's death. But if Del Brio somehow discovered that your father had helped Haley pull off this charade—"

"He would also have figured that my dad knew where Haley was," Dylan finished. "And he sent Black to find out where, only my dad wouldn't give Haley up and Black killed him.''

"That's how I figure it went down."

Dylan gripped the arms of his chair and leaned forward. "So when are you going to pick up the slime bag? Because I intend to be there when you haul him in for my father's murder."

"I wish it were that simple," Justin told the other man.

Dylan's eyes narrowed, glinted dangerously. "It looks simple enough to me. You said yourself that Haley Mercado was the connection."

"She is," Justin replied. He understood Dylan's frustration, felt some frustration of his own. "Unfortunately, all I have is a theory and no hard evidence."

"What about the e-mails?"

"It's circumstantial at best. Nothing here leads back to Del Brio. What I need is Haley Mercado herself. She's the key to all this. With her as a witness, I can prove Del Brio had motive and can nail him for your father's murder. But I've got to find her before Del Brio does." Justin picked up Carl's last e-mail again, stared at it. "I just wish I knew who this S.C. person was and what the situation is that they're supposed to be on top of."

"Maybe it's someone here in Mission Creek or in Del Brio's organization?"

"It's possible. But at the moment no one comes to mind," Justin admitted. "Maybe something in these old files will lead me to this S.C. or to Haley herself."

"And if it doesn't?" Dylan countered.

"Then start praying that we find that little girl soon. Because if Del Brio's behind her kidnapping and knows that she belongs to Haley, he'll use her to smoke Haley out. And once he has Haley, both she and her daughter are going to be in serious danger. I don't see Del Brio letting either one of them live.''

"Then we better find her," Dylan told him, the light of battle in his eyes. "What can I do to help?"

Justin shook his head. "I appreciate the offer, but you've already been a big help. Angela and I will take it from here."

"Angela?" Dylan said, and leaned back in his seat. "She the good-looking brunette with Ricky Mercado at the hospital dedication the other night? The one who's supposed to be some kind of psychic?"

Justin frowned, not sure which he objected to most— having Angela linked with Ricky or the skepticism in Dylan's voice about Angela being psychic. "Angela's a top profiler out of San Antonio who was brought in to help with the kidnapping case. She's got an impressive track record when it comes to locating missing people. Whether it's a psychic ability or just plain instinct, she's damned good at what she does."

"Hey, I meant no offense," Dylan told him. "I'm just surprised, that's all. Not about the psychic thing, but because Maddie told me she was your ex-wife."

"She was...is my ex-wife," Justin amended. "Anyway, the two of us make a good team." And he realized it was the truth. He and Angela did make a good team, both personally and professionally.

Dylan stood. "Then I'll leave it to you to nail Del Brio. But if there's anything I can do, and I mean anything at all, you let me know. I want that bastard to pay for killing my father."

"He will," Justin promised, and shook the other man's hand.

Dylan nodded, and the look he gave Justin said he

would hold him to it. "Then I guess I'll see you tonight at the country club."

"Tonight?" Justin repeated.

"At the fund-raiser for hurricane victims. Maddie told me you're giving the opening remarks."

"Damn! I forgot about that," Justin said. He looked at his watch, then swore again. It was late, much later than he'd realized. Where had the day gone? And what in the devil was Angela going to say about him never getting back to her as he'd promised?

"Excuse me. I need to make a call."

"Go ahead," Dylan said.

Justin grabbed the telephone, and after locating the slip of paper with Angela's number on it, he began to punch in the numbers.

Dylan chuckled and headed for the door. "Why don't you bring her with you tonight? I'd like to meet her."

But Justin barely heard Dylan and didn't notice him leave because he was too busy listening to the phone in Angela's condo ring. When it was picked up on the fourth ring, he felt a rush of relief. "Hey, it's Justin—"

"Hi, this is Angela. I'm unavailable to take your call. Leave a message and I'll call you back."

Irritated and telling himself he had no right to be, Justin said, "It's Justin. Sorry I didn't get back to you sooner. I'm at the office, and it looks like I'll be stuck here for at least another hour. Give me a call when you get back."

Angela slowed her car down to a crawl as she tried to determine where she was. For the most part she'd had little trouble locating the places on her list. And since her visit to the county records office that morning, where she'd obtained a list of all horse ranches within a hundred-mile radius of Mission Creek, she'd already found and ruled out six of them. But it had been at least twenty minutes since she'd pulled off the main highway in search of the next place on the list, and it had been almost as long since she'd last seen another vehicle.

Irritated with herself for getting lost, Angela turned off the radio, cutting off Faith Hill in the middle of her old hit "This Kiss." She pulled onto the side of the road and immediately began rummaging through the items on the passenger seat in search of the map she'd purchased at the gas station. "Ah, here it is," she murmured as she located the map. Smoothing it out with her fingers, she attempted to get her bearings.

A few minutes later she located the turnoff she'd taken on the map. Using her index finger, she traced the line marking the main road she'd taken to this one and frowned. That was odd, she thought. Where was the little squiggly line branching out from this spot to identify the road just below her? she wondered. But after checking again, she realized that the strip of road jutting out to her right wasn't listed on the map. Opening her door, she exited the car and walked a few yards along the shoulder of the roadway, seeking a better glimpse. Other than the fact that the road was narrow and curved and overgrown with brush, she saw little else. So she headed back to her vehicle.

Once inside her car, Angela checked her watch and was surprised to discover it was already after six o'clock. Even though it was June and darkness didn't set in until nearly eight o'clock most evenings, the sky had been overcast all day. Maybe she should just call it a day, go back to her condo and head out again in the morning. But thoughts of returning to her condo made her think of this morning and Justin. After he'd left her place, she'd waited nearly two hours for him to call and set up a time for them to meet and work out a strategy to locate the house in her sketches. And it had been two hours wasted when she could have been checking out the places on her list.

Maybe he tried to call after you left.

Maybe he had, she admitted, and retrieved her cell phone from her purse to check her machine for messages. But when she punched in the phone number for her condo, she got the annoying bleep that indicated no service was available in the area. Irritated, she tossed the phone onto the passenger seat and it landed beside the fluffy white lamb given to her by Josie Carson during her visit. Lena's favorite toy, Angela recalled with a pang. Picking up the stuffed animal, she remembered last night when she'd relived the little girl's moments of fear during the kidnapping. Her throat suddenly thick, her chest tight, Angela clutched the lamb to her and closed her eyes a moment. When she opened them again, her gaze fell onto the sketches on the neighboring seat. She picked up the one with the house and the winding road that led to it. Lifting her gaze, she stared in the direction of the road jutting off just ahead of her. From what she could see, that was a winding road.

She thought of the impending darkness, the cell phone that didn't work and the fact that no one knew where she was. The smart thing to do would be to go home and come back tomorrow with Justin.

But suppose that road led to the ranch where little Lena's being held?

Remembering how frightened the baby had been, Angela put aside the stuffed animal and restarted her car.

Fifteen minutes later dust swirled around her car like a cloud as she motored down the road. The sky had darkened considerably, giving the overgrown shrubbery and battered-looking trees an ominous appearance. But as she followed the next bend in the road, she spied a house approximately two hundred yards ahead. Pleased to at least see some sign of civilization, Angela continued forward when she hit another hole in the road and her car came to a sudden stop. The impact sent her lurching forward, then slamming back. Her head smacked the headrest so hard Angela was sure she heard her teeth rattle. Groaning, it took her a moment to clear the bells ringing in her head. And when she touched the area with her fingertips, she winced at the pain. She was going to have a doozy of a headache, she realized as she shoved the car into Park and shut off the engine before climbing out to examine her tires. All she needed was to get a blowout here, she thought, suddenly aware of how isolated she was.

Much to her relief, a quick check revealed the tire was okay—at least for the time being. But she had a sneaking suspicion that she was going to be in need of a new set of shocks really soon. Shoving back to her feet, she dusted her hands off and took a look around her.

Maybe it was because it was getting dark, she told herself, but the place gave her the creeps. She glanced back in the direction she'd just traveled, noting there wasn't a single road light of any kind to break the looming darkness. She'd spotted a discarded beer bottle and some cigarette butts as she'd driven along the road, but she hadn't seen another vehicle of any type. Uneasiness skittered down Angela's spine and she whipped around, looked over toward the house where she'd been headed. No lights burned in the distance, and she saw no sign of any movement whatsoever. Yet she had the oddest feeling that someone had been watching her.

When something slithered in the underbrush nearby, Angela scrambled back into her car and restarted the engine.

Probably just her imagination, she told herself as she carefully eased around the monster-size hole in the road and headed back the way she had come.

"It's all right now. She's leaving," the old woman said into the phone while she watched from behind the yellowing curtain inside the house as the car turned around and drove away.

"Are you sure she didn't see you?" Erica Clawson snapped at her mother in a harsh whisper. She'd been forced to keep her voice low so no one at the Lone Star Country club would hear her.

"I don't think so. I turned all the lights off just like you told me."

"What about the kid? She wasn't bawling again, was she?"

"No. Not at all. I was just about to give the little darling her bath, so she was playing with her plastic boat and waiting to get in the tub."

"All right. Well, I've got to go. You let me know if she comes back or if anyone else comes snooping around."

"Will you be coming to see us later?" Mary Lynn Clawson asked her daughter.

"I can't," Erica said, annoyed as much by the request as by the fact that she couldn't go to her mother's even if she'd wanted to do so. "There's some big fund-raiser here at the country club tonight, so I have to work."

"Do you think you could come tomorrow, then? I'm almost out of milk and Lena's getting low on diapers—"

"Jeez! Already?"

"She's a baby, Erica."

"I'm aware of that fact, Mother," Erica shot back. And she wished to hell that Frank had never insisted that they kidnap the kid. If she'd wanted a kid, she'd have had one of her own. At least she'd been able to dump the brat with her mother. After caring for the kid in that small rental near Goldenrod, as Frank had wanted her to do, she realized she wasn't cut out for motherhood—particularly to someone else's kid. As much as she hated waiting tables, at least her job had made it impossible for her to keep playing nursemaid to the brat. And even though Frank hadn't liked involving her mother, he'd agreed it was the only solution. It also helped put some distance between Frank and the kid. While Frank had said that he was using the kid to keep the Mercados in line, Erica was beginning to wonder if he was leveling with her. After all, she knew that he'd once been engaged to the brat's mother, Haley. She'd have to keep her eye on things, Erica told herself, because she fully intended to become Mrs. Frank Del Brio. And there was no way she was going to let an ex-girlfriend invade her turf.

"Erica? Did you hear me?"

"What?" Erica asked, realizing she'd tuned her mother out.

"I asked whether or not your friend Mr. Del Brio will be coming by to see his little girl."

Erica gritted her teeth, wishing now she could have come up with another story to explain showing up at her mother's with the kid half the town had been searching for for the past few months. Mary Lynn Clawson had bought her song and dance about Frank being the kid's father and how the mother was dead and the woman's family was trying to keep Frank away from his daughter. She could only be grateful that her mother was such a soft touch for a sob story and gullible enough not to find the holes in that story. "No. I told you the kid's relatives have detectives watching Frank. If he comes there to see Lena, they'll follow him and take her away. And Frank will never see her again."

"That's such a shame. Well, at least you'll see her when you come. Poor little thing, I think she misses having a mama. It'll be good when Frank gets custody and then you and he can get married and you'll be her mama."

Over her dead body, Erica thought. She intended to marry Frank, but no way was she going to play mama for his ex-girlfriend's kid.

"You will come by tomorrow with the things I need, won't you, honey?"

"Yeah. I'll come. But I've got to go now. Remember, if that woman comes back or anyone else shows up around the place, you make sure you and the kid stay out of sight and call me right away. Got it?"

"I understand. But don't you worry. I'm not going to let anyone take Mr. Del Brio's little girl."

"Thanks, Mom. I'll talk to you later." After ending the call, Erica opened the door of the office she'd snuck into in order to use the phone and checked to make sure she hadn't been missed yet. Then she closed the door and dialed Frank's private phone.

"Yeah."

"It's me. We've got a problem. That woman psychic that was with Ricky Mercado the other night at the hospital dedication was snooping around my mother's place a little while ago."

"Did she see the girl?" Frank asked, his voice deadly cold.

"No. My old lady turned off the lights and the woman must have thought the house was abandoned because she turned around and drove off."

"That place is in the middle of nowhere. There's no way she could have found it on her own. Someone must have followed you there," he accused. "I told you to be careful, that you might be tailed."

"I wasn't tailed," she fired back, resenting the fact that he thought she'd screwed up. "And no one followed me out there because I haven't been to my mother's for more than a week."

"Then how do you explain her finding it?"

"How do I know?" Erica countered, doing her best to keep the edge out of her voice. "Maybe that stuff about her being psychic is true. Anyway, I thought you ought to know, especially since she's so friendly with the Mercados. I know how much you'd hate for anyone to mess up your plans."

"You're right about that. I've got too much invested in this to let someone screw it up now," Frank told her, his voice hard and flat. "You just make sure your mother keeps her mouth shut and stays out of sight with the kid."

"She will, Frank. You don't have to worry about that," Erica assured him.

"Good. You keep trying to find out what you can on that waitress Daisy at the club. I need to know if she's Haley."

"I'm trying," Erica told him, annoyed by his obsession with Haley. "But it isn't easy. She doesn't talk very much."

"Then try harder," he ordered.

"What about that Mason woman? What if she goes snooping around my mother's place again?"

"You let me worry about Angela Mason. I'll see to it that she's taken care of."

Eight

"Angela, it's Justin again. Since I'm getting your machine, I guess you're still out." After a pause he continued, "Listen I'm sorry we haven't been able to connect all day, but I've been tied up. Anyway, I've got some info that could lead to a break in the case. It's too complicated to go into over the phone, so I'll explain everything when I see you tonight. Unfortunately, that's going to be later than I'd hoped. First, I've got to make a speech at a fund-raiser at the country club. But I'll get away as soon as I can and then meet you at your place."

After another pause and the closing of a door, he added, "Angel, I really am sorry that I left you hanging like this, especially after last night. But it just couldn't be helped. I promise, I'll explain everything when I see you. Bye."

Angela raced through the front door of her condo. Dumping her purse, keys and other items onto the counter, she hit the playback button on the answering machine even as she dashed up the stairs to change clothes. Ditching her jeans, shirt and boots, she grabbed the first dress in her closet while she listened for the second time to the messages on her machine that she'd retrieved via her cell phone less than thirty minutes ago. Two calls from Justin telling her he was tied up and one from Ricky advising her that he'd pick her up at eight o'clock for the fund-raiser tonight.

She pulled off her socks and tugged on panty hose, then

slid the dress over her head and zipped it up the back. Returning to her closet, she found her heels and was just stepping into them when she heard the new message from Justin.

Angela groaned. Grabbing the phone, she punched in the number at the Wainwright Ranch again, but the phone rang and rang with no answer. She ended the call and tried his office.

"Lone Star County Sheriff's Office."

"Hi, this is Angela Mason again. Is Sheriff Wainwright in?"

"Sorry, hon. He's not here. You might want to try him on his cell phone."

"I'm afraid I don't have that number, could you give it to me?"

"Can't do that, I'm afraid. But I'll tell him you called."

"Thanks," Angela said, and hung up, wishing she had thought to tell Justin this morning that she had committed to go to the fund-raiser tonight with Ricky. But then, this morning her head and her heart had been much too full of Justin making love with her to be able to think about anything else.

Angela freshened her lipstick. Sighing, she ran a brush through her hair and reminded herself once again that just because they'd spent the night together didn't mean that Justin felt the same way as she did. There were still problems between them that needed working out. But surely she wasn't wrong about them connecting on some new level last night.

She thought of how tentative their relationship was at the moment and worried at Justin's reaction to her arriving at the club with Ricky. She wasn't blind to the fact that Justin disliked Ricky and had never approved of her friendship with him. Maybe she should try the club, see if

Justin was there and explain that she'd said she'd attend
with Ricky before last night. And for the briefest of seconds she considered canceling on Ricky. Just as quickly
she dismissed the idea. She'd promised herself when she'd
left Mission Creek five years ago that she wasn't going to
ever again try to be someone she wasn't. If she and Justin
had any chance of ever making it together as a couple, he
would have to accept her for who she was. And she was
Ricky Mercado's friend.

At the sound of the doorbell announcing Ricky's arrival,
Angela gave herself a once-over in the mirror and decided
she would have to do. But as she headed downstairs to
greet Ricky, she was struck by a sense of foreboding about
the night ahead. Telling herself she was just nervous, she
dismissed the apprehension and hurried to answer the door.

"Hey, you look great," Ricky told her as she opened
the door for him.

"Thanks. So do you."

"We're running a little late. I got tied up with some
family business and wasn't able to get away sooner, so do
you mind if we just split?"

"No, not at all." Because the sooner she got to the club,
the sooner she could find Justin and explain.

"Is it too soon to ask if you've been able to come up
with anything about the kidnapper or where they might be
keeping the baby?" Ricky asked once they were inside the
car.

Angela felt a twinge of guilt as she thought about the
sketches she'd made last night and her promise to Justin
not to tell anyone. "I've already explained that I can't
share any information with you about this. It's one of the
conditions I agreed to."

"Just where does Wainwright get off dictating what you
and I can or can't talk about?"

"It's an official investigation," she reasoned.

"That's not why he's doing it, and you and I both know it. It's because the man hates my guts, and he doesn't like the fact that you and I are friends."

Angela suspected there was more than a small measure of truth in the accusation. But it didn't change the fact that she'd given Justin her word. "If my not sharing information with you about the kidnapping is going to be a problem, maybe you should turn the car around and take me back home."

Ricky whooshed out a breath. "It's not going to be a problem," he said. "I'm sorry if it seemed like I was pressuring you. It's just so frustrating…this not knowing if the kid is Haley's or not. Or if Haley really is alive or if I'm just deluding myself."

"I understand," she said, and she couldn't blame him for his frustration.

"I guess, regardless of whom she belongs to, the important thing is that you find the little girl."

"I intend to do everything I can to do just that. And so will Justin and the FBI," Angela promised as she leaned back against the seat while Ricky headed toward Mission Creek. She knew it wasn't much of an answer, and she suspected it did little to ease Ricky's concerns. And despite the fact that Ricky Mercado was a man who was used to demanding answers and getting them, he didn't press her further.

While they continued to speed toward the city in silence, Angela took the opportunity to study Ricky. He had changed since that summer when she had first met him when they were both in their teens. Her father had shipped her off to spend two months at the home of a former church member who had moved to Goldenrod and whose wife needed help with her children and home after surgery.

The Mercados had lived just down the road. She'd had a particularly rotten day, messing up by telling the people she was staying with where a missing paper was when she shouldn't have. It had freaked them out and made her feel more alone than ever. Ricky had happened upon her at the creek where she'd run off to. She'd been crying and feeling as though she had nothing to look forward to except a life of more rejection. But instead of making fun of her for sobbing and feeling sorry for herself, Ricky had comforted her. They had been friends ever since.

And even though they had remained friends all these years, she had never kidded herself about Ricky, Angela admitted. As a teenager he had been cocky, rough around the edges, a boy who danced on both sides of the law. The man was still cocky, still rough around the edges, and she suspected he still danced on both sides of the law. Yet he was different now. More serious, she decided, and wondered if that sober side had something to do with that mission in Central America that he had told her he'd been involved in with Luke Callaghan. Or was it caused by his concern for his father and Ricky's belief that the kidnapped child was his niece, a niece who could possibly lead him to a sister everyone thought dead? Maybe it was a combination of all those things, she conceded. Whatever the cause, the one thing that had not changed about Ricky was his love for his family and his loyalty to his friends. It was those qualities that enabled them to be friends despite their differences. They were also some of the same qualities that she'd admired in Justin. Unfortunately, it was a similarity between them that Justin either couldn't or wouldn't allow himself to see.

Thoughts of Justin had nerves dancing in her stomach again. She was anxious to see him, and almost afraid that she'd only imagined the magic between them the previous night. Once again she couldn't help wishing that they had talked, that she knew where this thing between them was going. Or if it was going anywhere at all.

"So how are you and Wainwright doing?"

Angela yanked her attention back to Ricky, worried for a moment that she had said something aloud. "What do you mean?"

He gave her a puzzled look. "I was just wondering if he was still giving you a bad time."

"No. No, not really."

"That's good, then," he said, and took the exit for Mission Creek. "I guess I should have warned you that there's supposed to be a big turnout for this thing tonight and Wainwright's probably going to be there."

"Yes, I know. He…left me a message."

"I really appreciate you coming with me. You have no idea how much I hate these things, but like I explained yesterday morning, Del Brio made a big deal about wanting to improve the company's image and how Mercado Brothers Paving and Contracting should turn out to support this fund-raiser. Of course, I didn't buy any of it. The man could care less about the company's image and community relations."

"Then why are you going?" she asked.

"Because I think Del Brio's up to something. I don't know what it is, but I intend to find out. I also didn't want to stir up suspicion by not showing up. As long as he thinks I'm part of his team, I can keep an eye on him."

"Ricky, if you think Del Brio is going to do something illegal or harmful, you really should go to the police. Or let me talk to Justin for you."

"No. I'll handle Del Brio myself," he insisted.

Not a wise move, Angela thought, but decided to remain silent. She knew Ricky was careful about what he told her and she was equally careful not to allow herself to get into a situation that would compromise her duty as an officer of the law. But she couldn't help thinking that Ricky would fare better were he not so determined to fight his battles with Del Brio alone.

"You know, I was thinking that since there are going to be so many people at the club tonight for that fundraiser, you might be able to pick up on something. You know, about the kidnapping."

"I'm sorry to disappoint you, but it doesn't work that way. I'm not going to walk into that country club tonight and suddenly know if someone there kidnapped Lena." But sometimes she wished it did work that way. It would make the frustration and confusion she often felt when struck by glimpses, as she had last night, easier for her to live with and easier for her to know what to do.

"I know. I know," Ricky told her as he turned into the entrance of the Lone Star Country Club. "I didn't mean that the way it sounded. I realize it's more complicated than that. All I'm saying is it can't hurt being in the same place where more than half of the people in town are going to be, because you never know if something or someone there will trigger something that might help."

But as they approached the four-story granite structure that served as the main clubhouse, Angela was struck once again by a sense of foreboding. Even after the valet attendant opened the car door and she'd started up the walkway lined with rose blooms and scented by the flowering shrubs, she couldn't shake the ominous feeling. And the moment she stepped inside the clubhouse, Angela knew with certainty that something terrible was going to happen. And whatever it was, it was going to happen at the Lone Star Country Club tonight.

* * *

Justin looked at his watch for the tenth time in as many minutes and wished that Maddie would pull the plug on the mayor so that he could give his spiel at the microphone and leave. Chastising himself for his own impatience, he reminded himself that holding this fund-raiser for storm victims at the start of each hurricane season had been his idea. He'd made the suggestion following a category-four hurricane that had nearly wiped out a nearby county last year. The people of Lone Star County had opened their hearts and their wallets to help the crippled community get back on its feet. It had been then that Justin had urged the townspeople to make the fund-raiser an annual event. They had agreed. The need for the fund-raiser was no less important now than it had been when he'd first suggested it, but his eagerness to see Angela made the waiting to get through the evening all the more difficult.

"Are you ready, Sheriff?"

"What?" Justin asked, dragging his thoughts back from Angela at the sound of Maddie Delarue Bridges's voice. Embarrassed, he stared at the events manager of the Lone Star Country Club, noting the twinkle in her eyes. "I'm sorry. Guess I wasn't listening."

She laughed. "I noticed. And somehow I doubt that it was hurricane relief that you had on your mind."

"You're right about that," he admitted with a smile. The truth was his head was already back at the condo with Angela, where it had been for a good part of the day. And Maddie wasn't the first person to notice his distracted manner. What was surprising was that he had ever managed to convince himself that he was over Angela in the first place, when here he was, after only one night with her, and he didn't seem able to go a full ten minutes without thinking about her and itching to be with her again.

Face it, Wainwright. You've got it bad. You may have

divorced Angela, but you never got over her. And you probably never will.

And for the first time in years, he could admit the truth to himself without feeling like an idiot. In fact, for the first time in a long time, he actually was looking forward to taking some time off for himself. For himself and Angela, he corrected.

"You're up, Sheriff," Maddie told him as the mayor finished his remarks and announced that the sheriff had a few words.

Justin moved over to the podium that had been set up for tonight's fund-raiser. "Thank you all again for coming, for taking time away from your families and your businesses to be here tonight. I've promised Maddie that I'll keep this short so she won't have to use that hook of hers to yank me off. She tells me that a number of our local businesses and some very generous members of our community have donated some really great items for tonight's silent auction, and Maddie's eager to get the bidding going."

"We're also eager to sample that food," someone called out, which resulted in an outbreak of laughter around the room.

"And you should be," Maddie added from her position beside him. "The Lone Star Country Club has generously donated all of tonight's food and liquor in the hopes that you will be equally generous when it comes to bidding on the wonderful items in our auction. Which is what I believe the sheriff wants to talk to you about."

At Maddie's nod, Justin delivered his speech, short but effective, he hoped. Then, amid a round of applause, he retreated from the podium and turned over the microphone to Maddie. Since he'd already made arrangements with Maddie to enter a generous bid on his behalf for the stud services of a champion stallion that was on the program, he felt comfortable taking his leave. All he wanted now was to get back to Angela.

"That was a nice speech you gave up there, son," Archy Wainwright told him.

"Thanks," Justin replied, his eyes darting toward the door.

"Your mother's here. She's bidding on some spa weekend."

"That's good. What about you? Aren't you going to check out some of the auction items?" Justin asked, hoping to hurry his father along.

"Sure am. But I figure there's plenty of time. Hang on," he told Justin, and called out to the waitress a few feet away. "Miss, I'd like to try one of those."

The blond waitress with the sad brown eyes whom Justin recognized as Daisy hurried over to them. "Of course," she said, and held out the tray and napkins.

"What are these?" Archy asked as he piled several onto a napkin.

"They're jalapeño poppers."

"Thank you, ma'am," he told her, and popped first one and then another of the batter-fried treats into his mouth.

"What about you, Sheriff?"

"Thanks, but I think I'll pass," he said, and wondered why the woman looked so unhappy. But before he could give it another thought, his father was whooshing out a breath and fanning his mouth.

"Whew! Those things are good, but they're hot as Hades. I need something to put out the fire. Come on, son. I'll buy you a cold one."

"They're free," Justin pointed out as his father made a path to one of the bars and he followed.

"Just a technicality. Since the club is donating the food

and liquor and the Wainwrights and Carsons run the club, I figure I'm buying." Once at the bar, he said, "Whiskey straight up for me. What about you, Justin?"

"I'll just have a club soda."

"I thought you were off duty," his father told him.

"I am, but I'm working on something and I'd just as soon keep a clear head."

His father looked at him over the rim of his glass. "That project you working on, does it involve Angela?"

Justin narrowed his eyes. "What makes you ask that?"

"I couldn't help noticing that she's back in Mission Creek. Truth is, I think the whole town noticed your little exchange with her the other night at the hospital. Judging by your reaction, I thought you might have some unresolved feelings where she's concerned."

"And if I do?" Justin demanded, remembering that his parents hadn't been thrilled when he'd announced that he and Angela had eloped.

"Then I suggest you resolve them."

"It's not that simple," Justin told him.

"It's not that hard, either." His father set down his glass and met Justin's gaze. "Listen, I know we didn't make things any easier on you when you told us you wanted to marry the girl."

"I don't want to get into this," Justin argued, not wanting to rehash with his father how Angela Mason wasn't good enough for him, that he needed to marry a woman who was better suited to be a Wainwright.

"We're going to get into it because you're going to let me say what I should have said a long time ago," his father told him. "I had no business telling you who to marry. And you were right to tell me to go to hell and marry the girl like you did."

"I appreciate you saying that. But Angela and I have

been divorced for five years," he reminded him. "So I think it's a little late for your blessing."

"It's not too late if you still love her and she's the woman you want to spend your life with," his father told him, surprising Justin again. "Take a lesson from your old man, son. Don't let pride keep you from what you really want, the way I let it keep me from going after your mother when she left me. You'll find pride a poor substitute for having the woman you love in your bed beside you at night and across the breakfast table from you in the morning."

"You sound like Hawk," Justin told him.

"You mean the boy sounds like me. After all, I'm his father. Not the other way around."

"Yeah, you're right," Justin said, and couldn't help but think about how much his father had changed. For that matter, so had he. "And speaking of Hawk, have you seen him yet? He and Jenny arrived a little while ago."

"That your way of telling your old man to butt out?"

"No, sir. I appreciate what you said," Justin told him honestly.

Archy nodded, apparently satisfied with his answer. "I'll go find Hawk and leave you in peace. Just make sure you say hello to your mother before you leave. And if you haven't seen her already, look for your sister Susan."

"Susan and Michael are here?"

His father nodded. "Michael arranged to get a few days off from the hospital, so he and your sister drove up from Houston for the weekend. I'm sure they'd appreciate seeing you before they head back."

"I'd like to see them, too," Justin said, and held out his hand to his father. "Thank you, sir."

"Anytime, son," he said, taking Justin's hand. And much to Justin's surprise, his father slapped him on the other arm and gave him a bear hug before he headed off into the crowd.

"Another club soda, Sheriff?" the pert redhead that he recognized as Erica asked him from behind the bar.

"No thanks," he said, and took another swallow of his drink as he scoured the crowd to see if he could spot his mother or sister and her husband.

"Looks like a good turnout tonight, and people are still coming in."

"Hopefully it means we'll raise a lot of money." Intent on finding his mother and sister, then splitting for Angela's, he polished off his drink and placed the glass on the counter.

"Did you see the dreamy diamond-and-sapphire necklace that's in the auction?" she asked him.

"No, I'm afraid I didn't."

"It's gorgeous. And Frank, my boyfriend, he says he's going to buy it for me. Sort of an early birthday present."

Justin paused, narrowed his eyes. "And the Frank you're referring to is Frank Del Brio, right?"

"Yes," she said proudly. "He and I...well, we're close. And someday we're going to get married."

Justin didn't bother commenting on the woman's choice in men, nor the fact that he suspected Frank wasn't likely to pop the question anytime soon.

"Frank really wanted to support this fund-raiser. Do you know that he bought twenty tickets and gave them to his employees?"

"That was real big of him," Justin said, and wondered how he had missed seeing Del Brio. Even in a crowd like this the man stuck out, especially with his thugs flanking him. But he no sooner asked himself the question when the answer came. He had probably missed Del Brio for the same reason he had been distracted all day. His thoughts were on Angela. Intent on doing his duty so he could leave for Angela's, he said, "Thanks for the drink, Erica. And good luck on getting that necklace."

"Sheriff, before you go, can I ask you a question? It's sort of personal."

He paused and said, "That depends on how personal the question is."

"Well, it's kind of personal, but not too personal, since you and her aren't married anymore."

"You're talking about Angela Mason?" Justin asked, trying to follow the thread of the woman's conversation and wondering why she would bring up Angela.

Erica nodded. "I heard she's here in Mission Creek to help find that little girl who was kidnapped. And since you used to be married to her, I figured you would know if it was true what they say about her. You know that stuff about her being psychic."

Justin frowned. Aware of the woman's relationship with Del Brio, his lawman's antenna went up. "What makes you ask?"

"Just curious," she said, all sweetness and light. "I mean, when I saw her come in, it made me wonder—"

"Angela's here?" Justin whipped his attention toward the club's entrance.

"Yes, I thought you saw her. She and Ricky Mercado are over there at the table where they're handing out the programs."

Then Justin did see her. She was standing at the check-in table in a dark blue dress that flowed over her curves and was anchored by tiny straps at her shoulders. And standing right behind her, with his hand at her back, was Ricky Mercado. Justin felt as though he'd been kicked in the gut. Everything inside him went white hot with pain. Then the rage took over, and not until he could feel the blood running cold in his veins did he start toward Angela.

Nine

Still unable to shake the uneasiness she'd felt from the moment she'd entered the country club's grounds, Angela turned to Ricky and asked, "Would you excuse me for a few minutes while I see if I can find Justin?"

"Sure. Why don't I go get us something to drink at the bar. Wine okay?"

"I'd rather have a soda," Angela told him. She was grateful Ricky hadn't pressed her for the reason she needed to see Justin. Scanning the room, she spotted him almost immediately. And when she noted he was coming toward her, she smiled and waved.

But as he drew closer, Angela noted the rigid set of his jaw. Her smile slipped a notch and her heart began to beat nervously. When he stopped in front of her, Angela sensed his barely checked anger. As she searched his face, her stomach dropped at the coldness in his eyes. Somehow managing to keep her voice calm, she said, "Hi. I'm glad I found you. I got your messages and tried to call you at the office and the ranch, but I must have missed you. And I didn't have your cell phone number."

"I guess we were both a little too distracted last night and this morning to get around to exchanging cell numbers," Justin said in a voice that was devoid of any warmth.

"Yes, I guess we were," Angela said. Swallowing, she met his gaze. "Listen, Justin, about my being here with

Ricky. I'd told him yesterday morning that I would come with him tonight and—''

''Save your explanations, Angela. I'm not interested in them. All I'm interested in is finding that little girl. I've got some new leads that I'll go over with you in the morning at my office.''

''Justin, wait. Please,'' she added when he continued to turn away.

''What?''

''What about us?'' she asked.

''There is no 'us' except in a professional sense and that's only until we find Lena.''

His words set off a roaring in her head, made her want to run away, to escape the pain. But they'd lost each other once because she'd run away. She didn't want to lose this second chance for them—not without at least trying. ''What about last night? Are you saying it didn't mean anything to you?''

''Last night I made a mistake. We both did. But you can rest assured that it's a mistake I won't be repeating.''

Chilled to the bone by his words, Angela clutched the program in her fist so tightly she could feel her nails digging into her palms. ''Justin, please—''

''If you want to go over the new info, be at my office at eight in the morning.''

He didn't bother saying goodbye; he simply turned and walked away from her. And as he did so, Angela realized, he took with him a piece of her heart and the last hope she had that the two of them might actually have a chance together.

''I see you found Wainwright,'' Ricky said, coming up behind her.

Wrapped in pain and grief, she couldn't bring herself to respond.

"Angie? Hey, Angie, you all right?" Ricky asked.

She could hear Ricky's voice, but could barely see him for the tears blurring her vision. Afraid to speak for fear she'd start blubbering, she nodded her head.

He set down the glass of soda on a passing tray, then slipped his arm around her shoulders and held the other glass to her lips. "Drink it," he ordered. And when she started to decline, he tightened his grip on her and repeated, "Drink it."

Angela took a sip, gasped and then coughed as the foul-tasting stuff burned a path from her throat to her stomach. "What is that?" she asked when she could finally catch her breath.

"Scotch," he informed her. "Better now?"

"Yes. Thank you."

"I take it your talk with Wainwright didn't go too well."

"No, it didn't." She should have laughed at the enormous understatement. Instead she felt the tears prickling at her eyes again.

"From the murderous looks he's shooting in my direction, my guess is I'm the reason. He's ticked off that you're with me, isn't he?"

"It's not your fault," she told him. "Justin and I..." How did she even begin to explain the complicated situation between her and Justin? "It's not your fault," she repeated.

"I'm sorry, Angie. Would it help if I went and talked to him, explained to the big jerk that you and I are just friends?"

She shook her head. "I'm afraid the problems between Justin and me go a lot deeper than his not approving of our friendship." It came down to Justin trusting and believing in her. "But thanks for offering."

Laughter flowed around them, voices swelled, glasses clinked in the gay party atmosphere. But Angela filtered it all through a haze of numbing pain.

"Come on, you're not up for this. I'll take you home."

"No. I'll be all right," she told Ricky. As much as she wanted to go home and nurse her aching heart, it wouldn't be fair to him. He'd told her that Del Brio had all but insisted that Ricky attend. "You go ahead and mingle. I'm going to go outside and get some air."

"I'll go with you."

"I'd really rather be alone."

"You sure you're all right?" Ricky asked.

"I'll be fine."

Justin stood out on the terrace where he'd gone to escape, unable to bear the sight of Angela with Ricky. At least everyone was too caught up in the auction fever to wander outdoors, he told himself, trying to be grateful that he had the space all to himself.

Kind of hard to feel grateful when he was feeling so stupid, he admitted, and mentally kicked himself again for being such a fool when it came to Angela. The sound of an owl in a nearby tree calling over and over for a mate that didn't answer sent another surge of hurt and loneliness pummeling through him. "I hear you, buddy," he muttered, and told himself again he was lucky no one was there to see him talking to himself. If they did, they'd probably have him committed.

He deserved to be committed for being a sucker, for thinking that he and Angela might have a shot at making things work between them. How did that old adage go? Something about make a fool of me once and it's shame on you. But make a fool of me twice, and the shame's on me. She'd made a fool of him twice now, Justin conceded.

Angry with himself for allowing it to happen and hating the fact that his fury did little to diminish the gut-wrenching ache inside him, he squeezed his eyes shut a moment.

Determined to get a grip on his emotions, he opened his eyes and drew in a breath. He caught the scents of the night—the hint of rain in the air, the smell of the freshly mowed lawn, the sweet perfume of the flowers. Somewhat calmer, Justin stared out across the manicured grounds, noted the gardens lush with blooms of red and yellow and white. But the sight of those flowers made him think of Angela again and how much she'd liked coming to the country club and strolling through these gardens. Of how she had planted that garden in front of their home.

Get a grip, Wainwright. You have to stop thinking about the woman. Get her out of your head.

He jammed a fist through his hair. Irritated with himself, he turned away and looked back toward the clubhouse. The French windows and doors that lined the terrace provided him with a glimpse of the party inside—a party he didn't want to join, he admitted. Deciding to go make his good-byes and leave, he headed back toward the clubhouse, not even bothering to put his suit jacket back on. He was just about to go inside when one of the French doors at the other end of the terrace opened and out walked Angela.

What little peace he'd been able to capture outdoors dissolved in an instant. Justin tensed, and though he hated to admit it, his heart ached at just the sight of her. Even though he told himself he should go inside, that Ricky would probably be joining her at any moment, he remained where he was.

As she began walking toward the center of the terrace, Justin thought she had spotted him and braced himself not to be moved by anything else she might say. But instead of continuing toward him, she veered to the right and stopped to stand before the railing that overlooked the gardens, where he had stood only moments earlier. A summer wind whistled across the terrace, making a mournful sound and ruffling the skirt of the dress she wore. If she noticed, she gave no indication; she simply leaned on the rail and stared out across the grounds.

Moonlight combined with the soft lighting on the terrace to cast a shimmering glow on her hair. The same hair that he had curled his fingers into last night when they'd made love. Her bare arms and shoulders looked even softer, creamier in the diminished light, he thought. He couldn't see her face, but there was a weariness in her stance, a slight slump to her shoulders that tugged at something inside him.

Realizing what he was doing, Justin silently cursed himself. He needed to get out of here, as far away from Angela as he could. He reached for the handle on the door, intent on leaving, when something, some instinct or lawman's sixth sense, kicked in, and he became aware that the night had gone silent. No owl hooted in search of a mate any longer. No squirrels chattered. No frogs from the distant ponds barked. He swung his gaze back in Angela's direction, panned the terrace.

And that was when he saw it. A movement in the darkness near one of the windows a few yards away and the shadow of an arm pointing a gun. "Angela, look out!" he shouted, and charged toward the arm pointing the gun.

He heard the muffled pop. Heard Angela's scream. Felt the burst of fire in his shoulder, followed by the sound of his own grunt as he hit the ground. The gunman had used a damned silencer, he thought as the world suddenly began to move in slow motion.

"Justin! Oh, my God, Justin!"

He could have sworn he heard Angela screaming at him, could have sworn he saw tears streaming down her face, felt her soft fingers holding his head in her hands and yelling for someone to help her. And just before the world went black, he could have sworn he heard Angela's voice pleading, "Justin? Justin, can you hear me? Please, Justin, open your eyes."

"Please, Justin, open your eyes," Angela pleaded, and he fought his way up through the shroud of darkness toward her voice.

Opening his eyes, he saw Angela's pale face. Then everything came back to him in a rush. The gunman aiming at her. The sound of the muffled shot. "Are you all right?" he demanded, and attempted to sit up, only to groan as white-hot pain seared his shoulder.

"Take it easy," Michael O'Day told him, and held him in place on the stone terrace with what Justin considered a surprisingly strong hand for a man who spent his days in a hospital operating room. The heart surgeon flashed him what Susan had termed the O'Day heartbreaker smile that had caused his ballerina sister to fall in love with the guy. "There's an ambulance on its way to take you to the hospital. Try to be still while I listen to your heart."

"I don't need an ambulance. And I'm not going to any hospital," Justin argued.

"You do, and you are if you want to get that bullet out of your shoulder," Michael told him as he removed the stethoscope tips from his ears.

Bullet?

Only then did Justin look at his shoulder and see the blood that had soaked his shirt and now covered the shawl that Angela had been carrying.

"Let me through. Let me through to my son," Kate

Wainwright cried out as she pushed her way through the circle of cops and people around him. "Oh, my God, Justin," she said as she knelt down beside him.

"I'm okay, Mother."

"Sheriff, we need to get a statement," his deputy, Hank, cut in. "Did you see who shot you?"

"No, I didn't," Justin began.

"Can't you see he's hurt?" Kate Wainwright demanded and the deputy mumbled an apology.

Ignoring Justin, she turned to Michael. "Is he going to be all right?"

"He should be his good old surly self in no time at all—once we get him to agree to go to the hospital and have that bullet removed."

"Of course he's going to the hospital," Kate informed them. "Archy, go see what's keeping the ambulance."

"Thanks a lot, O'Day."

"You're welcome, Sheriff," he told Justin as the ambulance siren blared and the EMTs came rushing through with a stretcher.

"I can walk," Justin argued.

"You'll do no such thing," Kate informed him.

Justin glared at the grinning O'Day as he allowed himself to be loaded onto the stretcher.

"You want to ride in the ambulance with him, Kate?" Michael asked.

"Please, Mrs. Wainwright," Angela cut in. "Would it be okay if I went in the ambulance with him?"

His mother's eyes widened at the request. She hesitated a moment, looked over at him with that same worried look clouding her eyes that he'd seen often when he was growing up. He recognized that look now for what it was—the concern of a mother for her child. But when she shifted her gaze back to Angela, her expression softened and she said, "Of course, you go ahead. Archy and I will meet you at the hospital."

For the last twelve of her thirty-two years she'd either been a cop or worked in law enforcement as a profiler. In that time she had seen her share of blood. While she would never become immune to the horrors of violence and its aftermath, she would never have been able to survive her chosen profession without developing a tolerance for bloodshed. Yet at the sight of Justin being shot, watching him go down and blood pooling around him, she'd nearly fallen apart. Had it not been for Justin's sister Susan calming her down and assuring her that Dr. O'Day would be able to take care of Justin, she had no doubt that she would have become hysterical. She still wasn't sure if her statement to Justin's deputy had even made sense. She knew she'd been of little help since she hadn't seen anything but Justin going down. And the blood. She shivered at the memory.

Sitting in the waiting room of the hospital now with her former in-laws and several of Justin's siblings and friends, she couldn't even begin to imagine what they thought of her plea to accompany Justin in the ambulance. And they probably were wondering why on earth she was even there, she admitted.

"Here, you look like you could use this."

Angela looked up at the slender blonde offering her the cup of coffee. "Thank you," she said, and tried to put a name with the face.

Apparently recognizing her confusion, the woman smiled at her and said, "I'm Jenny. Hawk's wife."

"Hello, I'm Angela Mason, Justin's...Justin and I used to be married."

"I know. Hawk told me," Jenny said. She motioned to the chair next to Angela. "May I?"

"Oh, yes. Please."

"I'm afraid your lovely dress is probably ruined," Jenny told her. "Blood is a tough one to get out, but I have this spot remover that's worked well on fabric stains in a few of the places I've done interior design work for. If you'd like to try it, I'd be happy to send you some."

Angela looked down at her clothes, saw the bloodstains on her dress. Justin's blood, she thought, and shivered as she recalled hearing him shout to her, then turning and seeing him get hit, his body falling to the ground and blood spilling from his shoulder.

"Try not to worry," Jenny told her, giving her arm a motherly pat. "He's going to be fine. Hawk tells me that Justin's much too stubborn to let a bullet keep him down for long."

Angela smiled at that. "Yes, he is stubborn," she murmured, unable to keep the wobble from her voice.

The doors from the hospital operating room swung open and Michael O'Day walked out. Angela stood at once. She was barely aware of Jenny taking her coffee cup from her fingers, putting it aside and then Jenny taking her hand and holding it in a show of support.

"How is he, Michael?" Kate Wainwright asked as she stood beside Archy, his arm around her shoulders.

"He's fine. No serious damage," the good-looking surgeon told her. "His upper arm is going to be sore for a few days and he'll need to wear a sling for a while, which he isn't too happy about, I might add. But that's really just to keep him from overusing the arm and to give the wound a chance to heal."

"Thank God," Kate said, and buried her face in Archy's shoulder.

"Doctor, could I see him?" Angela asked, and realized almost at once that as Justin's ex-wife her need to see him could in no way usurp his family's need. "I'm sorry," she told Justin's parents. "Of course, you'll want to see him first."

"It's all right," Archy told her. "Somehow I suspect Justin would much rather see your pretty face than mine. What do you say, Kate? Is it okay with you if Angela sees the boy first?"

Kate swiped the tears from her eyes with a lacy handkerchief. "Archy's right. You go ahead, dear. Now that I know my baby's going to be okay, I don't mind waiting."

"Your baby?" Michael O'Day repeated, his voice filled with humor. "You should have heard the colorful language that baby of yours was using when I was working on his shoulder."

But Angela didn't wait around to hear Kate's reply because she hurried through the doors, eager to see for herself that Justin was all right. Not sure what to expect after the crazed ride in the ambulance during which he'd drifted in and out of consciousness, Angela was relieved to see him sitting up in the hospital bed and glaring at the nurse who'd stuck a thermometer in his mouth and was taking his blood pressure.

"Much better," the sturdy-looking nurse said as she removed the blood-pressure cuff from his arm and took the thermometer from his mouth.

"I want my clothes," Justin informed the nurse, who didn't even look up from the chart on which she was writing. "Did you hear me? I want my clothes so I can get out of here."

"I heard you, Sheriff. And I'll tell you what I told you the last time—I'll let the doctor know."

"You tell O'Day I'm leaving—with or without my pants."

Unfazed, the nurse walked away from him, pausing only long enough to tell Angela, "He's supposed to rest quietly. If he gives you any trouble, ring for me."

"Angela," Justin said upon spying her standing there. "Good thing you're here. Come over here and help unhook me from this stuff," he told her, motioning to the IV bag and monitor hooked to him.

"I don't think you should do that," she told him as he struggled to get up.

He pinned her with serious green eyes—eyes that were all cop. "Did they catch the shooter?"

"No, I don't think so." Ricky had told her when he'd called her at the hospital that a search had been made, but with the huge crowd whoever had shot Justin had been able to get away.

"Then I need to get out of here so I can find him," he said, and resumed his efforts to untangle the sheets from around his legs.

"Your deputies are looking for him and Luke Callaghan called in some security people he works with to help."

When the IV line got in the way of his efforts to free himself from the sheets, Justin swore. He let out a breath. "Listen, I am not dead. I am not dying. I have what amounts to little more than a scratch on my shoulder. I'm fine. So will you come over here and give me a hand with these sheets?"

Angela went to him, assisted him with the sheets. And as she straightened and came to eye level with him, she couldn't help noticing the bandage that covered his shoulder—and the dark red stain beneath the thick gauze. He was too busy studying the IV lock in his hand to notice her scrutiny. Despite his attempt to downplay his condition, there was a gray cast beneath his sun-bronzed skin, and shadows stood out like faint bruises beneath his eyes. "Justin, please. You've been shot, and you've lost a lot of blood. What you need to do is rest."

"What I need to do is find my clothes so I can get out of here. Check that closet over there for me, will you, while I see if I can get this thing off?"

She found his suit hanging there. Evidently his blood-soaked shirt had been cut off of his body in order to remove the bullet. The knowledge of how close he'd come to being killed caused her stomach to pitch.

"You find them?"

Swallowing back the bile that had risen in her throat, she grabbed the pants, jacket and boots. "I found them."

He'd managed to remove the IV needle from the shunt in his hand and stood beside the bed clutching a hospital gown below his waist and staring down at the colored sensor leads on his chest. "Am I supposed to just rip these things off?"

"I think so." She suspected it was the prospect of him ripping out some chest hairs that made him hesitate. He made a grunting sound and tore the sensors off from his chest one by one.

"Thanks," he said when he took the pants from her. Still favoring his injured arm, he held the slacks out in front of him and looked up at her. "I may need a hand putting these on."

But even as she helped him, she argued, "Justin, you really shouldn't be doing this. You're in no condition to leave the hospital."

He zipped up the slacks and sat down on the bed. "I told you, I'm fine. You want to hand me my boots?"

"You're not fine. You were nearly killed. Why are you doing this?"

He slid on one boot. "Because I need to find that shooter."

"Why does it have to be you? Why can't you let someone else find him? Your deputies or Luke Callaghan's people."

"Because they're not the sheriff," he informed her as he slid on the other boot and stood. "I am. And it's my job."

"And what if it's his job to kill you?" she demanded, remembering that terrible sense of dread she'd had earlier that evening and realizing how close Justin had come to being killed. Maybe he was lost to her and they would never be together again. But she didn't want to even imagine a world without Justin somewhere in it. "Have you even stopped a minute to consider that? What if that gunman is out there somewhere?" she asked, pointing at the doors. "Suppose he's just waiting for you to walk out of this hospital so he can finish the job he started?"

Justin looked at her as though she'd lost her mind. And she supposed she couldn't blame him. She knew she must sound like a hysterical female, but even after all that had happened already, she couldn't shake the feeling that something worse was yet to come.

"Angela, look at me."

She lifted her gaze, stared into his, expecting to find annoyance or maybe even a return of the coldness that had been there when he'd walked away from her earlier that evening at the country club. What she hadn't expected to find was concern.

"That bullet wasn't meant for me. I'm not the one the gunman was after."

"But I don't understand," she said. She looked at his

shoulder, then back up at him. "I saw what happened. I saw you get hit."

"Because I tried to stop him. Angela, it wasn't me he intended to kill. I wasn't his target. You were."

Ten

"**Me?**"

"Yes, Angela. You. You were the gunman's target, not me," Justin told her. His stomach constricted again, just as it had constricted each time he realized that had he gone inside the clubhouse instead of lingering when he'd seen her come out onto the terrace, Angela would be dead now.

"Oh, my God. You were nearly killed because of me."

Her face, already pale, turned to the color of chalk. "Hey, you better sit down," he said, and caught her by the arm even though the movement sent a twinge of pain shooting through his shoulder. For once the woman didn't argue. She simply sank down onto the chair beside the bed.

"I'm sorry," she said, her voice barely a whisper. "I'm so sorry," she repeated, and covered her face with her hands.

The doors to the hospital room burst open and in walked O'Day. "It's all right, we haven't lost our patient," he said to the Attila-the-Hun nurse who was hot on his heels. "It seems the sheriff simply decided to disconnect himself from the monitor without telling anyone. You can go back to your station."

"Yes, Doctor," the nurse told him, but not before she'd tossed a glare in Justin's direction.

O'Day walked over to the machine, punched in some codes and all the lights went out. "You owe me, Wainwright," he said as he turned to face him. "If it weren't for me, she would have wrestled you down to the floor and hooked you back up to that monitor whether you wanted her to or not.''

Justin didn't doubt for a moment that it was true. "I'll buy you a beer," Justin offered.

"Think again. I want a split of champagne. Cristal or Dom Pérignon will do nicely."

"Take this thing out of my hand and lend me a shirt to wear out of here, and maybe I'll consider it."

After retrieving a wad of cotton and a bandage from the supply cupboard, O'Day took Justin's hand and expertly removed the shunt. As he pressed a cotton ball over the puncture, he said, "I suppose I'd be wasting my time if I were to tell you that you really should consider spending the night here and letting the staff monitor you."

"You're right. You'd be wasting your time," Justin told him.

O'Day finished off by applying the bandage. "Then I'll tell you that that hole in your shoulder is going to need to be cleaned twice a day and watched closely for infection."

"You're releasing him already?" Kate Wainwright asked Michael as she, Archy and several members of Justin's family filed into the room.

"I'd better go," Angela said, and started to get up.

"You stay there," Justin ordered. Either the command had surprised her or she was shaken because she obeyed him without argument.

"Michael, surely you're not letting Justin go already," Kate said. "He was shot, for heaven's sake."

"I'm afraid you'll have to take that up with your baby here, Kate," Michael said, a wicked gleam in his eyes. "He's the one who's refusing to stay."

"What do you mean he refuses?" Kate replied, and turned worried eyes upon her son. "Justin?"

"I'm fine, Mother. Michael did a great job of patching me up, and there's really no reason for me to stay in the hospital."

Kate's brow furrowed as it often had when she'd caught him up to mischief as a child. "Michael, is that true?"

"He should be okay, Kate. I've already explained that he'll need to clean the wound daily and take an antibiotic to ward off any infections. If he takes it easy and doesn't use the arm for a few days, he'll be fine."

"If you're sure," Kate said, a note of skepticism in her voice.

"He's sure," Justin told his mother, and snatched the prescriptions that O'Day held out to him. "Two?"

"One's an antibiotic. The other's for pain. When the shot I gave you wears off, that thing's going to hurt like hell—like the devil."

"Thanks," Justin told him as Michael left the room to prepare the paperwork. "Now, how about somebody lending me a shirt so I can blow this place?"

"I've got one in my truck you can use," Hawk offered. "Should fit okay."

"Thanks. I appreciate it," Justin told him.

Archy stepped forward. "Son, you have any idea who shot you and why?"

Justin rested his hand on Angela's shoulder, gently squeezed. "I didn't see his face. But I intend to find him. So don't worry."

"You gave us such a scare, Justin," his mother said, her eyes welling with tears. "Why, when I saw you lying on that terrace, I thought..."

Her sobs sent guilt ripping through him. "I'm sorry," he said, and meant it.

"Come on now, Kate," Archy said, taking her hand in a comforting gesture. "The boy's all right."

"Yes, I know," she said, swiping at the tears.

Hawk returned and this time Jenny was with him. "Here's that shirt."

"Thanks," Justin said, and took the chambray work shirt from him. When he began to slide it over his injured arm, Angela assisted him. Tender from the movement, he fastened only a handful of buttons. "I'll be sure to return it."

Hawk nodded.

"Okay, Wainwright, you're a free man," Michael said as he returned to the room. "The nurse will be here in a minute with a wheelchair to wheel you out."

"I can walk," Justin argued.

"Hospital policy, I'm afraid. You get a ride to the front door." Michael turned to Archy. "Is he going to ride with you, Archy?"

"Sure, I—"

"Actually, I'm not going to the ranch," Justin informed them all. "I'll be staying at Angela's."

It had taken Angela several moments before Justin's announcement sank in. By the time it had, he had been charging ahead and issuing commands like a field marshal. He'd gotten Hawk to give them a ride to her condo, made arrangements to have his truck and some of his things from the ranch delivered to her place, and given orders to his deputies about the pursuit of the shooter.

Now nearly two hours later they were alone for the first time. "You might have at least asked me before announcing to your family that you were going to stay here," Angela told him.

"If I'd asked, you would have said no."

It was true, Angela admitted. "All the more reason you

shouldn't have done it. You know how your family feels about me.''

"Yeah, I know. But I wonder if you do," Justin countered. "You always thought my parents didn't like you because they were against our getting married. But the truth is you never gave them a chance.''

"That's not true. I like your parents. I always have. But we both know that I didn't fit their ideal as a daughter-in-law.'' She'd been all too aware of the debutante daughter of a neighboring oilman that they had picked out as a potential wife for Justin. She had been a far cry from what they'd wanted for their son.

"Maybe not, but you're the woman I chose and they accepted you. But, then, you probably didn't notice because you were too busy building invisible walls around yourself, the ones you use to keep everyone out so that you can make sure nobody ever hurts you again. Maybe if you hadn't shut my folks out, they would have even loved you. But, then, I loved you and in the end you shut me out, too.''

Taken aback by his accusation, Angela started to argue that he was wrong. But the protest died on her lips as she wondered if Justin was right. Had she shut out the Wainwrights and Justin as he'd claimed?

"I don't even know why we're discussing this. It doesn't make any difference now, anyway,'' he told her, his voice filled with agitation. He walked over to the bar, poured himself some water and used it to chase down what she suspected was one of the pain pills Michael had given him from the hospital pharmacy until he could get the prescriptions filled in the morning. "I'll explain everything to my folks when all of this is over and you go back to San Antonio. But for now I want everyone in this county to know that I'm staying here.''

"Why?"

"Because I want the person who tried to kill you tonight to know that you're not alone. That way if he has any plans to come after you again, he'll know that he has to get through me first."

"I see," she murmured. "So you're here in your capacity as Sheriff of Lone Star County to protect me."

"That's right. This is business, Angela. Nothing else."

The coolness in his voice matched the coolness in his eyes. And hurt so much more than she'd ever dreamed it could. It was hard to believe that in the space of twenty-four hours they had gone from being lovers to polite strangers. "I understand," she said. And she did. Justin would tolerate her presence, even risk his own life to protect her. But it was strictly part of the job. Just as soon as they found Lena, he wanted her to pack her bags and get out of his town and his life.

He sank down onto the couch. "That pain pill is starting to kick in. Before my brain fuzzes over, I need to know if you have any idea who might want you dead."

"You mean besides you?"

Justin scowled at her. "Considering that I took a bullet for you a few hours ago, I think we can rule me out."

Ashamed that her hurt and anger had made her so petty, she said, "I'm sorry. That was very small of me when you saved my life."

"Forget it," he said. "Now, I need you to think. Were you working on anything before you came here that would cause someone to put a contract out on you?"

"No. I've been working kidnapping cases primarily for the past year or so. Mostly children. Several situations resulted in jail time for the perpetrators, but none are eligible for parole for a long, long time."

"All right," he said, and Angela could see him digesting that info. "Then it means the hit was generated by someone local."

"I haven't been back here long enough to generate that kind of dislike," she countered. Except from him, she added silently.

"A number of people know you're here working on the kidnapping. But except for the Carsons and Luke Callaghan, you haven't had time to ruffle any feathers with questions. So that leaves your association with Ricky Mercado. You've been seen in his company several times since you came back."

"I've been seen in your company, too," she pointed out. "And considering our history and your very vocal objection to my presence in Mission Creek a few days ago, if I was going to look for a suspect based on such flimsy evidence then you're a much better bet."

Justin glared at her. "I was thinking more in terms of someone who might have an ax to grind with Ricky."

Angela refused to defend her friendship with Ricky again. If after sharing her bed and her heart with Justin last night he still didn't believe her, he never would. And she wasn't going to put herself through the heartache of trying to convince him. "Why would someone who has a problem with Ricky come after me?"

"Maybe because they think you're more than friends. And maybe because they're worried he's told you something he shouldn't have."

Tired of the game and innuendos, she said, "All right, Justin. Why don't you just cut to the chase and tell me where you're going with this?"

"All right." He set down the water glass and leaned back against the chair. "Word on the street is that the Mercado family is about to make a really big score of some kind. I'm thinking that maybe Ricky said something to you in passing about this deal, and word got back to Del Brio about the slip. Del Brio's major paranoid. He has a thing about secrets. Even if he just thought you knew something you shouldn't and were a threat to him, he'd have you taken out.''

''There's one problem with your theory. Ricky hasn't told me anything about any deal, big or otherwise. The truth is he speaks very little about his family's business. And on those few occasions when Del Brio's name has come up, it's not with fondness. Ricky doesn't like him or trust him.''

''What makes you say that?''

''Well, take tonight, for instance. Ricky said the only reason he was going to the fund-raiser was to keep an eye on Del Brio because he thought he was up to something.''

Justin gave her a considering look. ''There's been some tension between Del Brio and Johnny Mercado. And for a while I thought there might be some trouble over Del Brio succeeding Carmine instead of Ricky. But there's no rumor of any schism or overthrow in the works, and as far as I can tell, Ricky has been firmly in Del Brio's corner since he came back to Lone Star County. According to my sources, Ricky's one of Del Brio's top lieutenants—which means he's up to his eyeballs in whatever this deal is that's supposed to go down.''

''Like I said, I wouldn't know. Ricky's never said anything about any deals to me. The only thing he's talked about is his father.''

''What does he say about him?''

''Mostly that he's worried about him. He says Mr. Mercado has been acting strange lately.''

''Strange in what way?'' Justin asked.

''Some of the things he says, mainly. Like the other

night at the hospital dedication, he said something about how if he had protected his wife, she'd still be alive.''

"Isadora died of a heart attack," Justin pointed out.

"I know. That's what Ricky said. But Ricky says his father's saying things like that, things that don't make sense, and that lately he's been acting secretive."

"Did he tell you anything else?" Justin asked.

"Only what I've already told you. That he and his father both think there's something to Del Brio's story that Haley is still alive. And both of them think that Lena might belong to Haley. Ricky believes it's the reason the little girl was kidnapped from the Carsons."

"Ricky is smarter than I'd given him credit for," Justin told her. "I suppose you told him we were pursuing that angle?"

"No, I didn't," she told him, hurt and angry that he would assume she'd broken her word. "I told you that I wouldn't discuss the case with Ricky, and I haven't. Believe it or not, I try to live up to my word."

A slight flush tinted his cheeks. Angela couldn't help being pleased to see a little more color in his face—even if the source of it was only embarrassment or irritation with her. While he no longer looked gray, as he had following the shooting, Justin also was a far cry from healthy. He looked tired and in pain. But she was sure if she suggested he get some rest, he would ignore her.

"Anyway, this stuff about Haley and the baby being hers, I think we were right. One of the reasons I tried to reach you today was to tell you that I found a connection linking Carl Bridges to a woman in London with a baby girl. Dylan Bridges was able to recover some e-mail exchanges between Carl and the woman, and it's a pretty safe bet that the woman was Haley using an alias. Carl warned her to be careful. It looks like he might have been murdered because he wouldn't give up her whereabouts. She was worried and scared, and after Carl didn't answer her last few messages, she apparently disappeared. Unfortunately, I haven't been able to find out where she is or even what name she's using now.''

"She's here, Justin," Angela told him. "She's here in Lone Star County. I'm sure of it." And she was. Angela knew instantly that Haley was there.

"What makes you say that?"

"Because she would have wanted to make sure her baby was all right. Think about it," she urged him. "It fits everything we already know. She would have known Luke was her baby's father, even if Luke didn't. If she was in trouble, she would have wanted her baby to be safe. Who could protect her child better than a man like Luke with his money and his connections?"

"All right, I'm listening."

"If Carl Bridges was helping her, he would have known about Luke's Sunday golf ritual. He may even have been the one to suggest leaving the baby on the golf course with a note for Luke. Only no one counted on Luke being away and the sprinkler system smearing the note so that Luke's name couldn't be read. So everything went wrong. But she wouldn't have left town until she was sure Lena was safely with her father.''

"And with Carl Bridges dead, the only way for her to be sure that happened was for her to remain in Lone Star County.''

"Exactly," Angela replied.

"If she's here, she'd have to be wearing a hell of a disguise to go unnoticed. Even the people who didn't know Haley well would remember seeing her picture splashed across the newspapers and TV during the trial.''

"It's not all that difficult for a woman to change her

appearance if she wants to. With a change of hair color, a new hairstyle, some colored contact lenses, the right makeup and clothes, I could walk through that door and you'd never know it was me.''

''Maybe you're right.''

''I am,'' she told him with a certainty that she felt in her bones. ''Haley's somewhere in Lone Star County, Justin. I know it.''

''You know what we haven't considered is that when Luke stayed away from Mission Creek for as long as he did that Haley might have decided to kidnap the little girl herself. That would explain there being no ransom note.''

Angela thought about the fear Lena had experienced when she'd been snatched and drugged. She shook her head. ''No, it wasn't Haley. It wasn't Lena's mother.''

''Then it comes back to Del Brio again. If he suspected Lena belonged to Haley, he might have swiped her to use as a bargaining chip or to flush Haley out.''

''That's my guess. From what I remember of him and everything I've heard about him since I've been back, he would fit the profile of the kidnapper.''

Justin scrubbed a hand down his face, and Angela suspected he was fighting the dulling effects of the pain pill in order to remain alert. ''All right, let's see what we've got, then. First, we have Carl Bridges murdered by a hit man presumably because he was trying to protect Haley Mercado. Second,'' he said, holding up a second finger, ''we have Haley Mercado, who's supposed to be dead, only she's alive and running around Lone Star County disguised as God knows who.''

Holding up another finger, he continued. ''Third, we have Haley's baby, whose father turns out to be Luke Callaghan, the result of a one-night stand with a woman he didn't know. Fourth,'' he added, ticking off another digit, "we have that same little girl kidnapped and probably being held somewhere by that sociopath Del Brio in order to flush Haley out."

"And finally," he said, his voice filled with exasperation or exhaustion or both, "we have someone trying to kill you, but we don't know who or why. Does that about cover it?"

"Actually, I think the person after me is the same person behind Carl Bridges's murder and Lena's kidnapping."

"Del Brio?"

Angela nodded.

"I'll admit the guy's a psycho and he's probably nervous if he knows you're working the kidnapping case. But it seems a bit extreme, even for Del Brio, to take a hit out on you at this stage. You've only been on the case a few days, and all you have is sketches and speculation. That's a long way from finding out where the girl is being held."

"But maybe I'm close."

"You mean the drawings?" Justin replied. "I tried to tell you that there are a lot of places that fit that picture."

"I know. I got a listing and started checking them out today."

"What?" he countered, instantly alert, his body tense. "This is my investigation, dammit. And I told you not to go off on your own."

"This is *our* investigation," she corrected him. "And if you learned nothing else about me during the time we were married, you should have learned that I don't take orders."

Justin clenched his hands into fists. The look he gave her was as hard as steel. "Suppose I hadn't been there tonight on that terrace when that gunman came looking for you? Do you have any idea what would have happened?"

"I'd probably be dead now and you wouldn't have a hole in your shoulder," she replied truthfully. "It was a very brave and foolish thing that you did tonight, Justin. I've already thanked you once but I'll say it again. Thank you for saving my life."

"I don't want your damn gratitude. I want you off this case."

"That, I'm afraid, is not going to happen."

"Why are you being so stupid about this? Are you that eager to get yourself killed? Or is it because you know I don't want you here or on this case, and it's your way of showing me that what I want doesn't count?"

Earlier today she might have thought his anger and concern meant that he still loved her. She knew better now. "I'm staying for the same reason you're here. Because it's my job. And as you've pointed out, this is business. Nothing else."

His shoulder hurt like hell and he'd barely slept a wink, Justin admitted the next morning as he stood at the sink in the bathroom and struggled to get a fresh bandage on his shoulder. The end result didn't look nearly as good as the one they'd put on him at the hospital, but it would have to do. No way did he intend to take Angela up on the offer of assistance she'd made last night. For once, he intended to follow his own advice, which she'd tossed back at him so nicely. Things between them would remain strictly business. And maybe by not muddying those waters, he'd keep the headstrong woman from getting herself killed and save himself a lot of grief.

Justin listened for sounds of movement from upstairs, and hearing none, he headed to the kitchen to put on the coffee. Angela had never been a morning person. Given the events of yesterday and their late conversation, he wasn't surprised she'd slept in this morning. He thought about her sleeping upstairs in that big bed, remembered how it had felt waking up there with her yesterday morning instead of alone in the guest room. Irritated with himself when he realized what he was doing, he poured himself coffee from the pot before it had finished brewing and headed into her workroom to make some calls.

Fifteen minutes later he'd put Hank in charge, left instructions for Bobby and went through the list of items needing his attention with Audrey Lou. "If anything comes up, you can reach me here or on my cell phone."

"So how long you planning to stay at your wife's place?" Audrey Lou asked him.

"Ex-wife," Justin corrected her, though he knew it was a waste of time. "And I don't know. Is there anything else?"

"No, I think we've about covered it all."

"All right. Tell Bobby to make sure he interviews the staff who were on duty at the club last night, too. One of them might have seen something. And if he comes up with any witnesses, I want to know about it right away."

He hung up the phone, punched in the number for his contact in the customs office again to see if she'd been able to find anything on a female and a child with the last names of Joseph who had arrived from London last year via the Dallas or the Houston ports of entry. It was a long shot that anything would turn up. They could even have come through a port of entry in another state. But it was a long shot he couldn't ignore, because if Haley had managed to disguise herself so well that she'd actually been in Lone Star County without being detected, matching her new face to a passport could save them a lot of time. When he got the voice mail, he left a message and gave numbers where to reach him.

After completing the call, he rubbed the back of his neck. He could feel a vicious headache coming on, his shoulder hurt something fierce, and it was just barely nine in the morning. Not the way to start the day, Justin thought. Opting to pass on the painkillers because of the fuzzy-headed feeling they gave him, he decided to see if aspirin would help and headed for the bathroom. He found a bottle in the medicine cabinet. After shaking out two tablets, he filled a glass with water and washed them down. When he exited the bathroom, he heard the water running upstairs.

Deciding to pour himself another cup of coffee while he waited for Angela, he was on his way to the kitchen when the doorbell rang. With the memory of the attempt on Angela's life so fresh, he checked the peephole in the door and scowled when he saw Ricky Mercado on the other side.

Justin opened the door. "What do you want, Mercado?"

If Mercado was surprised to see him, he gave no indication. He simply said, "I want to see Angela. Where is she?"

"In the shower. If you want to leave a message for her, I'll see that she gets it," Justin told him, and had the pleasure of seeing the other man's expression darken.

"No thanks, Wainwright. I'll wait and give her the message myself."

Justin blocked the doorway, dared Mercado with his body language to try to get past him. It was a dumb maneuver on his part, Justin admitted—especially considering he had a hole from a bullet in his shoulder and would probably have trouble holding his own even against a teenager at the moment. Ricky was no teenager and had never been a slouch when it came to handling himself. And judging by the deadly look in his dark eyes, the man would have loved nothing better than to plow him down. But for whatever reason, Ricky didn't press him. "When Angela comes downstairs, tell her I'll be in my car."

"She and I are liable to be tied up for a while," Justin taunted.

Ricky's lips thinned, but he didn't take the bait. "That's all right. Just tell her Bruno and I are waiting outside."

"Bruno?"

Ricky inclined his head in the direction of the dark sedan parked across the street with a bald hulk of a guy behind the wheel. "He's a bodyguard I've arranged for Angela."

"What makes you think she needs a bodyguard?"

"Because when she phoned me from the hospital last night, she said you claimed the shooter was after her. If that's the case, I want her protected."

"I intend to see that she is," Justin told him.

"No offense, Wainwright, but considering you were the reason she was so upset that she went out on that terrace alone in the first place, I don't want to count on you sticking around to take another bullet for her if it comes down to it. Besides, you've already done more damage to her than any bullet ever could."

"My relationship with Angela is none of your damn business, Mercado. Who in the hell do you think you are to talk to me about how I've hurt her?"

"I'm someone who cares about her. Apparently a lot more than you do."

Furious with Ricky for what he'd said and angry with himself because he suspected it was true, that he had hurt Angela last night when he'd cut off her explanations, Justin said, "Go to hell, Mercado. And take your bodyguard with you. If anyone's going to protect Angela, it's going to be me."

"Thanks, but I can take care of myself," Angela said

from behind him. "You want to tell me what's going on and what you're doing here, Ricky?"

"I've hired you a bodyguard," Ricky informed her.

"And I just finished telling Mercado you don't need his protection," Justin added. "That's why I'm here."

"Well, you've got part of that right," Angela told him. "I don't need a bodyguard. I also don't need you here standing guard over me. I can take care of myself. And I don't appreciate either one of you treating me like some female cream puff who needs a man to protect her."

"Don't pull that feminist crap on me. You were nearly killed last night," Justin pointed out.

"He's right," Ricky added.

"Which is why from now on, I'll be carrying this," she said, and held up the derringer. She made a point of checking the safety before strapping it inside her boot. "I appreciate the offer, Ricky, but tell your bodyguard he can go home. And I'd also appreciate it if you could move your car so I can get out." Picking up the tote bag resting on the floor beside her, she walked out the door past him.

"Where do you think you're going?" Justin asked.

She paused, looked back at him. "To do my job. I have a list of properties to check out."

"Not without me, you don't," Justin informed her. He pulled the door to her condo shut.

"I just finished telling you that I don't need a bodyguard or a baby-sitter."

"And you're not getting either. I'm doing my job, too. In case you've forgotten, this is my case. We'll take my truck," he told her, and fished his keys out of the pocket of his jeans.

"You're in no condition to drive. Dr. O'Day said you needed to take it easy," she argued.

"Then I won't drive," he told her. "You will." And he tossed the keys to Angela.

Eleven

"I warned you this would be like looking for a needle in a haystack," Justin told her as they called it a day and headed back to her condo.

"I still think we're on the right track. Otherwise, why would Del Brio have tried to have me killed?"

"It could have had something to do with the fact that you marched into the county clerk's office and asked for a listing of properties that he owned."

"I also asked for a listing of all the ranches in the area that specialized in the training and breeding of horses," she pointed out, then sighed at the give-me-a-break look he cast her way. "All right, so maybe it wasn't the smartest thing to do. But I felt that if it would help us find Lena quickly, it would be worth the risk."

"It would have been. But I've had Del Brio watched for a couple of weeks now, and if he's got the little girl stashed, he's playing it smart and not going anywhere near her. And so far there's no sign of a kid at any of his usual hangouts."

"Then maybe it was something about one of those places I visited that set him off. Like I told you, I had this creepy feeling that I was being watched, only…"

"Only what?" Justin prompted.

"Only maybe I was being overly sensitive," she admitted, no longer sure of herself and exhausted from the emotional roller coaster she'd been on for days now be-

cause of Justin. And until they found Lena, she'd no doubt
have more days like the one she'd just put in. "What I
mean is, I hadn't expected things to happen between us
the way they did, and we never had a chance to talk before
you left that morning."

"It's water under the bridge," he told her.

"I know that. I'm just trying to explain that maybe I
wasn't as focused as I should have been. I'd gotten lost.
It was getting late, and my cell phone wouldn't work.
Maybe I just imagined I was being watched."

"It's possible. But I don't think so. You're not the type
to get spooked or imagine things, Angela."

"Thanks. I think," she replied, somewhat surprised by
his compliment.

"Just stating the truth," he told her. "Anyway, I think
we ought to retrace your steps and take a second look at
those places. Maybe tonight you should put together a list
of where you went and we'll hit those places first thing
tomorrow," he said, and grabbed at his shoulder as she hit
an uneven stretch of road.

"I really don't need you to come with me," she told
him, noting how he held his shoulder and the way his lips
tightened each time she hit the slightest bump.

"We've already had this conversation. Where you go, I
go."

"Fine," she told him, exasperated by his stubbornness.
"And when the pain in that shoulder becomes unbearable
and you keel over, remember you have only yourself to
blame."

"My shoulder's fine. I just need some aspirin."

"Too macho to take the pain pills, huh?"

"I don't want to argue with you, Angela," he said, and
leaned his head back and closed his eyes.

The weariness in his voice, coupled with the shadows

beneath his eyes, sent guilt slicing through her with the swiftness of a bullet. As difficult as this situation was for her, it had to be even more so for Justin, she realized. Regardless of his feelings for her or lack thereof, he had insisted on staying at her place to protect her. That gallantry—as antiquated and maddening as it could be at times—was a part of who he was. And was one of the reasons she loved him, she admitted.

She glanced over at him asleep in the passenger's seat and sighed. There was no getting around it. She loved him, had always loved him and would probably go to her grave loving him. There was something so decent and solid about him, she thought. He was a man who had few secrets. A man who dealt in facts, in those things he could see with his own two eyes. While she…she lived in a world filled with secrets and shadows, and things that could never be explained.

Yet he had believed her about the sketches. Despite their history, despite how complicated things were now between them, Justin had believed her and in her. She took the exit that led to her condo and instead of dwelling on her own sense of loss, she contemplated what Justin must be feeling.

She knew from the notes in the file he'd given her to study that he had pushed himself unmercifully to recover the little girl long before she'd ever come onto the scene. Not succeeding would have left him frustrated and angry with himself, she reasoned. Her presence and his physical weakness now would have only magnified those feelings.

When she pulled into the driveway ten minutes later, she vowed to do her best not to add to Justin's troubles or her own. She'd get through this. They both would. Once they found little Lena—and she vowed that they would—she would return to her life in San Antonio and he would go back to his in Mission Creek. She simply prayed that when she left, she'd do so with at least her pride intact, if not her heart. Angela cut the engines and lights, and was wondering whether to wake him or not when he opened his eyes.

"I must have dozed off. Sorry," he said, and rubbed a hand down his face.

"No problem," she said. After unfastening her seat belt, she exited the truck. When she reached her condo door, she spied the envelope taped to it. "It's for you," she told him, and handed him the note with "Mr. Justin" scrawled across the front.

"It's from Mrs. Martinez. When we stopped for lunch, I called her at the ranch and asked her to pick up a few things at the grocery. She says she left them with your neighbors, the Collinses." He shoved the note into his shirt pocket and looked in the direction of her neighbors' condo, where a car was parked in the driveway. "I gave her quite a list and with my arm in this thing," he said, indicating the sling, "I may need you to give me a hand."

"I was planning to go to the store," she told him as she followed him across the lawn.

"Now you don't have to. And as long as I'm staying at your place, you'll be able to eat something besides junk food."

"I happen to like junk food," she countered, embarrassed that he'd had to ask his housekeeper to buy food for her place. She couldn't help wondering what the woman thought of her. Probably the same thing that his family thought of her. That she was all wrong for Justin.

"I don't," he informed her as they made their way to the neighbors' door. "That's why I asked Mrs. Martinez to go to the store."

"Well, I'll pay you for the groceries," she told him.

He rang the bell and then turned to face her. "Let's get something straight. I'm staying at your place until we find out who tried to kill you and I put him behind bars. As long as I'm here, I have to eat, and I prefer to eat real food. I don't expect you to pay for my food or to fix it because I'm not doing this for you. I'm doing it for me. Are we clear on that?"

"Crystal," she said, annoyed with him and herself.

The door opened and Angela got her first close look at her new neighbor. He was just under six feet, she guessed, but muscular with reddish hair, hazel eyes and a dusting of freckles across his nose. He narrowed his eyes as he looked at them. "Yeah?"

"Hi. I'm Angela Mason from two doors over."

"And I'm Justin Wainwright. Angela's friend. I understand some groceries were left here for us."

The man turned his head and glanced around. "Right. There's a box of stuff here," he said, and picked up the cardboard box sitting just inside the door.

"I'll take it," Justin said.

The man hesitated. "You sure you can handle it with that sling? I could bring it over for you."

"Thanks, but I've still got one good arm," Justin informed him as he took the box and anchored it under his arm.

"Thank you for holding it for us. We're sorry for any inconvenience," Angela said.

"Honey, is that our neighbor?" a woman called out from inside the condo.

"Yeah. They're picking up the groceries that were left here," he called back. "My wife, Annabelle. She was in the tub," he explained.

"Don't forget the stuff in the fridge that's theirs," Annabelle added.

The man frowned. "Hang on a second," he said. "There's apparently a bag of stuff in the kitchen that belongs to you, too. If you want to go on home, I'll bring it over."

"That's all right," Justin said before Angela could agree. "We'll wait."

"Suit yourself. I'll be right back with your stuff," Collins told him, and closed the door on them while he retreated into the house.

"Real friendly guy, isn't he? Wonder why he didn't invite us inside?" Justin commented. He nudged the door, which hadn't been firmly shut, and it opened slightly to reveal a living room with only a couple of chairs.

"Here you go," Mr. Collins told Angela as he returned, and practically shoved the bag of food at her. Evidently reading something in her expression, he said, "I'm afraid most of our stuff hasn't arrived from Kansas yet."

"I understand," she said. "Thanks again for holding this for us."

"Sure. No problem," he replied, and shut the door before she'd had a chance to offer him the use of some tray tables and a television set.

"How long ago did you say this guy and his wife moved in?" Justin asked her.

"About a week ago. They moved in the day after I did," she told him as they headed back to her condo. "Why?"

"And I bet before you went to bed your first night, you had your pictures on the walls, pillows and knickknacks scattered around to make the place feel like home."

It was true. She had. "So?"

"So Collins and his wife haven't put out so much as a snapshot," he pointed out as they went inside and headed for the kitchen.

"Well, he said most of their stuff hadn't arrived yet,"

she offered as she placed the bag of groceries on the counter and began to unpack. "Besides, what difference does it make?"

"Maybe none," he told her while he began shelving pasta and rice and canned goods in the pantry. "But something seemed off besides the guy's accent."

Angela turned from the refrigerator where she'd just stored milk, eggs, cheese, butter and enough bacon and cold cuts to feed an army. "What was wrong with his accent?"

"It was as New York as you can get."

"Did you have to say I was in the tub?"

"It was the first thing that came to mind," Sean Collins told Annabelle Harte, the female agent posing as his wife. "I sure didn't want to have to explain why my blushing bride had dirt smudges on her cheeks because she'd broken into their condo to snoop around."

Evidently choosing to ignore the remark, she asked, "You think they bought that bit about the furniture?"

"How do I know? You might have warned me that you'd accepted a delivery of groceries for them earlier."

"I didn't have a chance. I barely made it back over here before they pulled in the driveway."

"You're lucky you didn't get caught." But there had been a speculative look in Wainwright's eyes that Sean hadn't liked. He'd been an FBI agent too many years not to recognize that look Wainwright had given him—the look of a hunter on the trail of a scent.

"You believe that stuff about her being psychic, Collins?"

"Hell if I know. But if she is, you'd think she would have picked up on the fact that we're not newlyweds."

"Oh, I don't know about that," Annabelle told him, her

voice dropping to that sultry purr that had resulted in several erotic fantasies on his part—before the lady had informed him she wasn't interested in a relationship with him. "You were pretty convincing the other night in the driveway when you were pretending to be overcome with passion."

Sean gritted his teeth, remembered what a difficult time he'd had keeping an eye on the Mason woman and not losing himself in Annabelle. But he'd sooner cut out his heart than let her know she'd gotten to him. "Just doing my job, Harte," he said breezily, as if he hadn't gone to sleep that night hard and aching for her. What sin had he committed, he wondered, that had caused his boss to send her as the undercover agent posing as his wife?

"So you were acting?"

"That's right," he told her, and concluding that the Mason woman and Wainwright were still in the kitchen, he put down the binoculars he'd had trained on the windows of her den.

"Then I guess your body's, um, reaction was just your way of getting into the role?" she taunted, her dark eyes bright with sass.

He should have known she hadn't missed his obvious response to having her in his arms, Sean thought sourly. "Sure," he said. "The same way those little moaning sounds you were making were all for show."

"That's right," she told him, and he was pleased to see that flush in her cheeks.

"But anytime you want a real demonstration of my kissing technique, Harte, you just let me know."

"In your dreams, Collins," she huffed. "I'm going to check in and see if Hunter's been able to find out anything more about when that shipment is going to be moved."

"While you're at it, have them run another check on the Mason woman and Wainwright."

"Why? I thought the reports came back showing they were legit."

"They did. But have them checked again, anyway. It wasn't too long ago that they uncovered that group of corrupt officials calling themselves the Lion's Den down here. Just because the agency thinks they got rid of all the bad apples doesn't mean they did."

"I thought Bobby said the sheriff was on the level," Annabelle countered.

"Maybe he is. But the man's sleeping with his ex-wife and she's chummy with Ricky Mercado. Many a man has been known to do something stupid because of a woman."

"Speaking from experience, Collins?" Annabelle asked him.

"Not me, Harte. No way would I ever let a dame tie me up in knots the way Mason's done Wainwright." And even as he said it, Sean knew it was a lie because he'd let Annabelle Harte tie him up in so many knots he had trouble even looking at another woman.

"Did it ever occur to you that maybe he's still in love with her? And that she might still love him?"

"Nope."

"I forgot," she said, disdain in her voice. "You're the Ice Man. The guy who loves the ladies and leaves them."

"That's me," he said. "Now, why don't you be a good little agent and go see what the boys have got for us. Maybe we'll be lucky and wrap this case up in time to make it home for the weekend." And maybe he'd finish this assignment before he made an ass of himself and confessed that he was in love with her.

At the sound of her retreating, Sean sighed and picked up the binoculars again. He had a job to do, he reminded himself, and went into full agent mode. He'd worked too long and too hard setting up this operation and had practically forced Haley Mercado to help get this far. Having Haley's baby kidnapped had nearly derailed everything. That he and his people had been unable to find the little girl had been a major frustration. But having Callaghan pull strings to bring the Mason woman in for the case had been a bigger source of irritation. He didn't believe in psychics. It's why he'd told his boss he wasn't going to work with the woman—just as he hadn't worked with the sheriff. He couldn't afford to let anyone find out that Haley Mercado was the baby's mother. But that didn't mean he was going to sit back and let the woman or her ex-husband sheriff screw up everything now. He wasn't. Not when he was so close to putting cuffs on Del Brio. He was going to bring down Del Brio and the rest of the crime family and put an end to their new line of business—smuggling stolen Mayan artifacts out of Mexico. Thanks to Haley's taped conversations at the Lone Star Country Club, he knew a major shipment was being made soon. He'd also made sure that Del Brio himself would be on hand to make the exchange of goods for money. He was close, closer than they'd ever been before to nailing the crime lords. And no way did he intend to let some hick sheriff and the guy's ex-wife screw things up now.

"What is it?" Angela asked Justin late the next afternoon as he turned in his seat and looked through the rear window.

"There's been a green sedan following us for the last hour," Justin explained, and turned back around. "I wanted to see if he was still back there. He's not."

"We were being followed and you didn't tell me?"

It was late already, sunset less than thirty minutes away.

And so far, the day had been a complete bust, except for the spy game someone had been playing with them. "I figured it was probably your friend Mercado or one of those goons he hired to act as your bodyguard." Which was what he had assumed when he'd spotted the blue pickup truck tailing them for a good part of yesterday.

"If someone's been following us, it wasn't Ricky or anyone sent by him."

"How can you be so sure?"

"Because Ricky gave me his word that he would back off, and Ricky has never gone back on his word to me."

She said it with such conviction that Justin believed her. Which meant that someone else had been tailing them. But who?

"Just up ahead is where I took the wrong road and got lost."

"Go ahead and take it again. Let's see where it leads."

It led to nowhere, Justin soon discovered as they drove for another twenty minutes during which time the road itself became narrower and less traveled. By the time they'd pulled to a fork in the road, the condition of the roadway had diminished considerably, which the throbbing in his shoulder attested to. They also hadn't seen another vehicle for more than twenty miles.

"Right up ahead is where I pulled off."

"Let's do it, then," Justin told her, and she pulled the truck over to the side of the road. Exiting the truck, he walked down the road a piece, noted the overgrown brush and neglect. And all he could think of was how vulnerable Angela would have been all alone out here in the middle of nowhere.

"There's an old ranch house of some kind farther down this road," she told him. "It looked abandoned."

"It probably is. If I remember correctly, about twenty-five years ago there was talk of putting a highway through here. Most of the places along this stretch were bought up then and the people moved out. But politics being what they are, it all got changed and the highway was built somewhere else. As far as I know, this place has been uninhabited since then.''

''But I thought I saw tire tracks down here,'' Angela said, and continued ahead of him along the uneven path.

Justin stayed close on her heels and studied the tracks, noted the cigarette butts tossed in the brush. He looked up ahead and made out the shadows of an old place that appeared empty. It was too isolated, he thought, that lawman's instinct kicked in again. He didn't want Angela out here in the open. He'd have to come back another time—alone—to investigate. ''Probably just kids out joyriding,'' he told her. ''It's getting dark. We better get back.''

''We wasted a whole day because of me, didn't we?'' she asked once they were in the truck and headed home.

''Not wasted,'' Justin told her. ''We had to check it out.''

''I can't help feeling I've let her down.''

''Who?''

''Lena. She's counting on us to find her, Justin. We have to find her. Before it's too late.''

''We will,'' he told her, not wanting to be moved by the depth of her compassion and commitment, but moved all the same. He also didn't want to admit, even to himself, that he was just as worried about the little girl as Angela was. ''Maybe tomorrow. Don't worry. We'll find her.''

But they didn't find her the next day, or the next, or any of the days during that week or the next one. And with each passing day, Justin could feel an erosion of his resolve to keep things strictly business between Angela and himself. The days were tension filled and exhausting. But it was the nights that were the hardest. Because at night when he lay awake in bed, tired but too on edge to sleep, he thought of Angela upstairs, remembered that magical night of lovemaking they'd had before everything had gone to hell.

Justin splashed cold water on his face and stared at his reflection in the mirror. He couldn't keep this up much longer, he admitted as he dried his face with a towel and began to dress. He'd almost said to hell with it all several times the previous day and pulled Angela into his arms. He needed some space, a chance to get his head on straight, he reasoned as he tucked in his shirt, zipped his slacks and buckled his belt. Sitting on the edge of the bed, he grabbed his socks and boots and began pulling them on.

Besides, he needed to handle some things in his office without being distracted by Angela's presence and his feelings for her. He exited the room and headed for the kitchen and was surprised to find Angela already there. "You're up early," he commented, and tried not to notice how beautiful she was standing there barefoot in an ugly blue T-shirt that hit her midthigh.

"Actually, my stomach was bothering me. I came down to get some crackers to see if that would help."

"You weren't feeling so hot yesterday, either," he commented. He went to her and cupped her face in his hands. It was then that he noted the smudges under her eyes and that her skin was paler than normal. He placed a hand to her forehead. "You don't feel like you have a fever."

"I don't. I just have an upset stomach," she informed him, and nibbled on the cracker she was holding. "It's probably something I ate. Let me finish this and I'll go shower. I should be ready to go in fifteen minutes."

Concern for her warred with his responsibilities as sheriff. For a moment he considered changing his plans. Then he decided he couldn't. Too much was going on right now. Two of his sources had indicated that something strange was going on at Mercado Brothers Paving and Contracting. He needed to check it out without dragging Angela into it or risking her tipping off Ricky, even inadvertently. "Why don't you take the morning off? You said you were feeling tired yesterday, and it doesn't look like you're feeling any more energetic today."

"I'm okay."

"But why push it? The truth is, I'm not going to be able to hit that list of ranches with you until later, anyway. I've got some things I need to handle in the office. Bobby's on his way here now. When you're ready and feeling better, he'll bring you down to the office."

"Justin, I refused to let Ricky stick me with his bodyguard. What makes you think I'll allow you to stick one of yours on me?"

"Don't be stupid, Angela. Someone tried to kill you."

"Trust me, I'm aware of that fact. But I'm a big girl and can take care of myself. Go to work, Justin. And don't worry about me."

"I am worried, dammit. And I'm not leaving you alone here. I don't want you unprotected," he argued.

"But it's not what you want that counts. It's what I want. And I don't want a bodyguard or a baby-sitter. I'm not your concern anymore. I haven't been for a long time."

"Angela—"

"Go to your office, Justin. And don't worry about me."

But he did worry, Justin admitted as he drove to his office. He worried about her all morning, through the noon hour when he'd been positive someone had been listening on a phone extension while he'd been speaking with Dylan Bridges. He worried again at four o'clock that afternoon when he tried calling Angela at her condo and got her answering machine. And he was still worrying about her when he entered the restaurant at the Lone Star Country Club to meet with Luke Callaghan and saw her sitting at a table with Ricky.

Twelve

"Don't look now, but your ex just walked in, and he's heading this way."

Let him come, Angela thought. If he was angry, tough. So was she. When he stopped at the table where she was sitting, Angela glanced up at him and met his icy glare. "Hello, Justin."

"I tried to reach you at the condo to tell you I got tied up, but you didn't answer."

"That's because I wasn't there." She turned to Ricky, not wanting him to catch the brunt of this, and said, "Ricky, would you excuse us for a moment?"

"I'm going to go get a beer. Want one?" Ricky asked as he slid back his chair.

The thought of beer made her stomach pitch. "No. I'm fine."

"You didn't have to get rid of him on my account," Justin told her.

"I didn't do it for you," she countered. "I did it for him. This is between you and me, not Ricky. I don't want him caught in the cross fire."

Justin frowned at her and sat in the chair Ricky had vacated. "You want to tell me what you're talking about, because judging from the steam coming out of your ears you're ticked off at me."

"You've got that right. I am ticked off. And I'm sure you've got a pretty good idea why."

"I don't have a clue." He nearly spit out the words. "All I know is that I've been trying to reach you all day and when I couldn't, I sent Hank out to your place to check on you."

"You sent your deputy to check up on me?" she said, doing her best not to raise her voice.

"What did you expect me to do? You've been tired and complaining about your stomach the past couple of days, so I got worried." He took off his hat, set it on the tabletop and jammed a fist through his hair. "I thought maybe you were really sick or that something had happened to you when I couldn't get you at the condo or on your cell phone."

Angela hesitated. Her anger slipped a notch because she had forgotten to recharge her cell phone the previous night. As a result, it had been dead when she left the condo—a fact she hadn't discovered until she'd tried to use it. "So what's your excuse for having Bobby tail me today?"

Justin's frown deepened. "I didn't have Bobby tail you. He was out on patrol most of the morning, and I had him watching Del Brio this afternoon."

"Then what was he doing at two of the places I was checking out today?"

"I don't know, but you can bet I intend to find out," Justin told her, and from his thunderous expression, Angela couldn't help feel a little sad for Bobby Hunter.

"You really didn't have Bobby following me?"

"No. But if I'd known you'd planned to go off on your own again I might have."

Before she could respond, Ricky returned to the table with a dish of hot, golden, deep-fried onion rings. "I know how much you like these things, so I got us a batch," he said, and placed the dish in the center of the table. "You planning to join us for dinner, Wainwright?"

Justin slid his chair back and stood. He picked up his hat. "No, thanks. Unlike Angela, I'm a little more particular about whom I break bread with."

"Let it go, Ricky," Angela said, grabbing his arm for fear he would follow Justin and call him on the put-down. "Please."

"For you," he said, but the light of battle still gleamed like steel in his dark eyes. He shoved the plate of onion rings toward her. "How come you're not diving into these things yet?"

Angela's stomach swayed at the scent. "Thanks, but I'm really not very hungry. You go ahead," she managed to say, and grabbed the soda she'd been nursing earlier.

"That's a first. Since when have you ever needed to be hungry to eat onion rings?" Ricky teased, and popped one of the tasty treats into his mouth.

Ricky was right. What in the devil was wrong with her? She usually had enough energy to fuel a power plant, but she'd been lethargic and her stomach had been giving her fits for days now. As soon as she got back to San Antonio, she was going in for a full physical, she promised herself.

"Hey, Ricky, there you are. I've been looking everywhere for you," a burly guy with a cigar clamped in his jaw said upon entering the club and spying them. As he hurried over to their table, Angela remembered Ricky identifying him as Sal the night of the hospital dedication. He removed the cigar from his mouth and said, "Excuse me, ma'am, but I need to talk to Ricky for a minute. It's important."

"It's all right," Ricky said when she started to get up. "Angela's cool, Sal."

He hesitated a moment, then said, "Frank's looking for you, kid. He wants to see you right away."

"As you can see, Angela and I are about to have dinner. I'll give Frank a call later," Ricky said, his voice gruff.

"He wants to see you now."

"I'm busy now," Ricky countered. "Tell Frank I'll be by when I finish here."

Sal looked around and clamped a hand down on Ricky's shoulder. He leaned down and said in a loud whisper, "Don't be stupid, kid. Frank's in a real strange mood. You don't want to mess with him when he's like this."

Ricky shook off the older man's hand. "I'm not afraid of Del Brio."

"I know you're not. But think about your daddy, boy. You set Frank off, and you might not be the one who ends up paying for it," Sal told him. "Come on, kid. The lady will understand."

"Go ahead, Ricky," Angela interjected. "The truth is I'm not feeling all that well, anyway."

"All right," Ricky said, and Angela could see that it cost him to agree. "I'll give you a call later."

"Thanks, ma'am," Sal said, nodding his head. When he lifted the cigar to put it back in his mouth, the scent hit Angela.

"Excuse me," she said, and left the two men staring after her as she raced to the rest room, where she lost what little she had managed to keep in her stomach that day. When the worst of it was over, she exited the stall and went to the basin and rinsed out her mouth.

"Are you all right?"

Angela looked up from the sink and stared at the reflection of the curvy, blond waitress in the club's signature black pants and white shirt. "I think so," Angela said.

"Why don't you sit down a minute," she said, and led her to the bench against the wall. She wet a towel and brought it over to Angela. "You're still looking a little green."

"Probably because I feel a little green," Angela said, taking the cloth and using it to wipe her face. "Thanks." When she could breathe a little easier she said, "You seem familiar, but I'm afraid I don't remember your name."

"We haven't met before," she said a bit nervously. She smoothed her shirt where her name was stitched across the front of it. "I'm Daisy. Daisy Parker. I work here at the club."

"I'm Angela Mason. Thanks again, Daisy," she said, and attempted a smile. "Would you believe I never get sick? Not so much as a cold. And I usually have a cast-iron stomach. Although you'd never know it by the way I've been upchucking these past few days. Sometimes even just the smell of certain food has been setting it off. And just now when I smelled that cigar, well, I wasn't sure I'd make it to the bathroom in time."

Daisy gave her a thoughtful look. "You said you've been tired a lot lately, too?"

Angela's smile slipped. "Yes. Why?"

"Is it possible you're pregnant?"

"No, that's not possible. I can't..." Angela went still. "At least I don't think so," she corrected, but suddenly wondered if it could be true. Could she be pregnant?

"You might want to check with your doctor because when I—" Daisy paused, her expression grew sad and a haunted look came into her brown eyes. "When a friend of mine was pregnant, she was sleepy all the time and everything from cigar smoke to lemon oil made her queasy."

The door to the ladies' room burst open and in walked a petite, bubbly redhead. "Daisy, you're needed out front," she said as she eyed the two of them curiously.

"I'll be there in a minute," Daisy told the other woman. The redhead waited several beats, then flounced out. When they were alone again, she said, "I need to get back to my tables, but before I do, I just wanted to tell you that I heard about you coming to Mission Creek to try to find that little girl who was kidnapped. And I wanted you to know that I think it's a good thing you're doing, Ms. Mason. A real good thing. And I hope…I hope you can find her." She grabbed Angela's hand and squeezed it a moment, then stood. "I better go. Try chewing on ice and see if it helps your stomach."

Angela stared at the hand the woman had touched, squeezed it into a fist and tried to make sense of the swirl of grief and fear she picked up on from Daisy in their brief contact. But she felt confused and was unable to make sense of the source of Daisy's pain. Then her own situation hit her again. Recalling that night she and Justin had made love, she counted back and tried to determine where she'd been in her menstrual cycle. Since she'd never been regular, she'd paid little attention and didn't have a clue whether she was late now.

Could it be possible? After all this time and so many disappointments, could she possibly be pregnant with Justin's child?

The doctors had said there was always the possibility that she could get pregnant. It just wasn't likely to happen without her taking fertility drugs or going through the various high-tech procedures.

And if she was pregnant?

Angela smiled. She spread her fingers over her abdomen. She wanted the baby. More than wanted the baby, she welcomed it.

And Justin? How would Justin feel?

Her smile dimmed. Justin had made it clear that he

didn't want her in his life. How would he respond to her being pregnant with his child? It was a bridge she would have to cross if and when she came to it, she decided. First, she had to get one of those over-the-counter pregnancy tests and see if it confirmed her suspicions.

"Have you had any luck finding out who the woman is?" Luke asked Justin as they sat in the restaurant where the sheriff had agreed to meet him and give him an update.

"Not yet, but I've got some leads that I'm following," Justin told him.

Maybe the sheriff didn't know the identity of the mystery blonde he'd spent that night with, Luke thought. But Luke had a pretty good idea who she was. He thought about Daisy, the waitress at the club from whom he'd stolen a kiss the other night. The more he thought about her, the more Luke was convinced that Daisy was the mystery woman he'd met that night at the Saddlebag. Daisy was his daughter's mother.

His daughter.

Thoughts of the baby he'd fathered still rocked him. And his chest tightened each time he thought of missing this first year of her life, of learning that she'd been kidnapped. "What about the child? Have you been able to turn up anything about who might have her or where she's being held?" There was a long pause, which Luke found disturbing. "Justin?"

"Like I explained to you on the phone, Angela came up with a sketch of the place where she thinks Lena's being held."

"You believe she's right?"

"Yeah, I do," Justin told him. "Don't ask me to explain how she knows, because I can't. Hell, I find it hard to believe myself. But I think Angela's right about this. If we can find this place, we'll find your daughter.''

Luke leaned forward and wished he could see the other man's face. ''So why haven't you found her?''

''Because there are hundreds of places that could fit the one in her sketch,'' Justin said, and Luke could hear the exasperation in the other man's voice. ''I wish like hell I had better news, Luke, but the truth is for over two weeks we've been searching every ranch in Lone Star County that even comes close to matching the one in Angela's sketch. But so far we've struck out. We're going to find her. You have my word on that. It's just taking us a while to do it.''

''And while you're searching for my daughter, I'm sitting here doing nothing,'' Luke said with disgust.

''Come on, you're being a little rough on yourself, don't you think?''

''Hardly,'' Luke countered, unable to keep the bitterness from his voice. ''How would you feel if some sick bastard kidnapped your daughter and you were doing nothing to get her back?''

''You're hardly doing nothing. You have me and Angela searching for her plus the FBI. We're trained for this kind of work. You're not. Even if you had your sight, you'd probably just get in the way.''

But Justin's assurances did nothing to ease his guilt. The sheriff didn't know, couldn't know that he, too, had been trained to rescue. ''You think so?''

''Yes. This sort of thing is best left to the law, Luke. Not businessmen. Even one as successful as you.''

He'd done his job of acting the millionaire playboy well, Luke thought. ''Funny you should mention that. You know all those business trips I was always taking?''

''Yeah.''

"Well, they were business trips technically. But not the kind you and everyone thought they were."

"You sure you want to be telling me this? Don't forget I'm a lawman," Justin warned him.

Luke grinned wryly and imagined Justin was worried he was about to reveal some illegal activities he'd been involved in. "Yeah, I want to tell you, and your being a lawman doesn't matter. Those trips I took weren't for Callaghan Industries. They were special missions I handled for the United States government."

"You saying you're some kind of spy?"

"A secret agent, actually," Luke replied, and could almost imagine his friend's expression. "The last mission was in Central America. I won't bore you with the details, but it wasn't pretty. We were successful, but I ended up like this," he said, and tapped the side of the dark glasses he wore to shield his sightless eyes.

"Why are you telling me this now?" Justin asked.

"Because I want you to understand just how great a failure I am. As a man, as a father." He closed his eyes behind the glasses. "In the past ten years I've saved and rescued hundreds, probably thousands, of strangers. Yet now when the one person who has every right to expect me to protect her—my daughter—I can't help her. I can't save her from the sick bastard who's stolen her because I'm worthless. Without my eyes, I'm of no use to her or anyone."

"Luke, you—"

Someone barreled into the back of his chair, jolting him, and Luke's glasses fell from his face atop the table.

"Oh, heavens, I'm sorry. I wasn't watching where I was going," the woman said.

"Angela? Is that you?"

"Yes," she said, and scrambled to pick up his glasses. "I'm sorry, Luke. I should have been paying attention...."

But as he stared at her, he caught flickers of light bouncing off something around her neck. He rubbed his eyes, looked again and could just make out the image of a silver cross on a chain that reflected in the overhead lights.

"Here's your glasses," she told him.

Luke took the dark shades from her fingers, realized that he could make out the shape of her hand and the glasses he'd been hiding behind since he'd lost his sight.

"Are you all right?" she asked, worry in her voice, no doubt because he continued to stare at her.

"I'm fine," Luke assured her. He was better than fine, he realized. Because if those flickers of light and the shadowy images meant anything, his sight was coming back.

"You sure Del Brio is going to show for this swap meet you've got planned?"

"I'm sure," FBI agent Sean Collins told fellow agent Annabelle Harte as they sat out of sight and monitored the Texas road where more than a year's worth of work was finally going to pay off. Tonight he would finally put Del Brio and the Mercado crime family behind bars where they belonged. "You heard the tape Haley Mercado made. Del Brio said he would be on hand to make the exchange."

"I don't know, Collins. Why risk it? Why not let his men handle the exchange the way he's done in the past?"

"Maybe with a million bucks changing hands for those stolen artifacts, Frankie doesn't trust his homeboys. Whatever the reason, the minute he takes that money, we've got Del Brio where we want him." Sean trained his night-vision goggles on the road where the six trucks were lined up on opposite sides of the road—three containing smuggled Mayan treasures hidden inside bags of road-paving and concrete supplies from Mercado Brothers Paving and Contracting and three empty trucks, identical in appearance, that were to be driven away by Del Brio's people when the swap was made. Only, the drivers of the empty trucks had federal agents at the wheel who would take Del Brio and his men into custody when the money changed hands.

"I don't like this. Del Brio's late. The tape said he'd be here for eight-fifteen. It's eight-twenty now," Harte pointed out.

"Don't get your panties in a wad, Harte. He'll be here." But when another five minutes ticked by, Collins grew antsy himself. "Garrett, you all set?"

"Just sitting here in my big black sedan with my briefcase full of money waiting to buy me some genuine Mayan artifacts," the undercover agent replied.

Collins grimaced at the smart-mouthed reply. "Morrisey? Henderson? Wyatt? You and your partners all set?"

"All set," each team of drivers replied in turn.

"You forgot to ask about me, boss."

"You better hope you're right about Wainwright, Hunter. He and that Mason woman came real close to blowing this operation," Collins told the agent he'd sent in to work undercover in the county sheriff's office. Two nights ago when the pair had shown up at the door for their groceries, Collins had thought he'd have to haul them both in to salvage the operation. Just as he'd expected, Wainwright had picked up on something because he'd had Hunter check out Mason's new neighbors. Fortunately for Wainwright, he'd bought Hunter's story about the computer salesman and his wife from Kansas and hadn't pursued the matter.

"Heads up," Harte said, cutting into the chatter. "Looks like the big man's arrived. What is it with these

Texas guys and their trucks? Look at the tires on that green monster.''

''It's a guy thing,'' Hunter said with a good-old-boy chuckle that earned him a smart put-down from Harte.

''Looks like he's got someone with him,'' Collins noted as he watched the vehicle approach. ''Big gorilla of a guy.''

''Probably his bodyguard,'' Hunter supplied. ''Name's Alphonse Piccolo out of Jersey, but he goes by the name of Big Al.''

''Son of a— Big Al knows me,'' Wyatt informed them. ''I hauled him in about six years ago when I was working to crack a drug-smuggling ring back east. He was a real mean mother. Ended up cutting himself a deal with the D.A., squealed on some guys higher up the food chain and got himself a reduced sentence.''

''Can he make you?'' Collins asked.

''Yeah.''

''Well, it's too late to make like Casper now, Wyatt,'' Garrett informed him as the green truck pulled up beside the black sedan.

''Wyatt, you hang back as best you can and let Reynolds take the lead when it's time to exchange trucks,'' Collins ordered.

''You have my money, Mr. Garrett?'' Del Brio asked.

''Right here,'' the agent said, and, placing the black attaché case atop the hood of the sedan, he opened it to reveal neat stacks of one-hundred-dollar bills. But before allowing Del Brio to do more than look at it, he said, ''First, I want to see the merchandise.''

Del Brio went to each of the trucks, selecting random bags. Using a knife, he slit the canvas of one bag and out poured the chalky powder used to make concrete—along with ancient crosses, coins and religious artifacts from Mayan ruins in Mexico. "Satisfied?"

"Yes," Garrett told him.

"Excellent," Del Brio said. "Big Al, have our men switch trucks with Mr. Garrett's men while we conclude our business."

"Sure thing, boss."

"I'll take my money, Mr. Garrett," Del Brio told him, and they started back toward the sedan.

"Hey, what the—" Big Al shouted. "I know you. You're that lousy fed who..."

"He's made me," Wyatt said into his hidden microphone as Big Al came charging at him.

"Move in," Collins ordered.

And chaos erupted.

He was in a foul mood, Justin admitted as he drove his truck along the dark roadway. They'd spent another day searching for the ranch where Lena was being held and they had once again come up empty. He was tired, hungry and frustrated. He hadn't been pleased with Bobby's explanation for tailing Angela—that he'd just happened to find himself in the same vicinity while he'd been tracking Del Brio. Justin now found himself questioning his own wisdom in having Bobby check out Angela's neighbors, especially when the report that came back on Mr. and Mrs. Collins was clean.

Something had been off with Angela's neighbors. And something was off with his deputy, too, Justin surmised. The man was hiding something. But for the life of him, Justin couldn't figure out what. All the checks he'd run on Hunter had come back indicating that Bobby was just who he claimed to be—a young deputy eager to make good.

But Justin had a gut feeling there was more to Bobby Hunter than met the eye.

Turning off the main highway, Justin said, "Since it's so late, I thought I'd take an alternate route. There's an old road that's not used much anymore. It's a little longer distance-wise and the road has only one lane, but there's hardly any traffic."

"Hmm? Oh, fine," Angela said, and went back to gazing out the window.

"I don't know about you, but I'm hungry. What do you say we stop and have some Tex-Mex or maybe grab something at Coyote Harry's?"

"What?"

"I asked if you'd like to stop and have dinner," Justin repeated, irritated by Angela's continued distraction. She'd been acting as if she was only half there ever since that night at the country club when he'd run into her with Ricky.

"Thanks, but I'm really not very hungry."

Her answer did nothing to improve his lousy mood. Nor did Angela's silence for the next ten miles. It itched at him like a pesky mosquito bite, until he couldn't hold his tongue any longer. "Listen, I don't know what's going on, but—"

Lights flashed in the road up ahead, and Justin slowed the truck to a crawl. Suddenly sirens screamed. Shouts followed. Justin saw the group of trucks, surrounded by more trucks and sedans equipped with flashing lights and sirens.

In the space of a heartbeat, he heard the roar of an engine, the squeal of tires followed by the unmistakable burst of gunfire. And then he saw the dark green monster of a pickup racing away from the chaos—and heading straight for them.

"Hang on," Justin yelled to Angela as he cut his lights and shoved the Bronco into Reverse. The tires spun on the asphalt, and he jerked it to a stop and yelled, "Hurry! Get out!"

"Justin, no! You can't—"

He pushed her out of the passenger door and onto the road. And praying she wasn't hurt, that she would forgive him, he hit the gas and shot forward, then swerved the Bronco around so that it formed a blockade in the road. Quickly he shoved the gear into Park, and with the engine still running, he dove out the still-open passenger door. He had barely cleared the door before the green monster smashed into his Bronco. It was slowed by the impact but kept going, again picking up speed. Scrambling to his feet, Justin took aim at the fleeing truck and fired. But even as he did so, he knew there was little chance he'd hit his mark.

Then all he could think of was Angela. Spinning around, he searched the side of the road where he'd shoved her from the truck. When he spotted her lying there, his heart lurched. He raced over to her. "Angel, are you all right?" he asked as he knelt down beside her, helped her to sit up. He cupped her head in his hands and stared into her eyes. Relief flooded through him when she looked at him out of dazed blue eyes.

"Did I hurt you? Is anything broken?" He spit out the questions one after the other, all the while running his hands up and down her arms, her legs, checking her body to be sure she was okay.

What if she hadn't made it out of that truck in time? What if she had still been in that truck when it was hit?

The questions ran through his head, and for the first time in his life he realized he knew real fear. Shaken by her narrow escape and furious with himself for the chance he'd taken with her life, it took Justin several moments to register that Angela was yelling at him.

"Justin, I said I'm okay!"

Finally her words penetrated. "You're sure?"

"Yes," she assured him, her voice softening. "Now, will you help me up so we can see what's going on over there?"

Justin helped her to her feet. Doing his best not to look at what was left of his Bronco, he and Angela made their way over to where an army of vehicles had surrounded six trucks. In what looked like a circus, a horde of what he presumed were federal agents were running around, shouting orders. Justin recognized several members of Del Brio's crew spread-eagled and being cuffed while they were being read their rights. He also noted a number of cement bags imprinted with Mercado Brothers Paving and Contracting that were lying on the ground, slit open, and crosses, coins and other relics covered with powdery dust. He shot a look at Angela, realized she'd seen them, too, and had made the connection to her sketches. As he neared the heart of the melee, Justin shouted, "Who's in charge of this circus?"

"I am," came a familiar-sounding New York accent from the center of the fracas. When the man rose and turned to face him, Justin wasn't surprised to see Angela's neighbor Mr. Collins emerge from the group of agents. But he didn't expect to see the man who followed behind him—his own deputy, Bobby Hunter. Within seconds, Justin put two and two together, and a red haze of anger took charge.

"Listen, Justin, I'm sorry about this," Bobby began as he approached with the other agent.

Without preamble, Justin slugged him.

Two other agents grabbed him, restraining him before

he could go at the deputy again. "You just made a big mistake, pal," one of the agents said. "You just assaulted a federal officer."

"I just hit a lying bastard," Justin countered.

"Let him go," Bobby said as he wiped the blood from his mouth. "Given the circumstances, the sheriff has a right to be angry. I'm sorry I had to lie to you."

"You can take your apology and stuff it," Justin fired back as the agents released him. "What I want to know is where you guys get off conducting an undercover operation in my county without advising me."

"It was my call whether to tell you or not, and I chose not to," Collins told him.

"Then you better have a good reason."

"The Lion's Den that was operating out of here until a year ago seemed reason enough."

Knowing that the agent referred to the corruption within the former police chief's office, Justin resented the implication. "We both know that group was dismembered when the last police chief and his cronies were taken down."

"True. But we had no way of knowing whether or not the corruption was more widespread and included county law enforcement, too," Collins told him. "Agent Hunter here assures me that it doesn't."

"If you think that squares things, you're wrong," Justin informed the man. "I should have been told what was going on."

"I considered it. Until Ms. Mason showed up. Given her close…association with both you and Ricky Mercado, I felt we couldn't take the risk."

Justin narrowed his eyes, not liking the implication. He'd already figured out the reason Collins had posed as Angela's neighbor was because they considered her a suspect. "Careful, Collins. I've already hit one federal officer. I have no problem going two for two."

Collins's hazel eyes flashed. "You might want to think twice about threatening a federal agent."

Justin took a step forward, curling his hands into fists at his sides. "I don't need to think twice. Angela Mason is as honest as they come. To imply otherwise is an insult, and you owe the lady an apology."

"And are you speaking as a man or a sheriff?" Collins asked.

"Both."

"Then maybe I should point out that you might not be as objective considering that you were married to the woman and have been staying at her place for the past two weeks," Collins replied.

"What are you implying?" Justin demanded.

"Simply that since Ms. Mason here has an obvious relationship with Ricky Mercado, I couldn't tell you what we were doing because I had no way of knowing if she was using you to feed information to Mercado."

Furious with the federal agent, Justin took another step closer. "I don't give a damn what you think about me, Collins. But I better hear an apology to Angela tripping from that smart mouth of yours or I'm going to rip out your Yankee tongue and feed it to you."

"You're welcome to try, Wainwright."

"Justin, this isn't necessary," Angela said, grabbing at his arm.

He ignored her and the rumble coming from the other agents who watched the exchange. "Apologize. Now," he told Collins.

Collins met his steely gaze. "I don't take orders from small-town sheriffs, and I don't apologize for doing my job."

"That's enough," Angela said, stepping between the two men. "I'd suggest you both rein in the testosterone. The last time I checked, we were both on the same side."

"She's right, Collins," the blond female agent told him. "Try playing nice for a change. They might be able to help us locate Del Brio."

"Shut up, Harte. We'll find Del Brio," Collins said. He looked at Angela. "It's nothing personal, Mason. I'm just doing my job."

"So am I, Agent Collins. So I'll just let my record speak for itself," Angela said coolly. "And I certainly hope yours will be able to do the same for you."

"What's that supposed to mean?" Collins asked.

"It means that I intend to file in my report to the governor and the FBI how your failure to apprise the local law-enforcement agency of your activities here may very well have hindered our investigation and recovery of a kidnapped child—a child that we have every reason to believe belongs to Haley Mercado and is being held by Frank Del Brio. And thanks to your bungling of things here tonight, Del Brio is now on the run and our chances of recovering that little girl alive have just grown a lot slimmer."

Collins's eyes narrowed. "What makes you think the kid belongs to Haley Mercado? And why do you believe Del Brio has her?"

"Why, Agent Collins, you surprise me," Angela said. "I mean, a man who has gone to the lengths you have to check into my background and pry into my personal relationships. I'd have thought surely you had uncovered the fact that I'm psychic."

Thirteen

"Why don't we leave Agent Collins and his people to clean up their mess," Angela told Justin, and turned away before Collins could respond.

"Hang on a second," Justin told her. "I need a vehicle."

"Take mine," Bobby said, and tossed Justin the keys.

"Let's go," Justin said to her, and together they walked over to the deputy's navy-blue truck. Once they were inside, Justin turned to her and asked, "Are you all right?"

"Sure," she told him. "And thanks for sticking up for me back there."

"You didn't need any help from me," he told her. "You did fine all on your own. I suspect Agent Collins will think twice before tangling with another Texas gal."

Pleased by his comment and the fact that the arrogant agent had appeared shell-shocked by her claims, she grinned. "There's just one thing I need to know. Do you really believe what you told Collins? Or do you think that I would have warned Ricky about this bust if I'd known about it?"

"You wouldn't have told him."

"You're sure about that? After all, he and I have been friends a long time. I wouldn't have wanted to see him go to jail."

"You wouldn't have told him," he said firmly, and started the engine.

"Thank you for that," she murmured, trying to find solace in the fact that Justin believed her. If only she knew how he would respond when she told him she was pregnant. She still could hardly believe the over-the-counter test she'd done had come back positive all three times. She was pregnant with Justin's child.

As he drove past the mangled Bronco, he said, "I don't guess there's much point in trying to find my cell phone in that mess." He cut his glance to her. "I'm sorry about your bag and the drawings. But I don't want you giving up on finding Lena. I'm sure Collins has already cut off the roads out of Lone Star County but when I get to a phone, I'll give Hank a call. In the meantime, if I know Del Brio, he won't leave without getting the baby first. She's his link to Haley. And stopping to get her from wherever he's got her stashed will give us some time."

Angela didn't even want to look at the speedometer to see how fast they were going. She held onto the door's armrest as he swerved around a bend. "Justin—"

"We're going to find her. I promised Luke. In fact, I'll call him and ask for his help. I found out the other night that the man has more connections than I'd ever realized."

"Justin, I think I know where she is."

"And Luke can— What did you say?"

"I said I think I know where Lena is," she repeated.

"But back there, you told Collins—"

Angela wrinkled her nose. "I didn't see any point in telling the dumb fed I figured out where Lena was. I thought he deserved to stew awhile."

"Remind me never to play poker with you," he said dryly. "So are you going to fill me in on where we're going?"

"Remember that section where I got off the main highway and got lost the first day I went out on my own? The place where you said the property owners sold out to make room for a potential highway that wasn't built?''

''Yeah, I remember.''

''At that old ranch house, the one that we thought was abandoned, there was a rusted-out sign hanging from the hinges with a horse in the center of the letter *C*. When the truck that Del Brio was in sped past, there was a bumper sticker on it that read Carousel Gardens, and I made the connection.''

''I'm sorry, but you've lost me.''

''I know. I know it doesn't make sense to you, but it does to me. All this time, I was concentrating on finding a ranch with horses because I saw horses moving in circles in my vision. But seeing that bumper sticker made me wonder what if the horses weren't real horses, but horses on a carousel? Maybe the kind that you'd find atop a music box or a mobile in a child's room.'' Which made sense since she'd heard a lullaby.

Justin took the exit that led to the off road. ''So how does that tie in with the abandoned house?''

''Twenty-five, thirty years ago that house could have been the one in my vision. You said most of the homeowners sold out. What about the ones who didn't? Del Brio wouldn't have stashed Lena anywhere that we could trace to him. You said yourself he's too smart for that. But maybe he knew someone who still owned one of those abandoned home sites, and that's where he has Lena.''

''*C* for Clawson,'' Justin said, and smacked his forehead. ''I can't believe how stupid I was not to see it.''

''See what?''

''That Del Brio's girlfriend might be in on the kidnapping. He's been seeing one of the waitresses at the country club, a redhead by the name of Erica Clawson. I think it was Bobby who told me that she likes to ride because her daddy used to own a place with horses, but they lost the place when she was a little girl.'' He looked over at her, his green eyes solemn. ''What do you want to bet that Miss Butter-wouldn't-melt-in-her-mouth Erica Clawson's family still owns that land?'' He hit the steering wheel with the palm of his hand. ''I should have checked the place out. I should have checked her out more thoroughly and not bought into that bubbly innocent act of hers.''

She touched his arm. ''It doesn't matter now. We just need to get there before Del Brio gets Lena and leaves.'' Because she had a sick feeling in the pit of her stomach that the little girl was in real danger now.

When Justin turned off onto the road leading to the abandoned property, Angela was struck by how dark it was. Much darker than it had been that first time she'd been there at sunset, Angela realized. Without any highway or streetlights, the headlights of the truck and the moon provided their only source of illumination.

Justin came to the fork in the road, pulled over to the shoulder and cut the lights. ''If Del Brio's down there, I don't want him to spot us. Lock the doors and wait here while I go check the place out.''

Angela didn't even bother arguing. She exited the truck, and when he came around and saw her, she said, ''I'm going.''

''Then stay behind me.''

Her heart was in her throat as they made their way down the dirt road. The moment they reached the bend, they had no trouble seeing the house. It was lit up like a Christmas tree, unlike the last time she'd seen it. And while it still looked shabby and neglected, it no longer looked abandoned.

''Looks like you were right,'' Justin whispered.

When they reached the broken gate, they were saved the

task of climbing over it because it was open and hanging on its hinges. "Del Brio must have been in a hurry," she told Justin, and pointed to the rusted horse sign with the letter C that now lay in the dirt besides the gate.

"I don't see the truck, but there's a car near the front of the house. Come on." Angela followed Justin as he crept up toward the house. He hunkered down beside the car, felt the hood. "Still warm. You watch the front. I'm going to check around the back and see if I see anyone."

While Justin checked the rear, Angela kept herself low and eased up to the window at the front of the house. She looked inside, saw no one. But a chair was overturned and a lamp lay on its side. Inching her way up the steps to the door, she peered inside the broken window pane of the door. And seeing no one, she turned the knob and the door opened.

"What in the hell are you doing?" Justin said in a harsh whisper from behind her. He grabbed her around the waist and pulled her back against him. With one arm wrapped around her middle, he held her tightly in the cradle of his thighs. In his other hand he held his gun.

"It's empty," she told him. "They're gone."

Releasing her, he stepped in front of her and kicked the door. It swung open into the house, banging against a wall. After several seconds ticked by, during which no one came running or shouted, he lowered his gun and relaxed his stance. "All right. Let's check it out."

While Justin headed for the back of the house, Angela searched for the room where Lena had been kept. She found it. A tiny, dingy room with a crib and a small chest whose drawers had been emptied and tossed onto the floor. Angela's stomach constricted as she spied a little pink sock on the floor and stooped down to pick it up.

"Look. Over there by the table," Justin said upon entering the room. Lying on its side in the corner was a music box with a carousel of horses. "You were right all along."

As she held the baby's sock to her breast, the images hit her fast and hard. "The barn," she told him. "Hurry! We've got to find the barn."

"Around back," he told her.

They hurried out and ran around to the back of the house. And when Angela saw the big ugly red barn, she would have run across the field in the open to reach it, if Justin hadn't grabbed her.

"Stick to the shadows," he cautioned.

Though it nearly killed her to move so slowly, Angela did so. As they approached the barn, she spied the sliver of light from beneath the door. When Justin put a finger to his lips, urging her to be quiet, she nodded. He drew his weapon and nudged open the door of the barn with his foot. The squeaking sound echoed loudly in the quiet night and sent a shiver of fear down Angela's spine.

And then Angela heard it, the frightened cry of a baby coming from inside the barn. Unable to bear the heart-wrenching sounds, Angela stepped from behind Justin and saw Lena. The dark-haired little angel stood at the rail of a small playpen, clutching a stuffed bear while tears streamed down her cheeks. Angela didn't stop to think, she simply acted with a mother's instinct and raced inside the barn toward the child.

"Angela, no!"

She'd almost reached the playpen when Del Brio stepped out of the shadows with a gun in his hand. "That's close enough, Ms. Mason," he told her, and aimed the gun at her heart.

She stopped, gauged her chances of getting past him to Lena. "I wouldn't try it," he said as though he'd read her mind. ''You might as well come on out, Wainwright. I know you're there.''

Justin stepped out into the open.

''Drop the gun or I'll shoot her,'' he warned. Angela heard Justin's weapon hit the ground with a thud from some point behind her. ''Now kick it over there by that haystack, and then come join Ms. Mason here.''

As though Lena sensed the drama unfolding, her sobs increased. Big tears glistened in her eyes as she watched Angela.

''Put your hands up where I can see them,'' Del Brio told them as Justin moved beside her. Once they had done so, the man smiled at them and Angela shuddered at the glimpse of madness she read in his eyes.

''The two of you have caused me a great deal of trouble,'' he told them. ''I don't intend to allow either of you to cause me any more.''

Justin stepped in front of Angela and blocked her body with his. ''You kill us and you'll never get out of here alive. The feds are covering every road in and out of Lone Star County looking for you,'' Justin told him. ''Let Angela and the girl go, and take me as a hostage. It's your only chance to get out of here alive.''

An evil smile snaked across Del Brio's mouth. He released the safety on his pistol and aimed it at Justin. ''Very noble, Wainwright. But I'll take my chances. Me and Haley Mercado's baby.''

''I don't think so, Del Brio,'' a thready male voice said from the darkness.

Del Brio jerked his head to the left where Johnny Mercado stepped out of the dark corner of the barn with a gun trained on Del Brio. Since she'd seen him last, Johnny seemed to have shrunk several inches. His once silver-gray hair was now a dingy white. His hazel eyes were overbright, with huge shadows beneath them that Angela suspected were caused by lack of sleep and too much stress. The hand holding the gun on Del Brio was jumpy.

He looked like a man on the edge of breaking, Angela thought, and she knew he was no match for Del Brio. Fearful of what was about to happen, Angela gauged the chances of her getting to the weapon in her boot while Del Brio's attention was on Johnny.

"What's this all about, Johnny? You and me...we're family."

Johnny spit on the ground. "You're not my family. You killed my family."

"Johnny, you're talking crazy," Del Brio said. "Your wife died of a heart attack, remember? And Haley and I would have been married had it not been for that jerk Callaghan and his friends taking her out on that boat."

"Liar," Johnny shouted, his face growing red with rage.

With one eye on the baby and Johnny's jumpy gun hand, Angela tried easing her leg up to get access to her boot. She noted that Del Brio kept his gun trained on Justin, evidently recognizing that Justin, even unarmed, was a greater threat to him than Johnny with a weapon.

"You killed my Isadora! And because of you, my Haley pretended to die! But you found out, didn't you? That's why you kidnapped her baby. Now you think you can use my granddaughter to get Haley? Well, I'm not going to let you do it. This time I protect my family." Spittle flew from Johnny's mouth as he spoke, and even in the dim light there was no mistaking the sweat beading his brow as he waved his gun at Del Brio. "Now throw down your gun and step away from the baby."

"All right, Johnny," Del Brio said, and still holding the gun, he pointed the barrel toward the sky. "I'm going to put down my gun now. So take it easy. You don't want your gun to go off and hit your granddaughter, now do you?"

Looking confused a moment, Johnny relaxed, and Angela knew at once it was a setup. "Johnny, look out," she screamed.

Everything happened with dizzying speed. Del Brio fired his gun at Johnny. At the roar of the gunshot, Lena began to cry again. A look of shock spread across Johnny's face before he slid to the floor, where his body lay motionless while blood puddled around him.

Amid all the chaos, Angela went for her gun.

"Drop it, Ms. Mason," Del Brio said, swinging the gun back toward them. "Drop it, or I shoot Wainwright square between the eyes."

"Don't listen to him, Angela," Justin told her. "Think about Lena. She needs you. You give him your weapon and he's going to kill us both, anyway, and then who's going to save Lena?"

"Erica," Del Brio screamed out. "Erica, where in the hell are you?"

"I'm right here," the redhead said as she came rushing into the barn behind them.

"Relieve Ms. Mason of her weapon," Del Brio ordered.

Once Erica had taken her gun, she moved over to stand beside Del Brio. "I slit the tires on their truck like you said. And I got this guy who's sweet on me at the club to drive my mother to the bus station. I gave her money to go visit her sister down in New Orleans like you said. So we're all set to go."

"Can't you get that kid to stop crying?"

Erica picked up Lena, but the child continued to wail. "I told you the little brat doesn't like me."

"Then make her like you," Del Brio ordered. "Take her outside while I finish these two off."

"If you think you've got problems now, Del Brio," Justin told him, "try adding the murder of two cops to your list of crimes. And every law enforcement agency in Texas will be after you. And you, Ms. Clawson, will be an accomplice."

"Don't listen to him, Erica. Go outside."

When Erica hesitated, Angela added, "If he kills us, you'll go down for it just the same as if you pulled the trigger."

"Shut up! You think you two are the first cops I've ever killed?" Del Brio countered. "Now, do what I told you, Erica. Get the kid out of here."

When the woman started to leave, Angela grabbed her head and screamed.

Erica jumped, which made Lena wail louder. "What's wrong with her?" Erica asked. "Why's she holding her head like that?"

"How the hell do I know?" Del Brio fired back.

"It's the visions," Angela said on a gasp, and prayed she'd learned something from watching the phony psychics in carnival shows.

"What visions?" Erica asked.

"She's psychic," Justin explained. "Sometimes she gets these visions of things that happened or are going to happen. How do you think we knew where to find Lena? Angela saw this place in a vision."

"It's a bunch of hogwash," Del Brio claimed.

"What kind of vision are you seeing now?" Erica asked, her eyes wide.

"Blood. Lots and lots of blood. And dogs, big dogs hunting, chasing someone." Angela closed her eyes, covered her mouth as she feigned horror. "The screams! Oh, God," she said, opening her eyes. "They're tearing flesh from your bodies."

Erica paled. "Oh, God! Frank, I hate dogs. You know I hate dogs," a panicky Erica ranted. "Please, Frank. Let's get out of here. We've got enough trouble on our hands with this kid."

Del Brio hesitated a moment, then relented. "All right, go get in the truck with the kid while I lock them in here." After scooping up both Justin's gun and Johnny's, Del Brio closed them in the barn and locked it.

The moment the door closed, Angela raced over to Johnny. "He's unconscious and he's lost a lot of blood," she told Justin.

"See what you can do for him while I try to get us out of here."

She ripped off her jacket and used it to try to stem the flow of blood, while Justin found a rake and used it to break the lock on the rotting door. Within minutes her jacket was soaked and her fingers were bathed in the warm, sticky blood. "Hurry, Justin. If we don't get him to a hospital soon, I don't think he's going to make it."

"Did you get him?" Haley Mercado asked Agent Sean Collins when he entered the room where he'd instructed her to meet him. Finally, she would be free of Del Brio and the FBI, and she would get her precious baby girl back.

"Sit down, Haley."

"I don't want to sit down," she told him, not liking the look in the agent's eyes. "I want you to tell me you've put Frank Del Brio behind bars like you promised me."

"He got away."

"No," she cried out. "You promised me that if I helped you, that if I taped those conversations and got you the information you needed that you would lock Frank away," she said, tears of anger and frustration streaming down her face. "You promised me that if I did my part, you'd help me find my little girl, that you'd leave my father and brother alone, that you'd let me have my life back. Well, I did my part. I got you the information you needed. Now you have to keep your end of the bargain."

"I'm sorry," Collins told her and placed a comforting hand on her back as she sobbed. "I'm afraid I have more bad news for you."

Haley jerked her head up at that. "What? What is it?"

"Your father's been shot. He's lost a lot of blood and he's in a coma at Mission Creek Memorial Hospital. It doesn't look good."

She'd already lost her mother, and now her father. "But how? My father wasn't supposed to have anything to do with that shipment. How could your men—"

"It wasn't us. It was Del Brio."

Haley felt the color drain from her face. "How?"

"Your father apparently has been following Del Brio for some time, and when Del Brio escaped from us, your father knew where he'd go. So your father was waiting for him. According to Sheriff Wainwright and Angela Mason, Del Brio was going to kill them. Your father saved their lives, but Del Brio managed to get off a shot and your father was hit."

Haley wasn't sure how she knew. Perhaps it was something in Agent Collins's hazel eyes. Pity. Regret. She wasn't sure. But she knew there was more. "What is it you haven't told me?"

"Your daughter...Del Brio took her with him when he escaped."

"No!" Haley heard the anguished cry of an injured animal, and not until Agent Collins had called in agent Annabelle Harte did Haley realize that the cry had come from her.

"Feeling better?" Agent Harte asked after she'd calmed down.

Haley shook her head and forced herself to get a grip. "I'm okay." Or as okay as she could be knowing that Frank had her precious little girl. She stood and prepared to leave.

"Where do you think you're going?" Agent Collins asked.

"To find Frank and get my baby back," she told him honestly. What other option did she have? She couldn't leave Lena with Frank.

"I'm afraid I can't let you do that," Collins insisted.

"You can't stop me," Haley informed him, and started for the door.

"Wyatt! Henderson!" Collins called out and two tall, solid men that she recognized as other federal agents blocked her path.

"What do you think you're doing?" Haley demanded.

"I'm taking you into custody," Collins said.

"I'm not a prisoner. I haven't done anything wrong. You can't hold me."

"Actually, I can," Collins told her.

Furious and frustrated, she said, "You're going to hold me here while that—that monster is out there somewhere with my baby?"

"If I let you walk out that door, you're a dead woman, Haley. If Del Brio took your daughter, it means he knows you're alive. It's only a matter of time before he figures out that Daisy Parker is Haley Mercado."

"I don't care about me. I just want to get Lena back."

"Then you're going to have to trust me," Collins told her.

"I trusted you once, and look where's it's gotten me. My father's dying, and my daughter's with a madman."

"I won't let you down again, Haley. I promise. But if you want to stay alive and help your daughter, you've got to trust me. Will you do that?"

Haley nodded. But she didn't trust him, she admitted in silence. The man she should have trusted, wished she'd trusted, was Luke Callaghan. If only she had told him about their child, she thought. Somehow, someway, she would get Lena back, she vowed. Whatever it took, whatever she had to do, she would do it. She would get her daughter back.

"Has Angela called?" Justin asked Audrey Lou as he exited his office and dumped a stack of files on her desk.

"No, your missus hasn't called since the last time you asked me—which happened to be only ten minutes ago."

"It was fifteen minutes," he countered, and didn't bother correcting her about Angela no longer being his missus. "And since I was tied up on another call, you wouldn't have been able to put her through. So I was just checking."

"Uh-huh," she said, and fixed him with a you're-lying-through-your-teeth look. "Why don't you just call the woman and get it over with? Better yet, do us all a favor and go see her. You've been like a bear with a sore paw since you left her place and went back to your ranch."

"I don't need this kind of grief," Justin told her, and went back into his office and slammed the door. He didn't need it because he knew it was true. He'd been restless and miserable since he and Angela had agreed that, with Del Brio on the run, there was no longer any reason for him to continue staying at her condo. That had been two days ago, and he hadn't heard a word from her since. Feeling caged and restless, Justin grabbed his hat and headed out the door. "I'm going out for some lunch."

He hadn't planned to go to Angela's. But once he was behind the wheel of the new truck he'd bought to replace the Bronco, he found himself heading for her condo. When he turned onto her street, he still had no idea what he was going to say to her. And for once the sight of Ricky Mercado exiting Angela's driveway didn't infuriate him. In fact, when the other man passed him and tipped his head in acknowledgment, Justin did the same. With Ricky's father still in a coma and the situation with his sister and missing niece, he actually felt sorry for Ricky, he admitted.

Thinking of Ricky's family troubles made him take a look at his own family. The Wainwrights would never be the perfect family. But as messed up and maddening as they could be at times, at least he still had them alive and well and nearby, Justin conceded. Exiting the truck, he walked to the door of her condo and rang the bell. What he didn't have and wanted, he realized, was Angela.

"Justin," she said, her voice a breathless whisper as though she'd been rushing around.

He removed his hat and asked, "May I come in?"

"Of course," she said, and opened the door wider. "I was in the den, making a list of things I need to take care of. Any word yet on Del Brio?"

"Not yet," he said. "I came by to thank you for your help and tell you what a remarkable job you did, finding Lena the way you did."

"Not very remarkable," she murmured. "Del Brio still has her, and we don't know where they are."

"But thanks to you, we know it's Del Brio who has her." He took her hands, held them in his. "The other reason I came by was to tell you that the FBI is insisting that I leave the kidnapping case for them to handle. Haley really is alive and apparently she's been working with them for some time to help them nail Del Brio. I would have come by to let you know sooner, but they've had me buried in red tape because of that bust they bungled.''

"Yes, Ricky told me about Haley and the deal she cut with the FBI to save him and his father. The FBI promised her that they'll get Lena back," she said, her voice impossibly sad. "I can only imagine how poor Haley must feel. How worried she must be about her little girl. Why, if she were my baby, and someone had stolen her from me, I..." Angela's voice hitched, and the look in her blue eyes before she pulled her hands free and turned away nearly broke his heart.

"Hey, it's all right," Justin soothed. He placed his hands on her shoulders and gently squeezed. "Despite what happened the other night with Del Brio, those FBI guys are good. They'll find her," he said. He'd barely managed to finish the thought when he spied the two suitcases sitting on the floor beside the counter. Everything inside him went cold. A knot the size of Texas formed in his stomach. She was leaving. What a fool he'd been, he realized, to think that they might have a chance, that maybe they could make things work.

Angela turned around, gave him a puzzled look. "What's wrong?"

"Not a thing," he told her, unable to keep the bitterness from his voice. "I see you've decided not to stick around Lone Star County any longer than you have to."

"Actually, I'm going back to San Antonio to get some more of my things. Agent Collins has decided to allow me to work with him to locate Lena."

"I see," Justin said. She was sticking around but only long enough to help the FBI. "Well, I don't want to keep you, so I'll get out of your way. Goodbye, Angela. Take care of yourself," he said, and started for the door, afraid if he didn't get out of there, he'd make an even bigger fool of himself by begging her to stay for him.

Angela burst into tears, deep, gut-wrenching sobs.

Justin stopped cold and spun around. At the sight of her standing there, her shoulders heaving and tears flowing down her cheeks, he rushed to her. "Angel, what is it? What's wrong?" he asked, wiping her damp cheeks.

"What's wrong is that I—I'm p-pregnant with your child. And I love you," she said in hiccuping sobs while tears continued to fill her eyes and spill down her cheeks. "And...and the t-timing is all wrong because when you loved me and wanted me to have your b-baby, I couldn't get pregnant. And now that you don't love me and c-can't wait to get me out of your life, I'm pregnant."

Stunned, he needed a moment for her words to sink in. He cupped her face in his hands, forced her to look at him. "Repeat what you just said."

"I'm pregnant," she said on a sob. "I saw a doctor yesterday and she confirmed it."

Joy hit him first, pumped through him like an oil-well gusher. He felt like a man who'd been facing the firing squad and had just been granted a reprieve. A new life. A life with Angela. "No, no. Not the part about the baby," he said. "Although I'm thrilled about that part, too. I want you to repeat the other part, the part about you loving me. Tell me again, Angel. Tell me that you love me as much as I love you."

Her eyes lit up, the tears stopped. "I love you, Justin Wainwright," she said solemnly. "I always have."

"Then why did you leave me? If you loved me, why did you go?"

"Because I thought I'd failed you."

"Failed me how?" he asked, wanting to clear the problems of the past so that they would never impede their future. "Is this about your being psychic? Because if it is, I've already told you that I loved you because of who you are."

"It wasn't just that. It was knowing how badly you wanted children and knowing that I couldn't have them. It's the one basic thing a woman is supposed to be able to do, only I couldn't do it. So I knew I had to let you go. I had to let you find someone who could be a real wife to you, give you what you wanted most."

Justin kissed her hard. "You're an idiot, Angela Mason. Sure, I wanted kids, but I could live without kids. The one thing I wanted most, the one thing I didn't want to live without, don't want to live without is you."

"Oh, Justin," she said, laughing. She wrapped her arms around his neck. "We've both been such fools. All those years we've wasted. All that time we've lost."

When her smile dimmed and that worried look came back into her eyes, he asked, "What's wrong?"

"I was thinking of Haley Mercado and all the time she's lost with her little girl. And just when she was within reach, we lost her again to Del Brio."

Justin pressed a kiss to her lips. He, too, had been plagued by the idea of the little girl with Del Brio. But he was a firm believer that good eventually won out over evil. He believed it in this case, and he intended to do whatever he could to help make sure it did. "Haley's going to get her daughter back," Justin assured her. "I've already made plans to go see Luke."

"What about Agent Collins? You said he wanted you to back off."

"Tough," Justin said. "Between Luke and us and the FBI, we'll get Lena back. I feel it in my gut."

"Careful, Sheriff. You're beginning to sound like a man who could be psychic," she teased.

"Maybe I am. Or maybe it's the psychic I love rubbing off on me."

"I love you, Justin Wainwright."

"And I love you, Angela Mason." He picked her up and began spinning her around and around.

"Justin, stop, you're making me dizzy," she said, laughing.

He stopped spinning and kissed her deeply, thoroughly, with all the love in his heart. After all those lost years, they had found their way back to each other, he realized. He thought about the circle of life and fate. How Haley Mercado's night with Luke Callaghan had led to the birth of Lena. And how the little girl had led him and Angela back to each other. He and Angela were fated to be together, Justin reasoned. Just as Rose and Matt Carson had been fated to find each other. Just as Hawk and Jenny had found each other. The same way that Susan and Michael had found their way to each other. The way his father and mother were finding their way back to each other now.

Angela was his destiny, his life, Justin realized. He'd foolishly lost five years of the life he was meant to share with her. He didn't intend to waste another minute of that life ever again. Lifting his head, he looked into her dreamy eyes and smiled, then he headed for the stairs that led to her bedroom.

"Where are you going?" she asked.

"To make up for lost time."

Don't miss the next story from Silhouette's
LONE STAR COUNTRY CLUB:
TEXAS...NOW AND FOREVER
by Merline Lovelace

Available May 2003

*Turn the page for an excerpt from this
exciting romance...!*

One

A shrill buzz cut through the air-conditioned silence haunting the small farmhouse just outside Mission Creek, Texas. Like a deer speared by truck headlights, Haley Mercado froze. Her glance sliced to the FBI agent who'd acted as her controller for the past year.

Across the living room, Sean Collins met her desperate look. They'd been waiting for this call, she and Sean. So had the small army of agents guarding the safe house where the FBI had stashed Haley until they captured Frank Del Brio.

Frank Del Brio. The smooth, handsome head of the Texas mob who'd once shoved a square-cut, three-carat diamond on Haley's finger and announced that she was going to marry him. The ruthless thug who'd forced her to flee her home in South Texas and assume another identity abroad. The vicious killer whose horrific acts had brought Haley out of hiding a year ago and sent her undercover, determined to assist the FBI in bringing Del Brio down.

Frank Del Brio, who'd kidnapped the child she'd placed in safekeeping while she worked undercover and, only a few nights ago, who had escaped during a wild shootout that left her father in ICU and Haley under close protection at this secluded farmhouse.

The phone shrilled again, sending a jolt of desperate hope into her chest. They've got him! Please, God! Please let this call be from the FBI command center, advising that they've cornered Frank and rescued her baby! Her heart in her throat, she swiped her palms down the front of her jeans and kept her gaze locked on Sean as he reached for the cordless phone.

"Collins here."

When the FBI operative's face tightened, Haley's hope shattered into a thousand, knife-edged shards.

"How the hell did you get this number?"

It was Frank, she thought on a wave of sickening certainty. It could only be Frank.

Haley flew across the living room. "Let me talk to him."

"I'm warning you, Del Brio..."

"Let me talk to him!"

The agent relinquished the phone reluctantly, signaling for Haley to string out the conversation as long as she could. She understood. The communications technicians hooked into the line would need a few moments to trace the call. She understood, too, that the events of the past year were rapidly spiraling to a terrifying conclusion.

"Frank! Frank, are you there?"

"Hello, Daisy."

The deep, rich baritone made her skin crawl.

"You fooled me with that brassy hair and nose job, babe, but I have to admit I like the new look."

Haley didn't bother to comment on the fact that he'd penetrated the cover she'd been using for the past year. The long months she'd spent as Daisy Parker didn't matter anymore. All that mattered was her baby. Only her baby.

"Don't hurt her, Frank. Please, don't hurt her."

She hated to beg, hated hearing the abject pleading in her voice, almost as much as she hated Del Brio for the pain he'd caused her and her family.

"What do you want?" she whispered. "What do I have to do to get Lena back?"

"Two million just might do the trick. In unmarked, non-sequential bills. Nothing bigger than a hundred. I'll let you know where and when to deliver it."

His voice dropped to a low caress. Soft and husky, it scraped across Haley's raw nerves like a rusty nail.

"If I see one cop, if I smell their stink anywhere within a hundred miles when you deliver the ransom, you'll never see your baby again. You understand me?"

"Yes."

"Good. Talk to you soon, babe."

"Wait!" Her frantic shout bounced off the walls. "Don't hang up! Tell me how she's—"

The hum of the disconnected line thundered in Haley's ear. She wanted to scream, to shriek and batter the receiver against the phone. But she'd spent the past year living a dangerous lie. One long year undercover, risking her life every day to ferret out the details of the mob that had operated out of Mission Creek. If nothing else, those torturous months had taught her to subdue every natural impulse. To smile when she shook inside with fear. To hide her anguish as she watched another couple love and cherish the baby she'd been forced to give up temporarily for the child's own safety.

All those months had left their mark on Haley. Instead of shrieking or hurling the cordless phone at the wall, she merely handed it to Sean and listened in stony silence while he barked at the communications techs working the trace.

"Did you pinpoint the location?"

She knew. Even before she saw his mouth twist into a disgusted grimace, she knew. Frank was too smart to trip himself up with a simple phone call.

"Okay. Thanks."

His jaw tight, Sean punched the off button. Frustration gave a sharp edge to his broad New York accent when he confirmed what she already suspected.

"Del Brio used some kind of electronic scrambler. We couldn't confirm his location."

She nodded. "He'll kill her."

"Listen to me, Haley. Del Brio can't kill Lena. Not until he gets what he wants. He knows we'll demand proof she's still alive before we play his game."

The iron control she'd exercised for more than a year slipped and came close to shattering at that moment. "It's not a game!" she shot back furiously. "This is my child's life we're talking about!"

"Dammit, I know that."

Months of unrelenting tension sizzled and spit between them. With a little push, Haley could almost have hated Sean Collins, too.

"I'm sorry," he said finally, shagging a hand through his thick reddish hair. "You know I'll do whatever it takes to get Lena back. I want Del Brio as much as you do."

"No," she countered swiftly, her throat raw. "You couldn't. It wasn't your mother Frank murdered, Sean. Your father he tried to destroy. Your trusted friend and adviser he blew away."

She closed her eyes, aching for her mother. Grieving for the white-haired Texas judge who'd helped her arrange her escape and acted as her lifeline all those years she stayed in hiding. Aching, too, for the father who now lay in ICU, battling for every breath. And now her daughter...

Eyes closed, she pictured Lena the last time she'd seen her. The one-year-old was such a happy, bubbly child. All smiles and gurgles and bright blue eyes. With her mother's pointed chin and her father's black, curly hair.

Her father. Oh, God! Her father.

Luke Callaghan.

Swallowing the moan that tried to escape, Haley dug her hands into her sides. She had to tell Luke. Had to confirm what the DNA tests had already substantiated. He was Lena's father. When she admitted that, she'd have to confess, too, that the blond waitress he knew only as Daisy Parker was Lena's mother.

She cringed at the thought of having to explain to Luke the tangled web of lies and deceit she'd woven to protect herself and Lena, but every instinct told her he was now her only hope. Frank had warned her not to bring the feds when she delivered the ransom. He hadn't said anything about the baby's father.

Her mind worked feverishly. Del Brio was ruthless and totally without conscience. He also exercised an extensive network of contacts. He'd known how to reach Haley here, in this supposedly secure haven. He'd probably get word within minutes if she left it and went to Lena's father. He wouldn't worry, though. If there was a weak link in Del Brio's armor, it was his arrogance. He wouldn't doubt his ability to handle the combination of a terrified mother and blind father.

But could Haley handle it? After all this time, could she face the man who'd fathered her child? The man she'd loved as long as she could remember?

She could.

She had to!

Spinning on one heel, she bolted for the front door. Sean followed hard on her heels.

"Where are you going?"

"To find Luke Callaghan."

The secret is out!

Coming in May 2003 to SILHOUETTE BOOKS

Evidence has finally surfaced that a covert team
of scientists successfully completed experiments
in genetic manipulation.

The extraordinary individuals created by these
experiments could be anyone, living anywhere,
even right next door....

Enjoy these three brand-new FAMILY SECRETS
stories and watch as dark pasts are exposed
and passion burns through the night!

The Invisible Virgin by Maggie Shayne
A Matter of Duty by Eileen Wilks
Inviting Trouble by Anne Marie Winston

Five extraordinary siblings. One dangerous past.

If you missed the first exciting stories from the Lone Star Country Club, here's a chance to order your copies today!

0-373-61352-0	STROKE OF FORTUNE by Christine Rimmer	___ $4.75 U.S.	___ $5.75 CAN.
0-373-61353-9	TEXAS ROSE by Marie Ferrarella	___ $4.75 U.S.	___ $5.75 CAN.
0-373-61354-7	THE REBEL'S RETURN by Beverly Barton	___ $4.75 U.S.	___ $5.75 CAN.
0-373-61355-5	HEARTBREAKER by Laurie Paige	___ $4.75 U.S.	___ $5.75 CAN.
0-373-61356-3	PROMISED TO A SHEIK by Carla Cassidy	___ $4.75 U.S.	___ $5.75 CAN.
0-373-61357-1	THE QUIET SEDUCTION by Dixie Browning	___ $4.75 U.S.	___ $5.75 CAN.
0-373-61358-X	AN ARRANGED MARRIAGE by Peggy Moreland	___ $4.75 U.S.	___ $5.75 CAN.
0-373-61359-8	THE MERCENARY by Allison Leigh	___ $4.75 U.S.	___ $5.75 CAN.
0-373-61360-1	THE LAST BACHELOR by Judy Christenberry	___ $4.75 U.S.	___ $5.75 CAN.
0-373-61361-X	LONE WOLF by Sheri WhiteFeather	___ $4.75 U.S.	___ $5.75 CAN.

(Limited quantities available.)

TOTAL AMOUNT	$_____
POSTAGE & HANDLING	$_____
($1.00 for one book, 50¢ for each additional)	
APPLICABLE TAXES*	$_____
<u>TOTAL PAYABLE</u>	$_____

(Check or money order—please do not send cash)

To order, send the completed form along with your name, address, zip or postal code, along with a check or money order for the total above, payable to **Lone Star Country Club,** to:
In the U.S.: 3010 Walden Avenue, P.O. Box 9047, Buffalo, NY 14269-9047; **In Canada:** P.O. Box 616, Fort Erie, Ontario L2A 5X3

Name:_____
Address:_____ City:_____
State/Prov:_____ Zip/Postal Code:_____
Account Number (if applicable):_____
093 KJH DNC 3

*New York residents remit applicable sales taxes.
*Canadian residents remit applicable GST and provincial taxes.

Visit us at www.lonestarcountryclub.com   LSCCBACK-10

LONE STAR LSCC COUNTRY CLUB EST. 1923

Where Texas society reigns supreme—and appearances are *everything!*

Collect three (3) original proofs of purchase from the back pages of three (3) Lone Star Country Club titles and receive a free Lone Star book (regularly retailing at $4.75 U.S./$5.75 CAN.) that's not yet available in retail outlets!

Just complete the order form and send it, along with three (3) proofs of purchase from three (3) different Lone Star titles to: Lone Star Country Club, P.O. Box 9047, Buffalo, NY 14269-9047, or P.O. Box 613, Fort Erie, Ontario L2A 5X3.

Name (PLEASE PRINT)

Address   Apt. #

City   State/Prov.   Zip/Postal Code

Please specify which title(s) you would like to receive:

❑   0-373-61364-4   *Her Sweet Talkin' Man*
❑   0-373-61365-2   *Mission Creek Mother-To-Be*
❑   0-373-61366-0   *The Lawman*
❑   0-373-61367-9   *Doctor Seduction*

❑ Have you enclosed your proofs of purchase?

Remember—for each title selected, you must send three (3) original proofs of purchase. To receive all four (4) titles, just send in twelve (12) proofs of purchase, one from each of the 12 Lone Star Country Club titles.

LONE STAR LSCC COUNTRY CLUB EST. 1923

One Proof of Purchase
LSCCPOP11

Please allow 4 to 6 weeks for delivery. Offer good only while quantities last. Offer available in Canada and the U.S. only. Request should be received no later than July 31, 2003. Each proof of purchase should be cut out of the back-page ad featuring this offer.

Visit us at www.lonestarcountryclub.com   LSCCPOP11